In *The Gospel in Dickens*, Gina Dalf
glimpse into the mind and soul of Cha
and engagingly written, this volume follows Dickens's Christian thought through his oeuvre like no other book available. Dalfonzo's observations and assessments of the varied selections, based on her careful contextual reading, are astute and right on target—because she has a great sense of how Dickens thought, especially about his faith and how his faith came to bear on his life. Whether you've walked with Dickens for some time or you are just beginning to get to know him, you will want to own this delightful volume.

—*Gary Colledge, PhD, author of* God and Charles Dickens

George Orwell, the great English writer, observed that Charles Dickens was always preaching a sermon. *The Gospel in Dickens* provides an excellent framework for identifying the nature and content of these "sermons." Focusing on the key areas of repentance, grace, sin, redemption, and salvation, Gina Dalfonzo has provided a clear, insightful introduction to her selections. For those who are familiar with the works of Dickens, and for those who are keen to find out more, this book casts valuable light on an important aspect of the writer's life and work.

—*Keith Hooper, PhD, author of* Charles Dickens: Faith, Angels and the Poor

Though students of Dickens continue to debate whether he was a Christian, no one can debate that he relied upon Jesus Christ as the standard for humanity. Less an evangelist than a prophet, Dickens painted word pictures of common behavior to portray what it means to fall short of the glory of God. As these passages from his many novels make clear, Dickens never confused social and financial respectability with faithfulness to Christ. These passages reveal how closely Dickens had read the Gospels.

—*Harry Lee Poe, PhD, Charles Colson Professor of Faith and Culture, Union University*

The Gospel in Dickens

The Gospel in Dickens

Selections from His Works

Charles Dickens

Edited by Gina Dalfonzo

PLOUGH PUBLISHING HOUSE

Published by Plough Publishing House
Walden, New York
Robertsbridge, England
Elsmore, Australia
www.plough.com

Plough produces books, a quarterly magazine, and Plough.com to encourage people and help them put their faith into action. We believe Jesus can transform the world and that his teachings and example apply to all aspects of life. At the same time, we seek common ground with all people regardless of their creed.

Plough is the publishing house of the Bruderhof, an international Christian community. The Bruderhof is a fellowship of families and singles practicing radical discipleship in the spirit of the first church in Jerusalem (Acts 2 and 4). Members devote their entire lives to serving God, one another, and their neighbors, renouncing private property and sharing everything. To learn more about the Bruderhof's faith, history, and daily life, see Bruderhof.com. (Views expressed by Plough authors are their own and do not necessarily reflect the position of the Bruderhof.)

ISBN: 978-0-87486-841-8
24 23 22 21 20 1 2 3 4 5 6 7

Front cover photograph by Jeremiah Gurney

A catalog record for this book is available from the British Library.

Library of Congress Cataloging-in-Publication Data
Names: Dickens, Charles, 1812-1870, author. | Dalfonzo, Gina, 1975- editor. | Prior, Karen Swallow, other.
Title: The gospel in Dickens : selections from his works / Charles Dickens ; edited by Gina Dalfonzo ; foreword by Karen Swallow Prior ; introduction by Gina Dalfonzo.
Description: Walden, New York : Plough Publishing House, [2020] | Series: The gospel in great writers | Summary: "The most stirring Dickens scenes and characters in one concise volume"-- Provided by publisher.
Identifiers: LCCN 2020024609 (print) | LCCN 2020024610 (ebook) | ISBN 9780874868418 (paperback) | ISBN 9780874863437 (ebook)
Subjects: LCSH: Dickens, Charles, 1812-1870--Religion. | Dickens, Charles, 1812-1870--Characters. | Bible. Gospels--In literature. | Christianity in literature.
Classification: LCC PR4553 .D34 2020 (print) | LCC PR4553 (ebook) | DDC 823/.8--dc23
LC record available at https://lccn.loc.gov/2020024609 LC ebook record available at https://lccn.loc.gov/2020024610

Printed in the United States of America

Contents

Part II: Repentance and Grace

Part III: The Righteous Life

Appendix: Two Letters

Foreword

Good literature is fresh water for the soul. While some writers offer a sip ladled from the well, Dickens takes us to a mountain waterfall where rushing waters saturate, overwhelm, and put us at risk of drowning as we drink. But fear not. This book of selected readings is more like a gentle brook whose waters will quench the thirst of Dickens aficionados and neophytes alike. I know this volume will attract those who know and love Dickens already, but I hope it woos those who have yet to drink from his depths.

Dickens was, perhaps, the first real, grown up, *literary* author I fell in love with. I think that happened because I was allowed to wade into the stream gradually when I was first assigned *Great Expectations* by my junior high English teacher. By using an abridged, illustrated version for young readers, my teacher introduced us to the storytelling powers of Dickens without letting us get lost in the baroque style that is beyond the tastes and abilities of inexperienced readers. The images from that early immersion in an age-appropriate version have remained with me my whole life, deepened and enriched with each re-reading. The memories of the eccentric Miss Havisham, her decaying cake crawling with spiders, the sparring of the mysterious Pale Young Gentleman, and of course, the alternatingly endearing and annoying Pip are as vivid in my mind as memories of real-life people and events.

I was lucky enough to have a teacher who helped me develop that taste, not only for Dickens but for all of the demands that good literature makes upon readers. The difference between a great book and one written (and read) merely to entertain or pass the time is that good literature demands an investment from the reader in order to reap its rewards. Reading good literature well doesn't always come easily. Sometimes the challenge of literary art presents itself in its otherness (being by or about people from times and places vastly different from ours). Almost always the challenge comes from the artful use of language—words sparer, richer, less direct, or more resonant than those we use in everyday speech.

Both of these challenges—otherness and artfulness—are present in Dickens for today's readers. Dickens's style is difficult for those of us habituated to the plain, flat prose of cable news, blog posts, Twitter feeds, or Ernest Hemingway. To read Dickens well, not only for newcomers but even for me, a seasoned reader, requires deliberately arming ourselves against our usual hurry and our shortening attention spans. Readers of Dickens need to be willing to slow their reading pace, luxuriate in the circumlocutory sentences, re-read passages that take unexpected turns, and tune their ears to the cadence of the multiple voices that inhabit Dickens's busy, busy world. Whether the massive *Bleak House* or the short but still demanding *A Christmas Carol*, Dickens requires a commitment of time, attention, effort, and patience.

But that commitment is well worth it. For even beyond the literary merits of his works, Dickens puts forth, as Gina Dalfonzo explains in the introduction, a profoundly Christian view of the world. And while the redemptive elements are some of the strongest within the body of his work, perhaps what can speak most powerfully to our world today is the theme of guilt. Dickens is prophetic in the way he illuminates the distinctions we of a modern, increasingly secular world often fail to make between real guilt and false shame, between true repentance and cheap substitutions. More and more today—as in the world of these novels—the truly guilty feel no shame, those who feel greatly ashamed are the most innocent, and those who say they're sorry don't have the godly sorrow that brings repentance.

Thus, the division of the excerpts from Dickens's work into sections on sin, repentance, and righteousness is true not only to Dickens's major concerns but to ones we ought to have today as well. While this volume is a curated selection, this arrangement and the introduction offer a picture of Dickens's entire corpus. To return to my opening metaphor, the wide-ranging, insightfully arranged selections here encourage those whose souls thirst for more to follow the exhortation of Alexander Pope, a poet who lived a century before Dickens:

> Drink deep, or taste not the Pierian spring:
> There shallow draughts intoxicate the brain,
> And drinking largely sobers us again.

Karen Swallow Prior
Author, On Reading Well
January 2020

Introduction

I was fourteen years old, a ninth-grader in Mrs. Danelo's English class, when I encountered the works of Charles Dickens for the first time. (Aside from the beloved Disney animated short *Mickey's Christmas Carol*, that is.) We had an abridged version of *Great Expectations* in our literature books, and after reading it for class, I headed straight to the library for the real thing. No mere abridgment would do; I had to experience the full force of *all* of those words, those beguiling, downright magical words. And not just the words, but the spirit behind them—cynical and hopeful, knowing and questioning, wistful and hilarious, all in one. I've been entranced by those words and that spirit ever since.

As an avid reader of Dickens for thirty years now, I'm particularly sensitive to misunderstandings and misinterpretations of his work. Thus, I confess to feeling a twinge of irritation every time I hear someone say, "Well, you know he was paid by the word." There are a couple of reasons for that irritation. First, the charge simply isn't true; Dickens was not paid by the word but rather by installment for books that he published serially.[1]

The other, deeper reason for my irritation is the skeptical assumptions that tend to be bound up in the charge. More

1 "Was Dickens Really Paid by the Word?," The Dickens Project, University of California at Santa Cruz.

often than not, it's made by people who are finding Dickens overly wordy or just plain overwhelming—which, in an age much terser than that of the verbose Victorians, is not hard to understand. But it's become a sort of shorthand way to dismiss altogether what he has to offer, a way of accusing him of bloating what otherwise would have been much leaner, more comprehensible novels and stories for the sake of money, puffing his works up into monstrosities that no reasonable twenty-first-century reader should be expected to tackle.

This charge, too, is far from the truth, as anyone who has paid careful and loving attention to Dickens can tell you. This is simply who he was, a man and a writer overflowing with high spirits, given to wearing out himself and everyone else with thirty-mile walks, exuberant parties, and elaborate theatricals. He had what G. K. Chesterton, one of his most fervent admirers, called "an incomparable hunger for the vitality and the variety, for the infinite eccentricity of existence."[2] Dickens acted out scenes in the mirror as he wrote them and stunned audiences with the almost frightening intensity of his public readings. Words simply poured out of him, joyfully or at times mournfully (he confessed to weeping over the deaths of his own characters). He wore his heart on his sleeve, and the vivid creations of his pen *were* his heart.

There are those who express doubt about whether Dickens actually had any Christian faith to speak of, or whether the expressions of faith in his work arose simply from his being a man of his time, when such expressions were expected. Again, this arises from a fundamental misunderstanding of who Dickens was. There were parts of his life—from his early experiences with poverty and child labor to his marital troubles—that he carefully hid from view, or at least referred to in

---

2 G. K. Chesterton, *Charles Dickens* (New York: Dodd, Mead & Co., 1906), 289.

ways so oblique that only those closest to him had any idea of their significance. Charles Dickens was certainly not one to fake a religious enthusiasm or concoct fictitious spiritual insights or experiences for public consumption.

As a matter of fact, some of his supposedly Christian characters are so villainous as to throw many readers completely off the scent. As Peggy Fletcher Stack wrote in the *Washington Post* on the 200th anniversary of his birth, "Dickens, a member of the Church of England, believed deeply in Jesus as Savior and in his moral teachings, but many of the novelist's most avowedly Christian characters represent the worst in religion: greed, hypocrisy, indifference to human suffering, arrogance, self-righteousness and theological bullying." She quotes English professor Brian McCuskey as saying, "He was more interested in the general spirit than the specific letter of the faith. . . . Holding broad, loose beliefs, he had little patience for either institutional or evangelical Christianity."[3]

There is something to this view. Dickens is, after all, the man who made "beadle" (a church official who dealt with parish matters) a bad word thanks to his searing portrayal of the pompous Mr. Bumble in *Oliver Twist*, and a writer who mercilessly lampooned religious hypocrites every chance he got. Dickens worked tirelessly with Christians such as philanthropist Angela Burdett-Coutts to raise money, start schools, and run rehabilitation efforts for the destitute and fallen, but he wanted little to do with denominational or doctrinal disputes. He considered these worthless and divisive, and thought they took up time and energy that should have been used to help those in need. Indeed, he often warned his coworkers in these charitable endeavors against trying to force religion on the people they were helping, and in particular against too much emphasis

3 Peggy Fletcher Stack, "Dickens and Religion: A Tale of Two Views," *Washington Post*, February 7, 2012.

on divine wrath. He wrote a book about Christ, *The Life of Our Lord*, for his children, but focused more on the humanity of Christ than on his divinity. Much has been made of Dickens's involvement with Unitarianism, a faith that attracted him precisely because he saw its members putting the needs of the poor and oppressed above doctrinal nitpicking.

Still, there is ample evidence that in all this Dickens considered himself to be policing his own side, not joining the forces arrayed against religion. More than that, he had a deep and instinctive understanding of the gospel that, however unorthodox he could be at times, placed him firmly within the Christian tradition. As Gary Colledge puts it in *God and Charles Dickens*, "His narrative world emerged from his own uncompromising Christian worldview, and his characters were measured against the teaching and example of Jesus. As a result, Dickens wrote with a characteristic sense of Christian commitment and moral obligation that was firmly rooted in the Scriptures, particularly the New Testament, and with what Andrew Sanders so brilliantly refers to as the desire for a 'continued awakening of the Christian conscience.'"[4]

When Dickens satirizes or even condemns religious people, then, it is not because he is anti-religion, but because he is measuring them against the standard set by Jesus and finds them wanting. When, in *Bleak House*, he excoriates the missionary societies who preach loudly about the need to reach foreign peoples even as they allow an orphan to starve on their doorstep, it is with an anguished awareness of what they could and should be doing. In *Barnaby Rudge*, he harshly judges the anti-Catholic forces that sparked the Gordon Riots of 1780, not because he has any "sympathy" with the Catholic Church—he admits that

4 Gary L. Colledge, *God and Charles Dickens: Recovering the Christian Voice of a Classic Author* (Grand Rapids: Brazos Press, 2012), 3–4.

he has not[5]—but because he recognizes "that what we falsely call a religious cry is easily raised by men who have no religion, and who in their daily practice set at nought the commonest principles of right and wrong; that it is begotten of intolerance and persecution; that it is senseless, besotted, inveterate and unmerciful."[6]

It was religious hypocrisy that Dickens hated, not religion, and he was quite open about that fact. In 1861 he wrote to the Reverend David Macrae, who had failed to recognize the Christianity of his good characters:

> With a deep sense of my great responsibility always upon me when I exercise my art, one of my most constant and most earnest endeavours has been to exhibit in all my good people some faint reflections of the teachings of our great Master, and unostentatiously to lead the reader up to those teachings as the great source of all moral goodness. All my strongest illustrations are derived from the New Testament. All my social abuses are shown as departures from its Spirit. All my good people are humble, charitable, faithful, forgiving, over and over again. I claim them in expressed words as disciples of the Founder of our religion; but I must admit that to a man (or woman) they all arise and wash their faces, and do not appear unto men to fast.[7]

Those last words, a direct reference to Jesus' words in Matthew 6:17–18, signal what Dickens was trying to do—to create real characters who happened to be people of faith, not faith-based caricatures written solely to provide a moral message. (Perhaps

5 Charles Dickens, preface to the 1849 edition, *Barnaby Rudge*. Oddly enough, though, Dickens once had a vivid and realistic dream in which his beloved late sister-in-law Mary told him that Catholicism was "the best" religion for him. See Charles Dickens, letter to John Forster, September 30, 1844, *The Selected Letters of Charles Dickens*, ed. Jenny Hartley (Oxford: Oxford University Press, 2012), 144.

6 Charles Dickens, preface to the 1849 edition, *Barnaby Rudge*.

7 Charles Dickens, letter to David Macrae, 1861, *Selected Letters*, 364.

"real" is not quite the right word here, as so many of his characters were bigger than life! What I mean is that they were created first and foremost to be characters, not walking and talking moral lessons.)

Those words also, incidentally, signal something else: Dickens's immersion in Scripture. He knew it well and quoted and alluded to it frequently throughout his writings. Bible reading and prayer were both lifelong habits for him, habits that he also urged on others, especially his children. The teachings of the Bible were deeply ingrained in his mind—so deeply that they came out in all kinds of ways: not just in the actions of his characters, but in the words he chose, in his ability to show glimmers of hope in the midst of darkness, and in the very structure of his works. Even the coincidences he was so fond of putting into his books had their basis in his conception of Christianity. "In his writing," explains Keith Hooper in his book *Charles Dickens: Faith, Angels and the Poor*, "these coincidences more closely resemble providential appointments."[8]

Of course, like all of us, Dickens failed to live up to that perfect standard exhibited by Christ. He could be every bit as proud, stubborn, and selfish as he was compassionate, generous, and affectionate. And his marriage to Catherine Hogarth Dickens effectively ended in 1857 when he fell in love with actress Ellen Ternan. (Biographers still debate the exact nature and extent of his relationship with Ellen, but what no one disputes is that he made Catherine's life miserable.) He attempted to brazen things out in public, keeping Ternan's name quiet and portraying his critics as vicious rumormongers. As he himself had once written in *Little Dorrit*, "Only the wisdom that holds the clue to all hearts and all mysteries, can surely know to what extent a man . . . can

---

8 Keith Hooper, *Charles Dickens: Faith, Angels and the Poor* (Oxford: Lion Hudson, 2017), 27.

impose upon himself."[9] Privately, however, Dickens admitted to Burdett-Coutts, "I do not suppose myself blameless, but in this thing as in all others know, every day more and more, how much I stand in need of the highest of all charity and mercy."[10]

In his works, in spite of—or because of?—his own failings, Dickens never stopped expressing the fundamental truths of fall, repentance, redemption, and restoration found in the gospel. I have chosen excerpts from his work that exemplify these themes, and have followed that structure in laying them out. In some passages the Christian elements are explicit (for example, when particular characters pray for forgiveness in *Oliver Twist* and *A Tale of Two Cities*), in others implicit (some may be surprised to see the beating of the schoolmaster in *Nicholas Nickleby* included), but I believe that, as Dickens himself said, they all reflect in some way his understanding of and reverence for the gospel, and, more than that, his sense of his own great need for it.

Dickens could hide many things—even from himself—but he could not conceal or bury his own hunger for these truths. He wrote into his greatest works again and again the narratives of guilt and salvation that he knew he himself needed to remember. They still speak to us, all these years later, of our own greatest needs. With Pip, with Sydney Carton, with Nancy, with Charles Dickens himself, may we never stop reaching out for the truth that heals and restores; with the brusque but humane Betsey Trotwood, may we always come back to this prayer: "God forgive us all!"[11]

Gina Dalfonzo
January 2020

9 Dickens, *Little Dorrit*, Book the First, Chapter 19.

10 Dickens, letter to Angela Burdett-Coutts, April 8, 1860, *Selected Letters*, 353.

11 Dickens, *David Copperfield*, Chapter 54: "Mr. Micawber's Transactions."

A Dickens Bibliography

Major Works (with original dates of publication)

Sketches by Boz, 1836

The Pickwick Papers, 1836–7

Oliver Twist, 1837–9

Nicholas Nickleby, 1838–9

The Old Curiosity Shop, 1840–1

Barnaby Rudge, 1841

Martin Chuzzlewit, 1843–4

A Christmas Carol, 1843

Dombey and Son, 1846–8

David Copperfield, 1849–50

Bleak House, 1852–3

Hard Times, 1854

Little Dorrit, 1855–7

A Tale of Two Cities, 1859

Great Expectations, 1860–1

Our Mutual Friend, 1864–5

The Mystery of Edwin Drood, 1870

Minor Works Quoted in This Book

Sunday under Three Heads, 1836

The Haunted Man and the Ghost's Bargain, 1848

The Life of Our Lord, 1934

I

Sin and Its Victims

1. A Tight-Fisted Hand

A Christmas Carol

Dickens saved his greatest wrath for those who hardened their hearts against the poor. As this famous description of the miser Ebenezer Scrooge from A Christmas Carol *shows, he also saved for them some of his most striking and colorful imagery.*

Oh! But he was a tight-fisted hand at the grindstone, Scrooge! A squeezing, wrenching, grasping, scraping, clutching, covetous, old sinner! Hard and sharp as flint, from which no steel had ever struck out generous fire; secret, and self-contained, and solitary as an oyster. The cold within him froze his old features, nipped his pointed nose, shrivelled his cheek, stiffened his gait; made his eyes red, his thin lips blue; and spoke out shrewdly in his grating voice. A frosty rime was on his head, and on his eyebrows, and his wiry chin. He carried his own low temperature always about with him; he iced his office in the dog-days; and didn't thaw it one degree at Christmas.

External heat and cold had little influence on Scrooge. No warmth could warm, no wintry weather chill him. No wind that blew was bitterer than he, no falling snow was more intent upon its purpose, no pelting rain less open to entreaty. Foul weather didn't know where to have him. The heaviest rain, and snow, and hail, and sleet, could boast of the advantage over him in only one respect. They often "came down" handsomely, and Scrooge never did.

Nobody ever stopped him in the street to say, with gladsome looks, "My dear Scrooge, how are you? When will you come to see me?" No beggars implored him to bestow a trifle, no children asked him what it was o'clock, no man or woman ever once in all his life inquired the way to such and such a place, of Scrooge.

Even the blind men's dogs appeared to know him; and when they saw him coming on, would tug their owners into doorways and up courts; and then would wag their tails as though they said, "No eye at all is better than an evil eye, dark master!"

But what did Scrooge care! It was the very thing he liked. To edge his way along the crowded paths of life, warning all human sympathy to keep its distance, was what the knowing ones call "nuts" to Scrooge.

When two gentlemen ask him for a charitable donation, we get the chilling worldview behind Scrooge's formidable demeanor.

"At this festive season of the year, Mr. Scrooge," said the gentleman, taking up a pen, "it is more than usually desirable that we should make some slight provision for the Poor and destitute, who suffer greatly at the present time. Many thousands are in want of common necessaries; hundreds of thousands are in want of common comforts, sir."

"Are there no prisons?" asked Scrooge.

"Plenty of prisons," said the gentleman, laying down the pen again.

"And the Union workhouses?" demanded Scrooge. "Are they still in operation?"

"They are. Still," returned the gentleman, "I wish I could say they were not."

"The Treadmill[1] and the Poor Law[2] are in full vigour, then?" said Scrooge.

"Both very busy, sir."

---

1 Used as an instrument of punishment in prisons.

2 The Poor Law of 1834 "established the punitive workhouse system." ("Dickens, Scrooge and the Victorian poor," Special Collections Exhibitions, King's College London). Dickens staunchly opposed it.

"Oh! I was afraid, from what you said at first, that something had occurred to stop them in their useful course," said Scrooge. "I'm very glad to hear it."

"Under the impression that they scarcely furnish Christian cheer of mind or body to the multitude," returned the gentleman, "a few of us are endeavouring to raise a fund to buy the Poor some meat and drink, and means of warmth. We choose this time, because it is a time, of all others, when Want is keenly felt, and Abundance rejoices. What shall I put you down for?"

"Nothing!" Scrooge replied.

"You wish to be anonymous?"

"I wish to be left alone," said Scrooge. "Since you ask me what I wish, gentlemen, that is my answer. I don't make merry myself at Christmas and I can't afford to make idle people merry. I help to support the establishments I have mentioned—they cost enough; and those who are badly off must go there."

"Many can't go there; and many would rather die."

"If they would rather die," said Scrooge, "they had better do it, and decrease the surplus population. Besides—excuse me—I don't know that."

"But you might know it," observed the gentleman.

"It's not my business," Scrooge returned. "It's enough for a man to understand his own business, and not to interfere with other people's. Mine occupies me constantly. Good afternoon, gentlemen!"

Seeing clearly that it would be useless to pursue their point, the gentlemen withdrew. Scrooge resumed his labours with an improved opinion of himself, and in a more facetious temper than was usual with him.

Stave One: "Marley's Ghost"

But that night, taken on a Christmas Eve journey through his own past, present, and future, Scrooge comes to learn that his greed and selfishness will have tragic consequences both for others and for himself. In the company of the Ghost of Christmas Present, he sees his own self-centered philosophy play out in the life and potential death of his clerk's sickly youngest son, Tiny Tim.

Then Bob proposed:

"A Merry Christmas to us all, my dears. God bless us!"

Which all the family re-echoed.

"God bless us every one!" said Tiny Tim, the last of all.

He sat very close to his father's side upon his little stool. Bob held his withered little hand in his, as if he loved the child, and wished to keep him by his side, and dreaded that he might be taken from him.

"Spirit," said Scrooge, with an interest he had never felt before, "tell me if Tiny Tim will live."

"I see a vacant seat," replied the Ghost, "in the poor chimney-corner, and a crutch without an owner, carefully preserved. If these shadows remain unaltered by the Future, the child will die."

"No, no," said Scrooge. "Oh, no, kind Spirit! say he will be spared."

"If these shadows remain unaltered by the Future, none other of my race," returned the Ghost, "will find him here. What then? If he be like to die, he had better do it, and decrease the surplus population."

Scrooge hung his head to hear his own words quoted by the Spirit, and was overcome with penitence and grief.

"Man," said the Ghost, "if man you be in heart, not adamant,[3] forbear that wicked cant until you have discovered What the

---

3 Merriam-Webster defines *adamant* in this context as "a stone (such as a diamond) formerly believed to be of impenetrable hardness," or "an unbreakable or extremely hard substance."

surplus is, and Where it is. Will you decide what men shall live, what men shall die? It may be, that in the sight of Heaven, you are more worthless and less fit to live than millions like this poor man's child. Oh God! to hear the Insect on the leaf pronouncing on the too much life among his hungry brothers in the dust!"

Scrooge bent before the Ghost's rebuke, and trembling cast his eyes upon the ground.

Stave Three: "The Second of the Three Spirits"

Still later that night, guided by the Ghost of Christmas Yet to Come, Scrooge will see another death foreshadowed—a death that he does not yet know is his own.

He recoiled in terror, for . . . he almost touched a bed: a bare, uncurtained bed: on which, beneath a ragged sheet, there lay a something covered up, which, though it was dumb, announced itself in awful language.

The room was very dark, too dark to be observed with any accuracy, though Scrooge glanced round it in obedience to a secret impulse, anxious to know what kind of room it was. A pale light, rising in the outer air, fell straight upon the bed; and on it, plundered and bereft, unwatched, unwept, uncared for, was the body of this man.

Scrooge glanced towards the Phantom. Its steady hand was pointed to the head. The cover was so carelessly adjusted that the slightest raising of it, the motion of a finger upon Scrooge's part, would have disclosed the face. He thought of it, felt how easy it would be to do, and longed to do it; but had no more power to withdraw the veil than to dismiss the spectre at his side.

Oh cold, cold, rigid, dreadful Death, set up thine altar here, and dress it with such terrors as thou hast at thy command: for this is thy dominion! But of the loved, revered, and honoured

A Christmas Carol ✦ 7

John Leech, *The Last of the Spirits*

head, thou canst not turn one hair to thy dread purposes, or make one feature odious. It is not that the hand is heavy and will fall down when released; it is not that the heart and pulse are still; but that the hand WAS open, generous, and true; the heart brave, warm, and tender; and the pulse a man's. Strike, Shadow, strike! And see his good deeds springing from the wound, to sow the world with life immortal!

No voice pronounced these words in Scrooge's ears, and yet he heard them when he looked upon the bed. He thought, if this man could be raised up now, what would be his foremost thoughts? Avarice, hard-dealing, griping cares? They have brought him to a rich end, truly!

He lay, in the dark empty house, with not a man, a woman, or a child, to say that he was kind to me in this or that, and for the memory of one kind word I will be kind to him.

Stave Four: "The Last of the Spirits"

2. Cold, Cold Heart

Great Expectations

Scrooge is not the only Dickens villain to find his life poisoned by his own malice. Miss Havisham of Great Expectations, *jilted right before her wedding, raised her adopted daughter, Estella, to be heartless and unfeeling, so that she could "wreak revenge on all the male sex."*[4] *She failed to foresee the consequences for herself.*

We were seated by the fire . . . and Miss Havisham still had Estella's arm drawn through her own, and still clutched Estella's hand in hers, when Estella gradually began to detach herself. She had shown a proud impatience more than once before, and had rather endured that fierce affection than accepted or returned it.

"What!" said Miss Havisham, flashing her eyes upon her, "are you tired of me?"

"Only a little tired of myself," replied Estella, disengaging her arm, and moving to the great chimney-piece, where she stood looking down at the fire.

"Speak the truth, you ingrate!" cried Miss Havisham, passionately striking her stick upon the floor; "you are tired of me."

Estella looked at her with perfect composure, and again looked down at the fire. Her graceful figure and her beautiful face expressed a self-possessed indifference to the wild heat of the other, that was almost cruel.

"You stock and stone!" exclaimed Miss Havisham. "You cold, cold heart!"

"What?" said Estella, preserving her attitude of indifference as she leaned against the great chimney-piece and only moving her eyes; "do you reproach me for being cold? You?"

"Are you not?" was the fierce retort.

---

4 Chapter 22.

"You should know," said Estella. "I am what you have made me. Take all the praise, take all the blame; take all the success, take all the failure; in short, take me."

"O, look at her, look at her!" cried Miss Havisham, bitterly; "Look at her, so hard and thankless, on the hearth where she was reared! Where I took her into this wretched breast when it was first bleeding from its stabs, and where I have lavished years of tenderness upon her!"

"At least I was no party to the compact," said Estella, "for if I could walk and speak, when it was made, it was as much as I could do. But what would you have? You have been very good to me, and I owe everything to you. What would you have?"

"Love," replied the other.

"You have it."

"I have not," said Miss Havisham.

"Mother by adoption," retorted Estella, never departing from the easy grace of her attitude, never raising her voice as the other did, never yielding either to anger or tenderness, "Mother by adoption, I have said that I owe everything to you. All I possess is freely yours. All that you have given me, is at your command to have again. Beyond that, I have nothing. And if you ask me to give you what you never gave me, my gratitude and duty cannot do impossibilities."

"Did I never give her love!" cried Miss Havisham, turning wildly to me. "Did I never give her a burning love, inseparable from jealousy at all times, and from sharp pain, while she speaks thus to me! Let her call me mad, let her call me mad!"

"Why should I call you mad," returned Estella, "I, of all people? Does any one live, who knows what set purposes you have, half as well as I do? Does any one live, who knows what a steady memory you have, half as well as I do? I who have sat on this same hearth on the little stool that is even now beside you there, learning your lessons and looking up into your face, when your face was strange and frightened me!"

"Soon forgotten!" moaned Miss Havisham. "Times soon forgotten!"

"No, not forgotten," retorted Estella. "Not forgotten, but treasured up in my memory. When have you found me false to your teaching? When have you found me unmindful of your lessons? When have you found me giving admission here," she touched her bosom with her hand, "to anything that you excluded? Be just to me."

"So proud, so proud!" moaned Miss Havisham, pushing away her grey hair with both her hands.

"Who taught me to be proud?" returned Estella. "Who praised me when I learnt my lesson?"

"So hard, so hard!" moaned Miss Havisham, with her former action.

"Who taught me to be hard?" returned Estella. "Who praised me when I learnt my lesson?"

"But to be proud and hard to *me*!" Miss Havisham quite shrieked, as she stretched out her arms. "Estella, Estella, Estella, to be proud and hard to *me*!"

Estella looked at her for a moment with a kind of calm wonder, but was not otherwise disturbed; when the moment was past, she looked down at the fire again.

"I cannot think," said Estella, raising her eyes after a silence, "why you should be so unreasonable when I come to see you after a separation. I have never forgotten your wrongs and their causes. I have never been unfaithful to you or your schooling. I have never shown any weakness that I can charge myself with."

"Would it be weakness to return my love?" exclaimed Miss Havisham. "But yes, yes, she would call it so!"

"I begin to think," said Estella, in a musing way, after another moment of calm wonder, "that I almost understand how this comes about. If you had brought up your adopted daughter wholly in the dark confinement of these rooms, and had never let her know that there was such a thing as the daylight by which she has never once seen your face—if you had done that, and then, for a purpose, had wanted her to understand the daylight and know all about it, you would have been disappointed and angry?"

Miss Havisham, with her head in her hands, sat making a low moaning, and swaying herself on her chair, but gave no answer.

"Or," said Estella, "—which is a nearer case—if you had taught her, from the dawn of her intelligence, with your utmost energy and might, that there was such a thing as daylight, but that it was made to be her enemy and destroyer, and she must always turn against it, for it had blighted you and would else blight her;—if you had done this, and then, for a purpose, had wanted her to take naturally to the daylight and she could not do it, you would have been disappointed and angry?"

Miss Havisham sat listening (or it seemed so, for I could not see her face), but still made no answer.

"So," said Estella, "I must be taken as I have been made. The success is not mine, the failure is not mine, but the two together make me."

Miss Havisham had settled down, I hardly knew how, upon the floor, among the faded bridal relics with which it was strewn. I took advantage of the moment—I had sought one from the first—to leave the room, after beseeching Estella's attention to her with a movement of my hand. When I left, Estella was yet standing by the great chimney-piece, just as she had stood throughout. Miss Havisham's grey hair was all adrift upon the ground, among the other bridal wrecks, and was a miserable sight to see.

Chapter 38

3. Turtle Soup and Venison

Hard Times

As callous as Scrooge and Miss Havisham are, there is still something deep inside them that is willing to hear the call of redemption, as we will see. The same cannot be said of all Dickens's villains. Wealthy industrialist Josiah Bounderby of Hard Times *is well aware of the terrible conditions in which his factory workers, or "Hands," live and work, but as we see in his conversation with a guest, Mr. Harthouse, he pretends that those conditions are ideal and that any appeals for relief are little more than the demands of spoiled children.*

"Coketown, sir," said Bounderby, obstinately taking a chair, "is not the kind of place you have been accustomed to. Therefore, if you will allow me—or whether you will or not, for I am a plain man—I'll tell you something about it before we go any further."

Mr. Harthouse would be charmed.

"Don't be too sure of that," said Bounderby. "I don't promise it. First of all, you see our smoke. That's meat and drink to us. It's the healthiest thing in the world in all respects, and particularly for the lungs. If you are one of those who want us to consume it, I differ from you. We are not going to wear the bottoms of our boilers out any faster than we wear 'em out now, for all the humbugging sentiment in Great Britain and Ireland."

By way of "going in" to the fullest extent, Mr. Harthouse rejoined, "Mr. Bounderby, I assure you I am entirely and completely of your way of thinking. On conviction."

"I am glad to hear it," said Bounderby. "Now, you have heard a lot of talk about the work in our mills, no doubt. You have? Very good. I'll state the fact of it to you. It's the pleasantest work there is, and it's the lightest work there is, and it's the best paid work there is. More than that, we couldn't improve the mills themselves, unless we laid down Turkey carpets on the floors. Which we're not a-going to do."

"Mr. Bounderby, perfectly right."

"Lastly," said Bounderby, "as to our Hands. There's not a Hand in this town, sir, man, woman, or child, but has one ultimate object in life. That object is, to be fed on turtle soup and venison with a gold spoon. Now, they're not a-going—none of 'em—ever to be fed on turtle soup and venison with a gold spoon. And now you know the place."

Mr. Harthouse professed himself in the highest degree instructed and refreshed, by this condensed epitome of the whole Coketown question.

Book the Second: "Reaping," Chapter 2: "Mr. James Harthouse"

When Mr. Bounderby is confronted directly with the poverty and misery of these workers, his response, unlike Scrooge's, is to double down on his cruel insensitivity. We see this in his interactions with Stephen Blackpool, a Hand in particularly dire circumstances.

"Now, what do you complain of?" asked Mr. Bounderby.

"I ha' not coom here, sir," Stephen reminded him, "to complain. I coom for that I were sent for."

"What," repeated Mr. Bounderby, folding his arms, "do you people, in a general way, complain of?"

Stephen looked at him with some little irresolution for a moment, and then seemed to make up his mind.

"Sir, I were never good at showin o't, though I ha had'n my share in feeling o't. 'Deed we are in a muddle, sir. Look round town—so rich as 'tis—and see the numbers o' people as has been broughten into bein heer, fur to weave, an to card, an to piece out a livin', aw the same one way, somehows, twixt their cradles and their graves. Look how we live, an wheer we live, an in what numbers, an by what chances, and wi' what sameness; and look how the mills is awlus a goin, and how they never works us no nigher to ony dis'ant object—ceptin awlus, Death. Look how you considers of us, and writes of us, and talks of us, and goes up wi' yor deputations to Secretaries o' State 'bout us, and how yo are awlus right, and how we are awlus wrong, and never had 'n no reason in us sin ever we were born. Look how this ha growen an growen, sir, bigger an bigger, broader an broader, harder an harder, fro year to year, fro generation unto generation. Who can look on't, sir, and fairly tell a man 'tis not a muddle?"

"Of course," said Mr. Bounderby. "Now perhaps you'll let the gentleman know, how you would set this muddle (as you're so fond of calling it) to rights." . . .

"Sir, I canna, wi' my little learning an my common way, tell the genelman what will better aw this—though some working men o' this town could, above my powers—but I can tell him what I know will never do 't. The strong hand will never do 't. Vict'ry and triumph will never do 't. Agreeing fur to mak one side unnat'rally awlus and for ever right, and toother side unnat'rally awlus and for ever wrong, will never, never do 't. Nor yet lettin alone will never do 't. Let thousands upon thousands alone, aw leading the like lives and aw faw'en into the like muddle, and they will be as one, and yo will be as anoother, wi' a black unpassable world betwixt yo, just as long or short a time as sitch-like misery can last. Not drawin nigh to fok, wi' kindness and patience an cheery ways, that so draws nigh to one another in their monny troubles, and so cherishes one another in their distresses wi' what they need themseln—like, I humbly believe, as no people the genelman ha seen in aw his travels can beat—will never do 't till th' Sun turns t' ice. Most o' aw, rating 'em as so much Power, and reg'latin 'em as if they was figures in a soom, or machines: wi'out loves and likens, wi'out memories and inclinations, wi'out souls to weary and souls to hope—when aw goes quiet, draggin on wi' 'em as if they'd nowt o' th' kind, and when aw goes onquiet, reproachin 'em for their want o' sitch humanly feelins in their dealins wi' yo—this will never do 't, sir, till God's work is onmade."

Stephen stood with the open door in his hand, waiting to know if anything more were expected of him.

"Just stop a moment," said Mr. Bounderby, excessively red in the face. "I told you, the last time you were here with a grievance, that you had better turn about and come out of that. And I also told you, if you remember, that I was up to the gold spoon look-out."

"I were not up to 't myseln, sir; I do assure yo."

"Now it's clear to me," said Mr. Bounderby, "that you are one of those chaps who have always got a grievance. And you go about, sowing it and raising crops. That's the business of your life, my friend."

Stephen shook his head, mutely protesting that indeed he had other business to do for his life.

"You are such a waspish, raspish, ill-conditioned chap, you see," said Mr. Bounderby, "that even your own Union, the men who know you best, will have nothing to do with you. I never thought those fellows could be right in anything; but I tell you what! I so far go along with them for a novelty, that I'll have nothing to do with you either."

Stephen raised his eyes quickly to his face.

"You can finish off what you're at," said Mr. Bounderby, with a meaning nod, "and then go elsewhere."

"Sir, yo know weel," said Stephen expressively, "that if I canna get work wi' yo, I canna get it elsewheer."

The reply was, "What I know, I know; and what you know, you know. I have no more to say about it."

Stephen glanced at Louisa again, but her eyes were raised to his no more; therefore, with a sigh, and saying, barely above his breath, "Heaven help us aw in this world!" he departed.

Book the Second: "Reaping," Chapter 5: "Men and Masters"

4. Around Us Every Day

Bleak House

Dickens was particularly hard on Christians who failed to live up to Christ's call to care for the poor. Bleak House *is full of such types, and it goes into great, grim detail about the devastating effects of their callousness on those whom they neglect and condemn.*

One such negligent character is Mr. Chadband, the minister who makes an example of an impoverished young street sweeper known simply as Jo, who lives in a slum called Tom-all-Alone's.

"My friends," says Chadband, "we have partaken in moderation" (which was certainly not the case so far as he was concerned) "of the comforts which have been provided for us. May this house live upon the fatness of the land; may corn and wine be plentiful therein; may it grow, may it thrive, may it prosper, may it advance, may it proceed, may it press forward! But, my friends, have we partaken of anything else? We have. My friends, of what else have we partaken? Of spiritual profit? Yes. From whence have we derived that spiritual profit? My young friend, stand forth!"

Jo, thus apostrophised, gives a slouch backward, and another slouch forward, and another slouch to each side, and confronts the eloquent Chadband, with evident doubts of his intentions.

"My young friend," says Chadband, "you are to us a pearl, you are to us a diamond, you are to us a gem, you are to us a jewel. And why, my young friend?"

"*I* don't know," replies Jo. "I don't know nothink."

"My young friend," says Chadband, "it is because you know nothing that you are to us a gem and jewel. For what are you, my young friend? Are you a beast of the field? No. A bird of the air? No. A fish of the sea or river? No. You are a human boy, my young friend. A human boy. O glorious to be a human boy! And why glorious, my young friend? Because you are capable of receiving the lessons of wisdom, because you are capable of

Hablot Knight Browne, *Mr. Chadband "Improving" a Tough Subject*

profiting by this discourse which I now deliver for your good, because you are not a stick, or a staff, or a stock, or a stone, or a post, or a pillar.

> O running stream of sparkling joy
> To be a soaring human boy!

And do you cool yourself in that stream now, my young friend? No. Why do you not cool yourself in that stream now? Because you are in a state of darkness, because you are in a state of obscurity, because you are in a state of sinfulness, because you are in a state of bondage. My young friend, what *is* bondage? Let us, in a spirit of love, inquire."

At this threatening stage of the discourse, Jo, who seems to have been gradually going out of his mind, smears his right arm over his face, and gives a terrible yawn. Mrs. Snagsby indignantly expresses her belief that he is a limb of the arch-fiend.

"My friends," says Mr. Chadband, with his persecuted chin folding itself into its fat smile again as he looks round, "it is right that I should be humbled, it is right that I should be tried, it is right that I should be mortified, it is right that I should be corrected. I stumbled, on Sabbath last, when I thought with pride of my three hours' improving. The account is now favourably balanced: my creditor has accepted a composition. O let us be joyful, joyful! O let us be joyful!"

Great sensation on the part of Mrs. Snagsby.

"My friends," says Chadband, looking round him in conclusion, "I will not proceed with my young friend now. Will you come to-morrow, my young friend, and inquire of this good lady where I am to be found to deliver a discourse unto you, and will you come like the thirsty swallow upon the next day, and upon the day after that, and upon the day after that, and upon many pleasant days, to hear discourses?" (This, with a cow-like lightness.)

Jo, whose immediate object seems to be to get away on any terms, gives a shuffling nod. Mr. Guppy then throws him a penny, and Mrs. Snagsby calls to Guster to see him safely out of the house. But before he goes downstairs, Mr. Snagsby loads him with some broken meats from the table, which he carries away, hugging in his arms.

So, Mr. Chadband—of whom the persecutors say that it is no wonder he should go on for any length of time uttering such abominable nonsense, but that the wonder rather is that he should ever leave off, having once the audacity to begin—retires into private life. . . . Jo moves on, through the long vacation, down to Blackfriars Bridge, where he finds a baking stony corner wherein to settle to his repast.

And there he sits, munching and gnawing, and looking up at the great Cross on the summit of St. Paul's Cathedral, glittering above a red and violet-tinted cloud of smoke. From the boy's face one might suppose that sacred emblem to be, in his eyes, the crowning confusion of the great, confused city—so golden, so high up, so far out of his reach. There he sits, the sun going down, the river running fast, the crowd flowing by him in two streams—everything moving on to some purpose and to one end—until he is stirred up and told to "move on" too.[5]

Chapter 19: "Moving On"

It eventually falls to Allan Woodcourt, a compassionate young doctor, to give Jo what little spiritual guidance and comfort he can before the boy's death (probably from smallpox and pneumonia, according to Dickens's descriptions).

After watching him closely a little while, Allan puts his mouth very near his ear, and says to him in a low, distinct voice:

"Jo! Did you ever know a prayer?"

"Never knowd nothink, sir."

"Not so much as one short prayer?"

"No, sir. Nothink at all. Mr. Chadbands he wos a-prayin wunst at Mr. Sangsby's and I heerd him, but he sounded as if he wos a-speakin' to hisself, and not to me. He prayed a lot, but *I* couldn't make out nothink on it. Different times there was other genlmen come down Tom-all-Alone's a prayin, but they

5 The homeless Jo is frequently told by policemen to "move on" from wherever he happens to be.

all mostly sed as the t'other wuns prayed wrong, and all mostly sounded to be a-talking to theirselves, or a-passing blame on the t'others, and not a-talkin to us. *We* never knowd nothink. *I* never knowd what it wos all about."

It takes him a long time to say this; and few but an experienced and attentive listener could hear, or, hearing, understand him. . . .

"It's turned wery dark, sir. Is there any light a-comin?"

"It is coming fast, Jo."

Fast. The cart is shaken all to pieces, and the rugged road is very near its end.

"Jo, my poor fellow!"

"I hear you, sir, in the dark, but I'm a-gropin—a-gropin—let me catch hold of your hand."

"Jo, can you say what I say?"

"I'll say anythink as you say, sir, for I knows it's good."

"OUR FATHER."

"Our Father!—Yes, that's wery good, sir."

"WHICH ART IN HEAVEN."

"Art in heaven—is the light a-comin, sir?"

"It is close at hand. HALLOWED BE THY NAME!"

"Hallowed be—thy—"

The light is come upon the dark benighted way. Dead!

Dead, your Majesty. Dead, my lords and gentlemen. Dead, Right Reverends and Wrong Reverends of every order. Dead, men and women, born with Heavenly compassion in your hearts. And dying thus around us every day.

Chapter 47: "Jo's Will"

5. I Want Some More

Oliver Twist

Dickens calls out not just Christians who neglect the poor, but also those who pretend to care for them but leave them worse off than they were before. One of the most famous examples is Mr. Bumble, the beadle, and his heartless treatment of the hungry young orphans in the workhouse, with backup from its board.

Mr. Bumble walked on with long strides; little Oliver, firmly grasping his gold-laced cuff, trotted beside him, inquiring at the end of every quarter of a mile whether they were "nearly there." To these interrogations Mr. Bumble returned very brief and snappish replies; for the temporary blandness which gin-and-water awakens in some bosoms had by this time evaporated; and he was once again a beadle.

Oliver had not been within the walls of the workhouse a quarter of an hour, and had scarcely completed the demolition of a second slice of bread, when Mr. Bumble, who had handed him over to the care of an old woman, returned; and, telling him it was a board night, informed him that the board had said he was to appear before it forthwith.

Not having a very clearly defined notion of what a live board was, Oliver was rather astounded by this intelligence, and was not quite certain whether he ought to laugh or cry. He had no time to think about the matter, however; for Mr. Bumble gave him a tap on the head, with his cane, to wake him up: and another on the back to make him lively: and bidding him follow, conducted him into a large whitewashed room, where eight or ten fat gentlemen were sitting round a table. At the top of the table, seated in an arm-chair rather higher than the rest, was a particularly fat gentleman with a very round, red face.

"Bow to the board," said Bumble. Oliver brushed away two or three tears that were lingering in his eyes; and seeing no board but the table, fortunately bowed to that.

"What's your name, boy?" said the gentleman in the high chair.

Oliver was frightened at the sight of so many gentlemen, which made him tremble: and the beadle gave him another tap behind, which made him cry. These two causes made him answer in a very low and hesitating voice; whereupon a gentleman in a white waistcoat said he was a fool. Which was a capital way of raising his spirits, and putting him quite at his ease.

"Boy," said the gentleman in the high chair, "listen to me. You know you're an orphan, I suppose?"

"What's that, sir?" inquired poor Oliver.

"The boy *is* a fool—I thought he was," said the gentleman in the white waistcoat.

"Hush!" said the gentleman who had spoken first. "You know you've got no father or mother, and that you were brought up by the parish, don't you?"

"Yes, sir," replied Oliver, weeping bitterly.

"What are you crying for?" inquired the gentleman in the white waistcoat. And to be sure it was very extraordinary. What *could* the boy be crying for?

"I hope you say your prayers every night," said another gentleman in a gruff voice; "and pray for the people who feed you, and take care of you—like a Christian."

"Yes, sir," stammered the boy. The gentleman who spoke last was unconsciously right. It would have been *very* like a Christian, and a marvellously good Christian, too, if Oliver had prayed for the people who fed and took care of *him*. But he hadn't, because nobody had taught him.

"Well! You have come here to be educated, and taught a useful trade," said the red-faced gentleman in the high chair.

"So you'll begin to pick oakum to-morrow morning at six o'clock," added the surly one in the white waistcoat.

For the combination of both these blessings in the one simple process of picking oakum, Oliver bowed low by the direction of the beadle, and was then hurried away to a large ward: where, on a rough, hard bed, he sobbed himself to sleep. What a noble illustration of the tender laws of England! They let the paupers go to sleep!

Poor Oliver! He little thought, as he lay sleeping in happy unconsciousness of all around him, that the board had that very day arrived at a decision which would exercise the most material influence over all his future fortunes. But they had. And this was it:

The members of this board were very sage, deep, philosophical men; and when they came to turn their attention to the workhouse, they found out at once, what ordinary folks would never have discovered—the poor people liked it! It was a regular place of public entertainment for the poorer classes; a tavern where there was nothing to pay; a public breakfast, dinner, tea, and supper all the year round; a brick and mortar Elysium, where it was all play and no work. "Oho!" said the board, looking very knowing; "we are the fellows to set this to rights; we'll stop it all, in no time." So, they established the rule, that all poor people should have the alternative (for they would compel nobody, not they), of being starved by a gradual process in the house, or by a quick one out of it. With this view, they contracted with the water-works to lay on an unlimited supply of water; and with a corn-factor to supply periodically small quantities of oatmeal; and issued three meals of thin gruel a day, with an onion twice a week, and half a roll on Sundays. They made a great many other wise and humane regulations, having reference to the ladies, which it is not necessary to repeat; kindly undertook to divorce poor married people, in consequence of the great expense of a suit in Doctors' Commons; and, instead of compelling a man to support his family, as they had heretofore done, took his family away from him, and made him a bachelor! There is no saying how many applicants for relief, under these last two heads, might have started up in all classes of society, if it had not been coupled with the workhouse; but the board were long-headed men, and had provided for this difficulty. The relief was inseparable from the workhouse and the gruel; and that frightened people.

For the first six months after Oliver Twist was removed, the system was in full operation. It was rather expensive at first, in consequence of the increase in the undertaker's bill, and the necessity of taking in the clothes of all the paupers, which fluttered loosely on their wasted, shrunken forms, after a week or two's gruel. But the number of workhouse inmates got thin as well as the paupers; and the board were in ecstasies.

The room in which the boys were fed, was a large stone hall, with a copper at one end: out of which the master, dressed in an apron for the purpose, and assisted by one or two women, ladled the gruel at meal-times. Of this festive composition each boy had one porringer, and no more—except on occasions of great public rejoicing, when he had two ounces and a quarter of bread besides. The bowls never wanted washing. The boys polished them with their spoons till they shone again; and when they had performed this operation (which never took very long, the spoons being nearly as large as the bowls), they would sit staring at the copper, with such eager eyes, as if they could have devoured the very bricks of which it was composed; employing themselves, meanwhile, in sucking their fingers most assiduously, with the view of catching up any stray splashes of gruel that might have been cast thereon. Boys have generally excellent appetites. Oliver Twist and his companions suffered the tortures of slow starvation for three months: at last they got so voracious and wild with hunger, that one boy, who was tall for his age, and hadn't been used to that sort of thing (for his father had kept a small cook-shop), hinted darkly to his companions, that unless he had another basin of gruel *per diem*, he was afraid he might some night happen to eat the boy who slept next him, who happened to be a weakly youth of tender age. He had a wild, hungry eye; and they implicitly believed him. A council was held; lots were cast who should walk up to the master after supper that evening, and ask for more; and it fell to Oliver Twist.

The evening arrived; the boys took their places. The master, in his cook's uniform, stationed himself at the copper; his pauper assistants ranged themselves behind him; the gruel was served out; and a long grace was said over the short commons. The gruel disappeared; the boys whispered each other, and winked at Oliver; while his next neighbours nudged him. Child as he was, he was desperate with hunger, and reckless with misery. He rose from the table; and advancing to the master, basin and spoon in hand, said: somewhat alarmed at his own temerity:

"Please, sir, I want some more."

The master was a fat, healthy man; but he turned very pale. He gazed in stupefied astonishment on the small rebel for some seconds, and then clung for support to the copper. The assistants were paralysed with wonder, and the boys with fear.

"What!" said the master at length, in a faint voice.

"Please, sir," replied Oliver, "I want some more."

The master aimed a blow at Oliver's head with the ladle; pinioned him in his arms; and shrieked aloud for the beadle.

George Cruikshank, *Oliver Twist Causing a Sensation in the Children's Ward of the Workhouse*

The board were sitting in solemn conclave, when Mr. Bumble rushed into the room in great excitement, and addressing the gentleman in the high chair, said:

"Mr. Limbkins, I beg your pardon, sir! Oliver Twist has asked for more!"

There was a general start. Horror was depicted on every countenance.

"For *more*!" said Mr. Limbkins. "Compose yourself, Bumble, and answer me distinctly. Do I understand that he asked for more, after he had eaten the supper allotted by the dietary?"

"He did, sir," replied Bumble.

"That boy will be hung," said the gentleman in the white waistcoat. "I know that boy will be hung."

Nobody controverted the prophetic gentleman's opinion. An animated discussion took place. Oliver was ordered into instant confinement; and a bill was next morning pasted on the outside of the gate, offering a reward of five pounds to anybody who would take Oliver Twist off the hands of the parish. In other words, five pounds and Oliver Twist were offered to any man or woman who wanted an apprentice to any trade, business, or calling.

"I never was more convinced of anything in my life," said the gentleman in the white waistcoat, as he knocked at the gate and read the bill next morning: "I never was more convinced of anything in my life, than I am that that boy will come to be hung."

Chapter 2: "Treats of Oliver Twist's Growth, Education, and Board"

6. The Parish Beadle

Sketches by Boz

Mr. Bumble was not the first beadle held up to scorn in Dickens's works. He lampooned them as a class in one of the early essays that were collected into the book Sketches by Boz.

The parish beadle is one of the most, perhaps *the* most, important member of the local administration. He is not so well off as the churchwardens, certainly, nor is he so learned as the vestry-clerk, nor does he order things quite so much his own way as either of them. But his power is very great, notwithstanding; and the dignity of his office is never impaired by the absence of efforts on his part to maintain it. The beadle of our parish is a splendid fellow. It is quite delightful to hear him, as he explains the state of the existing poor laws to the deaf old women in the board-room passage on business nights; and to hear what he said to the senior churchwarden, and what the senior churchwarden said to him; and what "we" (the beadle and the other gentlemen) came to the determination of doing. A miserable-looking woman is called into the boardroom, and represents a case of extreme destitution, affecting herself—a widow, with six small children. "Where do you live?" inquires one of the overseers. "I rents a two-pair back, gentlemen, at Mrs. Brown's, Number 3, Little King William's-alley, which has lived there this fifteen year, and knows me to be very hard-working and industrious, and when my poor husband was alive, gentlemen, as died in the hospital"—"Well, well," interrupts the overseer, taking a note of the address, "I'll send Simmons, the beadle, to-morrow morning, to ascertain whether your story is correct; and if so, I suppose you must have an order into the House—Simmons, go to this woman's the first thing to-morrow morning, will you?"

Simmons bows assent, and ushers the woman out. Her previous admiration of "the board" (who all sit behind great books, and with their hats on) fades into nothing before her respect for her lace-trimmed conductor; and her account of what has passed inside, increases—if that be possible—the marks of respect, shown by the assembled crowd, to that solemn functionary. As to taking out a summons, it's quite a hopeless case if Simmons attends it, on behalf of the parish. He knows all the titles of the Lord Mayor by heart; states the case without a single stammer: and it is even reported that on one occasion he ventured to make a joke, which the Lord Mayor's head footman (who happened to be present) afterwards told an intimate friend, confidentially, was almost equal to one of Mr. Hobler's.

See him again on Sunday in his state-coat and cocked-hat, with a large-headed staff for show in his left hand, and a small cane for use in his right. How pompously he marshals the children into their places! and how demurely the little urchins look at him askance as he surveys them when they are all seated, with a glare of the eye peculiar to beadles! The churchwardens and overseers being duly installed in their curtained pews, he seats himself on a mahogany bracket, erected expressly for him at the top of the aisle, and divides his attention between his prayer-book and the boys. Suddenly, just at the commencement of the communion service, when the whole congregation is hushed into a profound silence, broken only by the voice of the officiating clergyman, a penny is heard to ring on the stone floor of the aisle with astounding clearness. Observe the generalship of the beadle. His involuntary look of horror is instantly changed into one of perfect indifference, as if he were the only person present who had not heard the noise. The artifice succeeds. After putting forth his right leg now and then, as a feeler, the victim who dropped the money ventures to make one or two distinct dives after it; and the beadle, gliding softly round, salutes his little round head, when it again appears above the seat, with divers double knocks, administered with the cane before noticed, to the intense delight of three young men in an adjacent pew, who cough violently at intervals until the conclusion of the sermon.

Such are a few traits of the importance and gravity of a parish beadle—a gravity which has never been disturbed in any case that has come under our observation, except when the services of that particularly useful machine, a parish fire-engine, are required: then indeed all is bustle. Two little boys run to the beadle as fast as their legs will carry them, and report from their own personal observation that some neighbouring chimney is on fire; the engine is hastily got out, and a plentiful supply of boys being obtained, and harnessed to it with ropes, away they rattle over the pavement, the beadle, running—we do not exaggerate—running at the side, until they arrive at some house, smelling strongly of soot, at the door of which the beadle knocks with considerable gravity for half-an-hour. No attention being paid to these manual applications, and the turn-cock having turned on the water, the engine turns off amidst the shouts of the boys; it pulls up once more at the workhouse, and the beadle "pulls up" the unfortunate householder next day, for the amount of his legal reward. We never saw a parish engine at a regular fire but once. It came up in gallant style—three miles and a half an hour, at least; there was a capital supply of water, and it was first on the spot. Bang went the pumps—the people cheered—the beadle perspired profusely; but it was unfortunately discovered, just as they were going to put the fire out, that nobody understood the process by which the engine was filled with water; and that eighteen boys, and a man, had exhausted themselves in pumping for twenty minutes, without producing the slightest effect!

Chapter 1: "The Beadle. The Parish Engine. The Schoolmaster."

7. A Moral Man

Martin Chuzzlewit

One of the most pompous and hypocritical Christians in all of Dickens's works is Mr. Pecksniff, who takes advantage of the truly good and decent Tom Pinch.

It has been remarked that Mr. Pecksniff was a moral man. So he was. Perhaps there never was a more moral man than Mr. Pecksniff: especially in his conversation and correspondence. It was once said of him by a homely admirer, that he had a Fortunatus's purse of good sentiments in his inside. In this particular he was like the girl in the fairy tale, except that if they were not actual diamonds which fell from his lips, they were the very brightest paste, and shone prodigiously. He was a most exemplary man: fuller of virtuous precept than a copy book. Some people likened him to a direction-post, which is always telling the way to a place, and never goes there: but these were his enemies; the shadows cast by his brightness; that was all. His very throat was moral. You saw a good deal of it. You looked over a very low fence of white cravat (whereof no man had ever beheld the tie, for he fastened it behind), and there it lay, a valley between two jutting heights of collar, serene and whiskerless before you. It seemed to say, on the part of Mr. Pecksniff, "There is no deception, ladies and gentlemen, all is peace, a holy calm pervades me." So did his hair, just grizzled with an iron-gray, which was all brushed off his forehead, and stood bolt upright, or slightly drooped in kindred action with his heavy eyelids. So did his person, which was sleek though free from corpulency. So did his manner, which was soft and oily. In a word, even his plain black suit, and state of widower, and dangling double eyeglass, all tended to the same purpose, and cried aloud, "Behold the moral Pecksniff!"

The brazen plate upon the door (which being Mr. Pecksniff's, could not lie) bore this inscription, "PECKSNIFF, ARCHITECT," to which Mr. Pecksniff, on his cards of business, added, "AND LAND SURVEYOR." In one sense, and only one, he may be said to have been a Land Surveyor on a pretty large scale, as an extensive prospect lay stretched out before the windows of his house. Of his architectural doings, nothing was clearly known, except that he had never designed or built anything; but it was generally understood that his knowledge of the science was almost awful in its profundity.

Mr. Pecksniff's professional engagements, indeed, were almost, if not entirely, confined to the reception of pupils; for the collection of rents, with which pursuit he occasionally varied and relieved his graver toils, can hardly be said to be a strictly architectural employment. His genius lay in ensnaring parents and guardians, and pocketing premiums. A young gentleman's premium being paid, and the young gentleman come to Mr. Pecksniff's house, Mr. Pecksniff borrowed his case of mathematical instruments (if silver-mounted or otherwise valuable); entreated him, from that moment, to consider himself one of the family; complimented him highly on his parents or guardians, as the case might be; and turned him loose in a spacious room on the two-pair front; where, in the company of certain drawing-boards, parallel rulers, very stiff-legged compasses, and two, or perhaps three, other young gentlemen, he improved himself, for three or five years, according to his articles, in making elevations of Salisbury Cathedral from every possible point of sight; and in constructing in the air a vast quantity of Castles, Houses of Parliament, and other Public Buildings. Perhaps in no place in the world were so many gorgeous edifices of this class erected as under Mr. Pecksniff's auspices; and if but one-twentieth part of the churches which were built in that front room, with one or other of the Miss Pecksniffs at the altar in the act of marrying the architect, could only be made available by the parliamentary commissioners, no more churches would be wanted for at least five centuries. . . .

"What is the domestic news since yesterday? John Westlock is gone, I hope?"

"Indeed no," said Charity.

"And why not?" returned her father. "His term expired yesterday. And his box was packed, I know; for I saw it, in the morning, standing in the hall."

"He slept last night at the Dragon," returned the young lady, "and had Mr. Pinch to dine with him. They spent the evening together, and Mr. Pinch was not home till very late."

"And when I saw him on the stairs this morning, Pa," said Mercy with her usual sprightliness, "he looked, oh goodness, *such* a monster! with his face all manner of colours, and his eyes as dull as if they had been boiled, and his head aching dreadfully, I am sure from the look of it, and his clothes smelling, oh it's impossible to say how strong, of"—here the young lady shuddered—"of smoke and punch."

"Now I think," said Mr. Pecksniff with his accustomed gentleness, though still with the air of one who suffered under injury without complaint, "I think Mr. Pinch might have done better than choose for his companion one who, at the close of a long intercourse, had endeavoured, as he knew, to wound my feelings. I am not quite sure that this was delicate in Mr. Pinch. I am not quite sure that this was kind in Mr. Pinch. I will go further and say, I am not quite sure that this was even ordinarily grateful in Mr. Pinch."

"But what can anyone expect from Mr. Pinch!" cried Charity, with as strong and scornful an emphasis on the name as if it would have given her unspeakable pleasure to express it, in an acted charade, on the calf of that gentleman's leg.

"Ay, ay," returned her father, raising his hand mildly: "it is very well to say what can we expect from Mr. Pinch, but Mr. Pinch is a fellow-creature, my dear; Mr. Pinch is an item in the vast total of humanity, my love; and we have a right, it is our duty, to expect in Mr. Pinch some development of those better qualities, the possession of which in our own persons inspires our humble self-respect. No," continued Mr. Pecksniff. "No! Heaven forbid that I should say, nothing can be expected from Mr. Pinch; or that I should say, nothing can be expected from any man alive (even the most degraded, which Mr. Pinch is not, no, really); but Mr. Pinch has disappointed me: he has hurt me: I think a little the worse of him on this account, but not of human nature. Oh no, no!"

"Hark!" said Miss Charity, holding up her finger, as a gentle rap was heard at the street-door. "There is the creature! Now mark my words, he has come back with John Westlock for his box, and is going to help him to take it to the mail. Only mark my words, if that isn't his intention!"

Even as she spoke, the box appeared to be in progress of conveyance from the house, but after a brief murmuring of question and answer, it was put down again, and somebody knocked at the parlour door.

"Come in!" cried Mr. Pecksniff—not severely; only virtuously. "Come in!"

An ungainly, awkward-looking man, extremely short-sighted, and prematurely bald, availed himself of this permission; and seeing that Mr. Pecksniff sat with his back towards him, gazing at the fire, stood hesitating, with the door in his hand. He was far from handsome certainly; and was drest in a snuff-coloured suit, of an uncouth make at the best, which, being shrunk with long wear, was twisted and tortured into all kinds of odd shapes; but notwithstanding his attire, and his clumsy figure, which a great stoop in his shoulders, and a ludicrous habit he had of thrusting his head forward, by no means redeemed, one would not have been disposed (unless Mr. Pecksniff said so) to consider him a bad fellow by any means. He was perhaps about thirty, but he might have been almost any age between sixteen and sixty: being one of those strange creatures who never decline into an ancient appearance, but look their oldest when they are very young, and get it over at once.

Keeping his hand upon the lock of the door, he glanced from Mr. Pecksniff to Mercy, from Mercy to Charity, and from Charity to Mr. Pecksniff again, several times; but the young ladies being as intent upon the fire as their father was, and neither of the three taking any notice of him, he was fain to say, at last,

"Oh! I beg your pardon, Mr. Pecksniff: I beg your pardon for intruding; but—"

"No intrusion, Mr. Pinch," said that gentleman very sweetly, but without looking round. "Pray be seated, Mr. Pinch. Have the goodness to shut the door, Mr. Pinch, if you please."

"Certainly, sir," said Pinch: not doing so, however, but holding it rather wider open than before, and beckoning nervously to somebody without: "Mr. Westlock, sir, hearing that you were come home—"

"Mr. Pinch, Mr. Pinch!" said Pecksniff, wheeling his chair about, and looking at him with an aspect of the deepest melancholy, "I did not expect this from you. I have not deserved this from you!"

"No, but upon my word, sir—" urged Pinch.

"The less you say, Mr. Pinch," interposed the other, "the better. I utter no complaint. Make no defence."

"No, but do have the goodness, sir," cried Pinch, with great earnestness, "if you please. Mr. Westlock, sir, going away for good and all, wishes to leave none but friends behind him. Mr. Westlock and you, sir, had a little difference the other day; you have had many little differences."

"Little differences!" cried Charity.

"Little differences!" echoed Mercy.

"My loves!" said Mr. Pecksniff, with the same serene upraising of his hand; "My dears!" After a solemn pause he meekly bowed to Mr. Pinch, as who should say, "Proceed"; but Mr. Pinch was so very much at a loss how to resume, and looked so helplessly at the two Miss Pecksniffs, that the conversation would most probably have terminated there, if a good-looking youth, newly arrived at man's estate, had not stepped forward from the doorway and taken up the thread of the discourse.

"Come, Mr. Pecksniff," he said, with a smile, "don't let there be any ill-blood between us, pray. I am sorry we have ever differed, and extremely sorry I have ever given you offence. Bear me no ill-will at parting, sir."

"I bear," answered Mr. Pecksniff, mildly, "no ill-will to any man on earth."

"I told you he didn't," said Pinch, in an under tone; "I knew he didn't! He always says he don't."

"Then you will shake hands, sir?" cried Westlock, advancing a step or two, and bespeaking Mr. Pinch's close attention by a glance.

"Umph!" said Mr. Pecksniff, in his most winning tone.

"You will shake hands, sir."

"No, John," said Mr. Pecksniff, with a calmness quite ethereal; "no, I will not shake hands, John. I have forgiven you. I had already forgiven you, even before you ceased to reproach and taunt me. I have embraced you in the spirit, John, which is better than shaking hands."

"Pinch," said the youth, turning towards him, with a hearty disgust of his late master, "what did I tell you?"

Poor Pinch looked down uneasily at Mr. Pecksniff, whose eye was fixed upon him as it had been from the first: and looking up at the ceiling again, made no reply.

"As to your forgiveness, Mr. Pecksniff," said the youth, "I'll not have it upon such terms. I won't be forgiven."

"Won't you, John?" retorted Mr. Pecksniff, with a smile. "You must. You can't help it. Forgiveness is a high quality; an exalted virtue; far above *your* control or influence, John. I *will* forgive you. You cannot move me to remember any wrong you have ever done me, John."

"Wrong!" cried the other, with all the heat and impetuosity of his age. "Here's a pretty fellow! Wrong! Wrong I have done him! He'll not even remember the five hundred pounds he had with me under false pretences; or the seventy pounds a-year for board and lodging that would have been dear at seventeen! Here's a martyr!"

"Money, John," said Mr. Pecksniff, "is the root of all evil. I grieve to see that it is already bearing evil fruit in you. But I will not remember its existence. I will not even remember the conduct of that misguided person"—and here, although he spoke like one at peace with all the world, he used an emphasis that plainly said "I have my eye upon the rascal now"—"that misguided person who has brought you here to-night, seeking to disturb (it is a happiness to say, in vain) the heart's repose and peace of one who would have shed his dearest blood to serve him."

The voice of Mr. Pecksniff trembled as he spoke, and sobs were heard from his daughters. Sounds floated on the air, moreover, as if two spirit voices had exclaimed: one, "Beast!" the other, "Savage!"

"Forgiveness," said Mr. Pecksniff, "entire and pure forgiveness is not incompatible with a wounded heart; perchance when the heart *is* wounded, it becomes a greater virtue. With my breast still wrung and grieved to its inmost core by the ingratitude of that person, I am proud and glad to say that I forgive him. Nay! I beg," cried Mr. Pecksniff, raising his voice, as Pinch appeared about to speak, "I beg that individual not to offer a remark: he will truly oblige me by not uttering one word, just now. I am not sure that I am equal to the trial. In a very short space of time, I shall have sufficient fortitude, I trust, to converse with him as if these events had never happened. But not," said Mr. Pecksniff, turning round again towards the fire, and waving his hand in the direction of the door, "not now."

"Bah!" cried John Westlock, with the utmost disgust and disdain the monosyllable is capable of expressing. "Ladies, good evening. Come, Pinch, it's not worth thinking of. I was right and you were wrong. That's a small matter; you'll be wiser another time."

So saying, he clapped that dejected companion on the shoulder, turned upon his heel, and walked out into the passage, whither poor Mr. Pinch, after lingering irresolutely in the parlour for a few seconds, expressing in his countenance the deepest mental misery and gloom, followed him. Then they took up the box between them, and sallied out to meet the mail.

That fleet conveyance passed, every night, the corner of a lane at some distance; towards which point they bent their steps. For some minutes they walked along in silence, until at length young

Westlock burst into a loud laugh, and at intervals into another, and another. Still there was no response from his companion.

"I'll tell you what, Pinch!" he said abruptly, after another lengthened silence—"You haven't half enough of the devil in you. Half enough! You haven't any."

"Well!" said Pinch with a sigh, "I don't know, I'm sure. It's a compliment to say so. If I haven't, I suppose, I'm all the better for it."

"All the better!" repeated his companion tartly: "All the worse, you mean to say."

"And yet," said Pinch, pursuing his own thoughts and not this last remark on the part of his friend, "I must have a good deal of what you call the devil in me, too, or how could I make Pecksniff so uncomfortable? I wouldn't have occasioned him so much distress—don't laugh, please—for a mine of money: and Heaven knows I could find good use for it too, John. How grieved he was!"

"*He* grieved!" returned the other.

"Why didn't you observe that the tears were almost starting out of his eyes!" cried Pinch. "Bless my soul, John, is it nothing to see a man moved to that extent and know one's self to be the cause! And did you hear him say that he could have shed his blood for me?"

"Do you *want* any blood shed for you?" returned his friend, with considerable irritation. "Does he shed anything for you that you *do* want? Does he shed employment for you, instruction for you, pocket money for you? Does he shed even legs of mutton for you in any decent proportion to potatoes and garden stuff?"

"I am afraid," said Pinch, sighing again, "that I am a great eater: I can't disguise from myself that I'm a great eater. Now, you know that, John."

"*You* a great eater!" retorted his companion, with no less indignation than before. "How do you know you are?"

There appeared to be forcible matter in this inquiry, for Mr. Pinch only repeated in an under-tone that he had a strong misgiving on the subject, and that he greatly feared he was.

"Besides, whether I am or no," he added, "that has little or nothing to do with his thinking me ungrateful. John, there is scarcely a sin in the world that is in my eyes such a crying one as ingratitude: and when he taxes me with that, and believes me to be guilty of it, he makes me miserable and wretched."

"Do you think he don't know that?" returned the other scornfully. "But come, Pinch, before I say anything more to you, just run over the reasons you have for being grateful to him at all, will you? Change hands first, for the box is heavy. That'll do. Now, go on."

"In the first place," said Pinch, "he took me as his pupil for much less than he asked."

"Well," rejoined his friend, perfectly unmoved by this instance of generosity. "What in the second place?"

"What in the second place!" cried Pinch, in a sort of desperation, "why, everything in the second place. My poor old grandmother died happy to think that she had put me with such an excellent man. I have grown up in his house, I am in his confidence, I am his assistant, he allows me a salary; when his business improves, my prospects are to improve too. All this, and a great deal more, is in the second place. And in the very prologue and preface to the first place, John, you must consider this, which nobody knows better than I: that I was born for much plainer and poorer things, that I am not a good hand for his kind of business, and have no talent for it, or indeed for anything else but odds and ends that are of no use or service to anybody."

He said this with so much earnestness, and in a tone so full of feeling, that his companion instinctively changed his manner as he sat down on the box (they had by this time reached the finger-post at the end of the lane); motioned him to sit down beside him; and laid his hand upon his shoulder.

"I believe you are one of the best fellows in the world," he said, "Tom Pinch."

"Not at all," rejoined Tom. "If you only knew Pecksniff as well as I do, you might say it of him, indeed, and say it truly."

"I'll say anything of him, you like," returned the other, "and not another word to his disparagement."

"It's for my sake, then; not his, I am afraid," said Pinch, shaking his head gravely.

"For whose you please, Tom, so that it does please you. Oh! He's a famous fellow! *He* never scraped and clawed into his pouch all your poor grandmother's hard savings—she was a housekeeper, wasn't she, Tom?"

"Yes," said Mr. Pinch, nursing one of his large knees, and nodding his head: "a gentleman's housekeeper."

"*He* never scraped and clawed into his pouch all her hard savings; dazzling her with prospects of your happiness and advancement, which he knew (and no man better) never would be realised! *He* never speculated and traded on her pride in you, and her having educated you, and on her desire that you at least should live to be a gentleman. Not he, Tom!"

"No," said Tom, looking into his friend's face, as if he were a little doubtful of his meaning; "Of course not."

"So I say," returned the youth, "of course he never did. *He* didn't take less than he had asked, because that less was all she had, and more than he expected; not he, Tom! He doesn't keep you as his assistant because you are of any use to him; because your wonderful faith in his pretensions is of inestimable service in all his mean disputes; because your honesty reflects honesty on him; because your wandering about this little place all your spare hours, reading in ancient books and foreign tongues, gets noised abroad, even as far as Salisbury, making of him, Pecksniff the master, a man of learning and of vast importance. *He* gets no credit from you, Tom, not he."

"Why, of course he don't," said Pinch, gazing at his friend with a more troubled aspect than before. "Pecksniff get credit from *me*! Well!"

"Don't I say that it's ridiculous," rejoined the other, "even to think of such a thing?"

"Why, it's madness," said Tom.

"Madness!" returned young Westlock. "Certainly it's madness. Who but a madman would suppose he cares to hear it said on Sundays, that the volunteer who plays the organ in the church, and practises on summer evenings in the dark, is Mr. Pecksniff's young man, eh, Tom? Who but a madman would suppose it is the game of such a man as he, to have his name in everybody's mouth, connected with the thousand useless odds and ends you do (and which, of course, he taught you), eh, Tom? Who but a madman would suppose you advertised him hereabouts, much cheaper and much better than a chalker on the walls could, eh, Tom? As well might one suppose that he doesn't on all occasions pour out his whole heart and soul to you; that he doesn't make you a very liberal and indeed rather an extravagant allowance; or, to be more wild and monstrous still, if that be possible, as well might one suppose," and here, at every word, he struck him lightly on the breast, "that Pecksniff traded in your nature, and that your nature was to be timid and distrustful of yourself, and trustful of all other men, but most of all, of him who least deserves it. There would be madness, Tom!"

Mr. Pinch had listened to all this with looks of bewilderment, which seemed to be in part occasioned by the matter of his companion's speech, and in part by his rapid and vehement manner. Now that he had come to a close, he drew a very long breath; and gazing wistfully in his face as if he were unable to settle in his own mind what expression it wore, and were desirous to draw from it as good a clue to his real meaning as it was possible to obtain in the dark, was about to answer, when the sound of the mail guard's horn came cheerily upon their ears, putting an immediate end to the conference; greatly as it seemed to the satisfaction of the younger man, who jumped up briskly, and gave his hand to his companion.

Chapter 2: "Wherein Certain Persons Are Presented to the Reader, with Whom He May, If He Please, Become Better Acquainted"

8. He That Is without Sin

Bleak House

In this passage, "a good, good woman"—a woman who trusts in her own self-righteousness and bears an unending grudge against the mother of the illegitimate child she is raising—literally does not survive an encounter with the Jesus of the Scriptures.

I was brought up, from my earliest remembrance—like some of the princesses in the fairy stories, only I was not charming—by my godmother. At least I only knew her as such. She was a good, good woman! She went to church three times every Sunday, and to morning prayers on Wednesdays and Fridays, and to lectures whenever there were lectures; and never missed. She was handsome; and if she had ever smiled, would have been (I used to think) like an angel—but she never smiled. She was always grave, and strict. She was so very good herself, I thought, that the badness of other people made her frown all her life. I felt so different from her, even making every allowance for the differences between a child and a woman; I felt so poor, so trifling, and so far off; that I never could be unrestrained with her—no, could never even love her as I wished. It made me very sorry to consider how good she was, and how unworthy of her I was; and I used ardently to hope that I might have a better heart; and I talked it over very often with the dear old doll; but I never loved my godmother as I ought to have loved her, and as I felt I must have loved her if I had been a better girl. . . .

It was my birthday. There were holidays at school on other birthdays—none on mine. There were rejoicings at home on other birthdays, as I knew from what I heard the girls relate to one another—there were none on mine. My birthday was the most melancholy day at home, in the whole year. . . .

Dinner was over, and my godmother and I were sitting at the table before the fire. The clock ticked, the fire clicked; not another sound had been heard in the room, or in the house, for I don't know how long. I happened to look timidly up from my stitching, across the table, at my godmother, and I saw in her face, looking gloomily at me, "It would have been far better, little Esther, that you had had no birthday; that you had never been born!"

I broke out crying and sobbing, and I said, "O, dear godmother, tell me, pray do tell me, did mama die on my birthday?"

"No," she returned. "Ask me no more, child!"

"O, do pray tell me something of her. Do now, at last, dear godmother, if you please! What did I do to her? How did I lose her? Why am I so different from other children, and why is it my fault, dear godmother? No, no, no, don't go away. O, speak to me!"

I was in a kind of fright beyond my grief; and I caught hold of her dress, and was kneeling to her. She had been saying all the while, "Let me go!" But now she stood still.

Her darkened face had such power over me, that it stopped me in the midst of my vehemence. I put up my trembling little hand to clasp hers, or to beg her pardon with what earnestness I might, but withdrew it as she looked at me, and laid it on my fluttering heart. She raised me, sat in her chair, and standing me before her, said, slowly, in a cold, low voice—I see her knitted brow and pointed finger:

"Your mother, Esther, is your disgrace, and you were hers. The time will come—and soon enough—when you will understand this better, and will feel it too, as no one save a woman can. I have forgiven her"—but her face did not relent—"the wrong she did to me, and I say no more of it, though it was greater than you will ever know—than any one will ever know, but I, the sufferer. For yourself, unfortunate girl, orphaned and degraded from the first of these evil anniversaries, pray daily that the sins of others be not visited upon your head, according to what is written. Forget your mother, and leave all other people to forget her who will do her unhappy child that greatest kindness. Now, go!"

She checked me, however, as I was about to depart from her—so frozen as I was!—and added this:

"Submission, self-denial, diligent work, are the preparations for a life begun with such a shadow on it. You are different from other children, Esther, because you were not born, like them, in common sinfulness and wrath. You are set apart."

I went up to my room, and crept to bed, and laid my doll's cheek against mine wet with tears, and holding that solitary friend upon my bosom, cried myself to sleep. Imperfect as my understanding of my sorrow was, I knew that I had brought no joy, at any time, to anybody's heart, and that I was to no one upon earth what Dolly was to me. . . .

It must have been two years afterwards, and I was almost fourteen, when one dreadful night my godmother and I sat at the fireside. I was reading aloud, and she was listening. I had come down at nine o'clock, as I always did, to read the Bible to her, and was reading from St. John, how our Saviour stooped down, writing with his finger in the dust, when they brought the sinful woman to him.

"So when they continued asking him, he lifted up himself and said unto them, 'He that is without sin among you, let him first cast a stone at her!'"

I was stopped by my godmother's rising, putting her hand to her head, and crying out, in an awful voice, from quite another part of the book:

"'Watch ye therefore! lest coming suddenly he find you sleeping. And what I say unto you, I say unto all, Watch!'"

In an instant, while she stood before me repeating these words, she fell down on the floor. I had no need to cry out; her voice had sounded through the house, and been heard in the street.

She was laid upon her bed. For more than a week she lay there, little altered outwardly, with her old handsome resolute frown that I so well knew, carved upon her face. Many and many a time, in the day and in the night, with my head upon the pillow by her that my whispers might be plainer to her, I kissed her, thanked her, prayed for her, asked her for her blessing and forgiveness, entreated her to give me the least sign that she knew or heard me. No, no, no. Her face was immoveable. To the very last, and even afterwards, her frown remained unsoftened.

Chapter 3: "A Progress"

9. A Troublesome Bad Child

Our Mutual Friend

Villainy is not always deliberate in Dickens's works; sometimes the worst consequences arise from weaknesses of character rather than from abuse of power or from hypocrisy. The unforgettable character of Jenny Wren, the disabled young doll's dressmaker in Our Mutual Friend, *suffers deeply from her father's drunkenness and neglect. Forced to play parent to the man who should be acting as a parent to her, Jenny takes her role very literally, with results that are both grotesque and touching. We see her first in the company of her housemate Lizzie and Lizzie's would-be suitor Eugene, rising to heights of mysticism that are completely forgotten when her father makes his entrance.*

"Talking of ideas, my Lizzie," they were sitting side by side as they had sat at first, "I wonder how it happens that when I am work, work, working here, all alone in the summer-time, I smell flowers."

"As a common-place individual, I should say," Eugene suggested languidly—for he was growing weary of the person of the house—"that you smell flowers because you *do* smell flowers."

"No I don't," said the little creature, resting one arm upon the elbow of her chair, resting her chin upon that hand, and looking vacantly before her; "this is not a flowery neighbourhood. It's anything but that. And yet, as I sit at work, I smell miles of flowers. I smell roses till I think I see the rose-leaves lying in heaps, bushels, on the floor. I smell fallen leaves, till I put down my hand—so—and expect to make them rustle. I smell the white and the pink May in the hedges, and all sorts of flowers that I never was among. For I have seen very few flowers indeed, in my life."

"Pleasant fancies to have, Jenny dear!" said her friend: with a glance towards Eugene as if she would have asked him whether they were given the child in compensation for her losses.

"So I think, Lizzie, when they come to me. And the birds I hear! Oh!" cried the little creature, holding out her hand and looking upward, "how they sing!"

There was something in the face and action for the moment quite inspired and beautiful. Then the chin dropped musingly upon the hand again.

"I dare say my birds sing better than other birds, and my flowers smell better than other flowers. For when I was a little child," in a tone as though it were ages ago, "the children that I used to see early in the morning were very different from any others that I ever saw. They were not like me; they were not chilled, anxious, ragged, or beaten; they were never in pain. They were not like the children of the neighbours; they never made me tremble all over, by setting up shrill noises, and they never mocked me. Such numbers of them, too! All in white dresses, and with something shining on the borders, and on their heads, that I have never been able to imitate with my work, though I know it so well. They used to come down in long bright slanting rows, and say all together, 'Who is this in pain! Who is this in pain!' When I told them who it was, they answered, 'Come and play with us!' When I said 'I never play! I can't play!' they swept about me and took me up, and made me light. Then it was all delicious ease and rest till they laid me down, and said, all together, 'Have patience, and we will come again.' Whenever they came back, I used to know they were coming before I saw the long bright rows, by hearing them ask, all together a long way off, 'Who is this in pain! Who is this in pain!' And I used to cry out, 'O my blessed children, it's poor me. Have pity on me. Take me up and make me light!'"

By degrees, as she progressed in this remembrance, the hand was raised, the late ecstatic look returned, and she became quite beautiful. Having so paused for a moment, silent, with a listening smile upon her face, she looked round and recalled herself.

"What poor fun you think me; don't you, Mr. Wrayburn? You may well look tired of me. But it's Saturday night, and I won't detain you."

"That is to say, Miss Wren," observed Eugene, quite ready to profit by the hint, "you wish me to go?"

"Well, it's Saturday night," she returned, "and my child's coming home. And my child is a troublesome bad child, and costs me a world of scolding. I would rather you didn't see my child."

"A doll?" said Eugene, not understanding, and looking for an explanation.

But Lizzie, with her lips only, shaping the two words, "Her father," he delayed no longer. He took his leave immediately. At the corner of the street he stopped to light another cigar, and possibly to ask himself what he was doing otherwise. If so, the answer was indefinite and vague. Who knows what he is doing, who is careless what he does!

A man stumbled against him as he turned away, who mumbled some maudlin apology. Looking after this man, Eugene saw him go in at the door by which he himself had just come out.

On the man's stumbling into the room, Lizzie rose to leave it.

"Don't go away, Miss Hexam," he said in a submissive manner, speaking thickly and with difficulty. "Don't fly from unfortunate man in shattered state of health. Give poor invalid honour of your company. It ain't—ain't catching."

Lizzie murmured that she had something to do in her own room, and went away up-stairs.

"How's my Jenny?" said the man, timidly. "How's my Jenny Wren, best of children, object dearest affections broken-hearted invalid."

To which the person of the house, stretching out her arm in an attitude of command, replied with irresponsive asperity: "Go along with you! Go along into your corner! Get into your corner directly!"

The wretched spectacle made as if he would have offered some remonstrance; but not venturing to resist the person of the house, thought better of it, and went and sat down on a particular chair of disgrace.

"Oh-h-h!" cried the person of the house, pointing her little finger. "You bad old boy! Oh-h-h you naughty, wicked creature! *What* do you mean by it?"

The shaking figure, unnerved and disjointed from head to foot, put out its two hands a little way, as making overtures of peace and reconciliation. Abject tears stood in its eyes, and stained the blotched red of its cheeks. The swollen lead-coloured under-lip trembled with a shameful whine. The whole indecorous threadbare ruin, from the broken shoes to the prematurely-grey scanty hair, grovelled. Not with any sense worthy to be called a sense, of this dire reversal of the places of parent and child, but in a pitiful expostulation to be let off from a scolding.

"*I* know your tricks and your manners," cried Miss Wren. "*I* know where you've been to!" (which indeed it did not require discernment to discover). "Oh, you disgraceful old chap!"

The very breathing of the figure was contemptible, as it laboured and rattled in that operation, like a blundering clock.

"Slave, slave, slave, from morning to night," pursued the person of the house, "and all for this! *What* do you mean by it?"

There was something in that emphasized "What," which absurdly frightened the figure. As often as the person of the house worked her way round to it—even as soon as he saw that it was coming—he collapsed in an extra degree.

"I wish you had been taken up, and locked up," said the person of the house. "I wish you had been poked into cells and black holes, and run over by rats and spiders and beetles. *I* know their tricks and their manners, and they'd have tickled you nicely. Ain't you ashamed of yourself?"

"Yes, my dear," stammered the father.

"Then," said the person of the house, terrifying him by a grand muster of her spirits and forces before recurring to the emphatic word, "*what* do you mean by it?"

"Circumstances over which had no control," was the miserable creature's plea in extenuation.

"*I*'ll circumstance you and control you too," retorted the person of the house, speaking with vehement sharpness, "if you talk in that way. I'll give you in charge to the police, and have you fined five shillings when you can't pay, and then I won't pay the money for you, and you'll be transported for life. How should you like to be transported for life?"

"Shouldn't like it. Poor shattered invalid. Trouble nobody long," cried the wretched figure.

"Come, come!" said the person of the house, tapping the table near her in a business-like manner, and shaking her head and her chin; "you know what you've got to do. Put down your money this instant."

The obedient figure began to rummage in its pockets.

"Spent a fortune out of your wages, I'll be bound!" said the person of the house. "Put it here! All you've got left! Every farthing!"

Marcus Stone, *The Person of the House and the Bad Child*

Such a business as he made of collecting it from his dog's-eared pockets; of expecting it in this pocket, and not finding it; of not expecting it in that pocket, and passing it over; of finding no pocket where that other pocket ought to be!

"Is this all?" demanded the person of the house, when a confused heap of pence and shillings lay on the table.

"Got no more," was the rueful answer, with an accordant shake of the head.

"Let me make sure. You know what you've got to do. Turn all your pockets inside out, and leave 'em so!" cried the person of the house.

He obeyed. And if anything could have made him look more abject or more dismally ridiculous than before, it would have been his so displaying himself.

"Here's but seven and eightpence halfpenny!" exclaimed Miss Wren, after reducing the heap to order. "Oh, you prodigal old son! Now, you shall be starved."

"No, don't starve me," he urged, whimpering.

"If you were treated as you ought to be," said Miss Wren, "you'd be fed upon the skewers of cats' meat; only the skewers, after the cats had had the meat. As it is, go to bed."

When he stumbled out of the corner to comply, he again put out both his hands, and pleaded: "Circumstances over which no control——"

"Get along with you to bed!" cried Miss Wren, snapping him up. "Don't speak to me. I'm not going to forgive you. Go to bed this moment!"

Seeing another emphatic "What" upon its way, he evaded it by complying, and was heard to shuffle heavily up-stairs, and shut his door, and throw himself on his bed. Within a little while afterwards, Lizzie came down.

"Shall we have our supper, Jenny dear?"

"Ah! bless us and save us, we need have something to keep us going," returned Miss Jenny, shrugging her shoulders.

Lizzie laid a cloth upon the little bench (more handy for the person of the house than an ordinary table), and put upon it such plain fare as they were accustomed to have, and drew up a stool for herself.

"Now for supper! What are you thinking of, Jenny darling?"

"I was thinking," she returned, coming out of a deep study, "what I would do to Him, if he should turn out a drunkard."[6]

"Oh, but he won't," said Lizzie. "You'll take care of that, beforehand."

"I shall try to take care of it beforehand, but he might deceive me. Oh, my dear, all those fellows with their tricks and their manners do deceive!" With the little fist in full action. "And if so, I tell you what I think I'd do. When he was asleep, I'd make a spoon red hot, and I'd have some boiling liquor bubbling in a saucepan, and I'd take it out hissing, and I'd open his mouth with the other hand—or perhaps he'd sleep with his mouth ready open—and I'd pour it down his throat, and blister it and choke him."

"I am sure you would do no such horrible thing," said Lizzie.

"Shouldn't I? Well; perhaps I shouldn't. But I should like to!"

"I am equally sure you would not."

"Not even like to? Well, you generally know best. Only you haven't always lived among it as I have lived—and your back isn't bad and your legs are not queer."

As they went on with their supper, Lizzie tried to bring her round to that prettier and better state. But, the charm was

---

6 Jenny refers to her prospective future husband, an unknown "Him" of whom she often speaks, stipulating how he is to behave.

broken. The person of the house was the person of a house full of sordid shames and cares, with an upper room in which that abased figure was infecting even innocent sleep with sensual brutality and degradation. The doll's dressmaker had become a little quaint shrew; of the world, worldly; of the earth, earthy.

Poor doll's dressmaker! How often so dragged down by hands that should have raised her up; how often so misdirected when losing her way on the eternal road, and asking guidance! Poor, poor little doll's dressmaker!

Book the Second: "Birds of a Feather," Chapter 2: "Still Educational"

10. The Father of the Marshalsea

Little Dorrit

Similarly, William Dorrit, who has lived in the Marshalsea debtor's prison since before his daughter Amy was born, is unhealthily dependent on her and manipulative of her, to the point of trying to use a guard's son's interest in her to curry favor with the guard.

There was a great deal of leave-taking going on in corners, as was usual on Sunday nights; and here and there in the dark, some poor woman, wife or mother, was weeping with a new Collegian.[7] The time had been when the Father[8] himself had wept, in the shades of that yard, as his own poor wife had wept. But it was many years ago; and now he was like a passenger aboard ship in a long voyage, who has recovered from sea-sickness, and is impatient of that weakness in the fresher passengers taken aboard at the last port. He was inclined to remonstrate, and to express his opinion that people who couldn't get on without crying, had no business there. In manner, if not in words, he always testified his displeasure at these interruptions of the general harmony; and it was so well understood, that delinquents usually withdrew if they were aware of him.

On this Sunday evening, he accompanied his brother to the gate with an air of endurance and clemency; being in a bland temper and graciously disposed to overlook the tears. In the flaring gaslight of the Lodge, several Collegians were basking; some taking leave of visitors, and some who had no visitors, watching the frequent turning of the key, and conversing with one another and with Mr. Chivery. The paternal entrance made

7 Prisoner.

8 William Dorrit is frequently referred to as "the Father of the Marshalsea," because of the length of his stay there and the stately manner that has earned him the respect of the other prisoners.

a sensation of course; and Mr. Chivery, touching his hat (in a short manner though) with his key, hoped he found himself tolerable.

"Thank you, Chivery, quite well. And you?"

Mr. Chivery said in a low growl, "Oh! *he* was all right." Which was his general way of acknowledging inquiries after his health, when a little sullen.

"I had a visit from Young John to-day, Chivery. And very smart he looked, I assure you."

So Mr. Chivery had heard. Mr. Chivery must confess, however, that his wish was that the boy didn't lay out so much money upon it. For what did it bring him in? It only brought him in Wexation. And he could get that anywhere for nothing.

"How vexation, Chivery?" asked the benignant father.

"No odds," returned Mr. Chivery. "Never mind. Mr. Frederick going out?"

"Yes, Chivery, my brother is going home to bed. He is tired, and not quite well. Take care, Frederick, take care. Good night, my dear Frederick!"

Shaking hands with his brother, and touching his greasy hat to the company in the Lodge, Frederick slowly shuffled out of the door which Mr. Chivery unlocked for him. The Father of the Marshalsea showed the amiable solicitude of a superior being that he should come to no harm.

"Be so kind as to keep the door open a moment, Chivery, that I may see him go along the passage and down the steps. Take care, Frederick! (He is very infirm.) Mind the steps! (He is so very absent.) Be careful how you cross, Frederick. (I really don't like the notion of his going wandering at large, he is so extremely liable to be run over.)"

With these words, and with a face expressive of many uneasy doubts and much anxious guardianship, he turned his regards upon the assembled company in the Lodge: so plainly indicating that his brother was to be pitied for not being under lock and key, that an opinion to that effect went round among the Collegians assembled.

But he did not receive it with unqualified assent; on the contrary, he said, No, gentlemen, no; let them not misunderstand him. His brother Frederick was much broken, no doubt, and it might be more comfortable to himself (the Father of the Marshalsea) to know that he was safe within the walls. Still, it must be remembered that to support an existence there during many years, required a certain combination of qualities—he did not say high qualities, but qualities—moral qualities. Now, had his brother Frederick that peculiar union of qualities? Gentlemen, he was a most excellent man, a most gentle, tender, and estimable man, with the simplicity of a child; but would he, though unsuited for most other places, do for that place? No; he said confidently, no! And, he said, Heaven forbid that Frederick should be there in any other character than in his present voluntary character! Gentlemen, whoever came to that College, to remain there a length of time, must have strength of character to go through a good deal and to come out of a good deal. Was his beloved brother Frederick that man? No. They saw him, even as it was, crushed. Misfortune crushed him. He had not power of recoil enough, not elasticity enough, to be a long time in such a place, and yet preserve his self-respect and feel conscious that he was a gentleman. Frederick had not (if he might use the expression) Power enough to see in any delicate little attentions and—and—Testimonials[9] that he might under such circumstances receive, the goodness of human nature, the fine spirit animating the Collegians as a community, and at the same time

9 Mr. Dorrit's euphemism for the money he solicits from visitors.

no degradation to himself, and no depreciation of his claims as a gentleman. Gentlemen, God bless you!

Such was the homily with which he improved and pointed the occasion to the company in the Lodge, before turning into the sallow yard again, and going with his own poor shabby dignity past the Collegian in the dressing-gown who had no coat, and past the Collegian in the sea-side slippers who had no shoes, and past the stout greengrocer Collegian in the corduroy knee-breeches who had no cares, and past the lean clerk Collegian in buttonless black who had no hopes, up his own poor shabby staircase, to his own poor shabby room.

There, the table was laid for his supper, and his old grey gown was ready for him on his chair-back at the fire. His daughter put her little prayer-book in her pocket—had she been praying for pity on all prisoners and captives!—and rose to welcome him.

Uncle had gone home, then? she asked as she changed his coat and gave him his black velvet cap. Yes, uncle had gone home. Had her father enjoyed his walk? Why, not much, Amy; not much. No! Did he not feel quite well?

As she stood behind him, leaning over his chair so lovingly, he looked with downcast eyes at the fire. An uneasiness stole over him that was like a touch of shame; and when he spoke, as he presently did, it was in an unconnected and embarrassed manner.

"Something, I—hem!—I don't know what, has gone wrong with Chivery. He is not—ha!—not nearly so obliging and attentive as usual to-night. It—hem!—it's a little thing, but it puts me out, my love. It's impossible to forget," turning his hands over and over and looking closely at them, "that—hem!—that in such a life as mine, I am unfortunately dependent on these men for something, every hour in the day."

Her arm was on his shoulder, but she did not look in his face while he spoke. Bending her head she looked another way.

"I—hem!—I can't think, Amy, what has given Chivery offence. He is generally so—so very attentive and respectful. And to-night he was quite—quite short with me. Other people there too! Why, good Heaven! if I was to lose the support and recognition of Chivery and his brother officers, I might starve to death here." While he spoke, he was opening and shutting his hands like valves; so conscious all the time of that touch of shame, that he shrunk before his own knowledge of his meaning.

"I—ha!—I can't think what it's owing to. I am sure I cannot imagine what the cause of it is. There was a certain Jackson here once, a turnkey of the name of Jackson (I don't think you can remember him, my dear, you were very young), and—hem!—and he had a—brother, and this—young brother paid his addresses to—at least, did not go so far as to pay his addresses to—but admired—respectfully admired—the—not the daughter, the sister—of one of us; a rather distinguished Collegian; I may say, very much so. His name was Captain Martin; and he consulted me on the question whether it was necessary that his daughter—sister—should hazard offending the turnkey brother by being too—ha!—too plain with the other brother. Captain Martin was a gentleman and a man of honour, and I put it to him first to give me his—his own opinion. Captain Martin (highly respected in the army) then unhesitatingly said, that it appeared to him that his—hem!—sister was not called upon to understand the young man too distinctly, and that she might lead him on—I am doubtful whether lead him on was Captain Martin's exact expression: indeed I think he said tolerate him—on her father's—I should say, brother's—account. I hardly know how I have strayed into this story. I suppose it has been through being unable to account for Chivery; but as to the connection between the two, I don't see—"

His voice died away, as if she could not bear the pain of hearing him, and her hand had gradually crept to his lips. For a little while, there was a dead silence and stillness; and he remained shrunk in his chair, and she remained with her arm round his neck, and her head bowed down upon his shoulder.

His supper was cooking in a saucepan on the fire, and, when she moved, it was to make it ready for him on the table. He took his usual seat, she took hers, and he began his meal. They did not, as yet, look at one another. By little and little he began; laying down his knife and fork with a noise, taking things up sharply, biting at his bread as if he were offended with it, and in other similar ways showing that he was out of sorts. At length he pushed his plate from him, and spoke aloud. With the strangest inconsistency.

"What does it matter whether I eat or starve? What does it matter whether such a blighted life as mine comes to an end, now, next week, or next year? What am I worth to anyone? A poor prisoner, fed on alms and broken victuals; a squalid, disgraced wretch!"

"Father, father!" As he rose she went on her knees to him, and held up her hands to him.

"Amy," he went on in a suppressed voice, trembling violently, and looking at her as wildly as if he had gone mad. "I tell you, if you could see me as your mother saw me, you wouldn't believe it to be the creature you have only looked at through the bars of this cage. I was young, I was accomplished, I was good-looking, I was independent—by God I was, child!—and people sought me out, and envied me. Envied me!"

"Dear father!" She tried to take down the shaking arm that he flourished in the air, but he resisted, and put her hand away.

"If I had but a picture of myself in those days, though it was ever so ill done, you would be proud of it, you would be proud of it. But I have no such thing. Now, let me be a warning! Let no man," he cried, looking haggardly about, "fail to preserve at least that little of the times of his prosperity and respect. Let his children have that clue to what he was. Unless my face, when I am dead, subsides into the long departed look—they say such things happen, I don't know—my children will have never seen me."

"Father, father!"

"O despise me, despise me! Look away from me, don't listen to me, stop me, blush for me, cry for me—even you, Amy! Do it, do it! I do it to myself! I am hardened now, I have sunk too low to care long even for that."

"Dear father, loved father, darling of my heart!" She was clinging to him with her arms, and she got him to drop into his chair again, and caught at the raised arm, and tried to put it round her neck.

"Let it lie there, father. Look at me, father, kiss me, father! Only think of me, father, for one little moment!"

Still he went on in the same wild way, though it was gradually breaking down into a miserable whining.

"And yet I have some respect here. I have made some stand against it. I am not quite trodden down. Go out and ask who is the chief person in the place. They'll tell you it's your father. Go out and ask who is never trifled with, and who is always treated with some delicacy. They'll say, your father. Go out and ask what funeral here (it must be here, I know it can be nowhere else) will make more talk, and perhaps more grief, than any that has ever gone out at the gate. They'll say your father's. Well then. Amy! Amy! Is your father so universally despised? Is there nothing to redeem him? Will you have nothing to remember him by but his ruin and decay? Will you be able to have no affection for him when he is gone, poor castaway, gone?"

He burst into tears of maudlin pity for himself, and at length suffering her to embrace him, and take charge of him, let his grey head rest against her cheek, and bewailed his wretchedness. Presently he changed the subject of his lamentations, and clasping his hands about her as she embraced him, cried, O Amy, his motherless, forlorn child! O the days that he had seen her careful and laborious for him! Then he reverted to himself, and weakly told her how much better she would have loved him if she had known him in his vanished character, and how he would have married her to a gentleman who should have been proud of her as his daughter, and how (at which he cried again) she should first have ridden at his fatherly side on her own horse, and how the crowd (by which he meant in effect the people who had given him the twelve shillings he then had in his pocket) should have trudged the dusty roads respectfully.

Thus, now boasting, now despairing, in either fit a captive with the jail-rot upon him, and the impurity of his prison worn into the grain of his soul, he revealed his degenerate state to his affectionate child. No one else ever beheld him in the details of his humiliation. Little recked the Collegians who were laughing in their rooms over his late address in the Lodge, what a serious picture they had in their obscure gallery of the Marshalsea that Sunday night.

There was a classical daughter once—perhaps—who ministered to her father in his prison as her mother had ministered to her. Little Dorrit, though of the unheroic modern stock, and mere English, did much more, in comforting her father's wasted heart upon her innocent breast, and turning to it a fountain of love and fidelity that never ran dry or waned, through all his years of famine.

She soothed him; asked him for his forgiveness if she had been, or seemed to have been, undutiful; told him, Heaven knows truly, that she could not honour him more if he were the favourite of Fortune and the whole world acknowledged him. When his tears were dried, and he sobbed in his weakness no longer, and was free from that touch of shame, and had recovered his usual bearing, she prepared the remains of his supper afresh, and, sitting by his side, rejoiced to see him eat and drink. For, now he sat in his black velvet cap and old grey gown, magnanimous again; and would have comported himself towards any Collegian who might have looked in to ask his advice, like a great moral Lord Chesterfield, or Master of the ethical ceremonies of the Marshalsea.

To keep his attention engaged, she talked with him about his wardrobe; when he was pleased to say, that Yes, indeed, those shirts she proposed would be exceedingly acceptable, for those he had were worn out, and, being ready-made, had never fitted him. Being conversational, and in a reasonable flow of spirits, he then invited her attention to his coat as it hung behind the door: remarking that the Father of the place would set an indifferent example to his children, already disposed to be slovenly, if he went among them out at elbows. He was jocular, too, as to the heeling of his shoes; but became grave on the subject of his cravat, and promised her that when she could afford it, she should buy him a new one.

While he smoked out his cigar in peace, she made his bed, and put the small room in order for his repose. Being weary then, owing to the advanced hour and his emotions, he came out of his chair to bless her and wish her Good-night. All this time he had never once thought of her dress, her shoes, her need of anything. No other person upon earth, save herself, could have been so unmindful of her wants.

He kissed her many times with "Bless you, my love. Good-night, my dear!"

But her gentle breast had been so deeply wounded by what she had seen of him, that she was unwilling to leave him alone, lest he should lament and despair again. "Father, dear, I am not tired; let me come back presently, when you are in bed, and sit by you."

He asked her, with an air of protection, if she felt solitary?

"Yes, father."

"Then come back by all means, my love."

"I shall be very quiet, father."

"Don't think of me, my dear," he said, giving her his kind permission fully. "Come back by all means."

He seemed to be dozing when she returned, and she put the low fire together very softly lest she should awake him. But he overheard her, and called out who was that?

"Only Amy, father."

"Amy, my child, come here. I want to say a word to you."

He raised himself a little in his low bed, as she kneeled beside it to bring her face near him; and put his hand between hers. O! Both the private father, and the Father of the Marshalsea were strong within him then.

"My love, you have had a life of hardship here. No companions, no recreations, many cares I am afraid?"

"Don't think of that, dear. I never do."

"You know my position, Amy. I have not been able to do much for you; but all I have been able to do, I have done."

"Yes, my dear father," she rejoined, kissing him. "I know, I know."

"I am in the twenty-third year of my life here," he said, with a catch in his breath that was not so much a sob as an irrepressible sound of self-approval, the momentary outburst of a noble consciousness. "It is all I could do for my children—I have done it. Amy, my love, you are by far the best loved of the three; I have had you principally in my mind—whatever I have done for your sake, my dear child, I have done freely and without murmuring."

Only the wisdom that holds the clue to all hearts and all mysteries, can surely know to what extent a man, especially a man brought down as this man had been, can impose upon himself. Enough, for the present place, that he lay down with wet eyelashes, serene, in a manner majestic, after bestowing his life of degradation as a sort of portion on the devoted child upon whom its miseries had fallen so heavily, and whose love alone had saved him to be even what he was.

That child had no doubts, asked herself no question, for she was but too content to see him with a lustre round his head. Poor dear, good dear, truest, kindest, dearest, were the only words she had for him, as she hushed him to rest.

She never left him all that night. As if she had done him a wrong which her tenderness could hardly repair, she sat by him in his sleep, at times softly kissing him with suspended breath, and calling him in a whisper by some endearing name. At times she stood aside, so as not to intercept the low fire-light, and, watching him when it fell upon his sleeping face, wondered did he look now at all as he had looked when he was prosperous and happy; as he had so touched her by imagining that he might look once more in that awful time. At the thought of that time, she kneeled beside his bed again, and prayed, "O spare his life! O save him to me! O look down upon my dear, long-suffering, unfortunate, much-changed, dear dear father!"

Not until the morning came to protect him and encourage him, did she give him a last kiss and leave the small room. When she had stolen downstairs, and along the empty yard, and had crept up to her own high garret, the smokeless housetops and the distant country hills were discernible over the wall in the clear morning.

As she gently opened the window, and looked eastward down the prison yard, the spikes upon the wall were tipped with red, then made a sullen purple pattern on the sun as it came flaming up into the heavens. The spikes had never looked so sharp and cruel, nor the bars so heavy, nor the prison space so gloomy and contracted. She thought of the sunrise on rolling rivers, of the sunrise on wide seas, of the sunrise on rich landscapes, of the sunrise on great forests where the birds were waking and the trees were rustling; and she looked down into the living grave on which the sun had risen, with her father in it, three-and-twenty years, and said, in a burst of sorrow and compassion, "No, no, I have never seen him in my life!"

Book the First: "Poverty," Chapter 19: "The Father of the Marshalsea in Two or Three Relations"

11. Safe with the Parish

Our Mutual Friend

As we've seen, in Dickens's time, many efforts by both the government and the church that were ostensibly for the good of the poor served only to terrorize and traumatize them. Dickens demonstrates this in the character of Betty Higden, an elderly woman who, once she no longer has the health and strength to support herself, flees everyone she knows—even the friends who would willingly care for her—because of her overwhelming dread of ending up in a parish workhouse.

The old abhorrence grew stronger on her as she grew weaker, and it found more sustaining food than she did in her wanderings. Now, she would light upon the shameful spectacle of some desolate creature—or some wretched, ragged groups of either sex, or of both sexes, with children among them, huddled together like the smaller vermin, for a little warmth—lingering and lingering on a doorstep, while the appointed evader of the public trust did his dirty office of trying to weary them out and so get rid of them. Now, she would light upon some poor decent person, like herself, going afoot on a pilgrimage of many weary miles to see some worn-out relative or friend who had been charitably clutched off to a great, blank, barren Union House, as far from old home as the County Jail (the remoteness of which is always its worst punishment for small rural offenders), and in its dietary, and in its lodging, and in its tending of the sick, a much more penal establishment. Sometimes she would hear a newspaper read out, and would learn how the Registrar General cast up the units that had within the last week died of want and of exposure to the weather: for which that Recording Angel seemed to have a regular fixed place in his sum, as if they were its halfpence.

All such things she would hear discussed, as we, my lords and gentlemen and honourable boards, in our unapproachable magnificence never hear them, and from all such things she would fly with the wings of raging Despair.

This is not to be received as a figure of speech. Old Betty Higden, however tired, however footsore, would start up and be driven away by her awakened horror of falling into the hands of Charity. It is a remarkable Christian improvement, to have made a pursuing Fury of the Good Samaritan; but it was so in this case, and it is a type of many, many, many.

Two incidents united to intensify the old unreasoning abhorrence—granted in a previous place to be unreasoning, because the people always are unreasoning, and invariably make a point of producing all their smoke without fire.

One day she was sitting in a market-place on a bench outside an inn, with her little wares for sale, when the deadness that she strove against came over her so heavily that the scene departed from before her eyes; when it returned, she found herself on the ground, her head supported by some good-natured market-women, and a little crowd about her.

"Are you better now, mother?" asked one of the women. "Do you think you can do nicely now?"

"Have I been ill then?" asked old Betty.

"You have had a faint like," was the answer, "or a fit. It ain't that you've been a-struggling, mother, but you've been stiff and numbed."

"Ah!" said Betty, recovering her memory. "It's the numbness. Yes. It comes over me at times."

Was it gone? the women asked her.

"It's gone now," said Betty. "I shall be stronger than I was afore. Many thanks to ye, my dears, and when you come to be as old as I am, may others do as much for you!"

They assisted her to rise, but she could not stand yet, and they supported her when she sat down again upon the bench.

"My head's a bit light, and my feet are a bit heavy," said old Betty, leaning her face drowsily on the breast of the woman who had spoken before. "They'll both come nat'ral in a minute. There's nothing more the matter."

"Ask her," said some farmers standing by, who had come out from their market-dinner, "who belongs to her."

"Are there any folks belonging to you, mother?" said the woman.

"Yes sure," answered Betty. "I heerd the gentleman say it, but I couldn't answer quick enough. There's plenty belonging to me. Don't ye fear for me, my dear."

"But are any of 'em near here?" said the men's voices; the women's voices chiming in when it was said, and prolonging the strain.

"Quite near enough," said Betty, rousing herself. "Don't ye be afeard for me, neighbours."

"But you are not fit to travel. Where are you going?" was the next compassionate chorus she heard.

"I'm a-going to London, when I've sold out all," said Betty, rising with difficulty. "I've right good friends in London. I want for nothing. I shall come to no harm. Thankye. Don't ye be afeard for me."

A well-meaning bystander, yellow-legginged and purple-faced, said hoarsely over his red comforter, as she rose to her feet, that she "oughtn't to be let to go."

"For the Lord's love don't meddle with me!" cried old Betty, all her fears crowding on her. "I am quite well now, and I must go this minute."

She caught up her basket as she spoke and was making an unsteady rush away from them, when the same bystander checked her with his hand on her sleeve, and urged her to come with him and see the parish-doctor. Strengthening herself by the utmost exercise of her resolution, the poor trembling creature shook him off, almost fiercely, and took to flight. Nor did she feel safe until she had set a mile or two of by-road between herself and the market-place, and had crept into a copse, like a hunted animal, to hide and recover breath. Not until then, for the first time, did she venture to recall how she had looked over her shoulder before turning out of the town, and had seen the sign of the White Lion hanging across the road, and the fluttering market booths, and the old grey church, and the little crowd gazing after her, but not attempting to follow her.

The second frightening incident was this. She had been again as bad, and had been for some days better, and was travelling along by a part of the road where it touched the river, and in wet seasons was so often overflowed by it that there were tall white posts set up to mark the way. A barge was being towed towards her, and she sat down on the bank to rest and watch it. As the tow-rope was slackened by a turn of the stream and dipped into the water, such a confusion stole into her mind that she thought she saw the forms of her dead children and dead grandchildren peopling the barge, and waving their hands to her in solemn measure; then as the rope tightened and came up, dropping diamonds, it seemed to vibrate into two parallel ropes and strike her, with a twang, though it was far off. When she looked again, there was no barge, no river, no daylight, and a man whom she had never before seen held a candle close to her face.

"Now, Missis," said he; "where did you come from and where are you going to?"

The poor soul confusedly asked the counter-question where she was?

"I am the Lock," said the man.

"The Lock?"

"I am the Deputy Lock, on job, and this is the Lock-house. (Lock or Deputy Lock, it's all one, while the t'other man's in the hospital.) What's your Parish?"

"Parish!" She was up from the truckle-bed directly, wildly feeling about her for her basket, and gazing at him in affright.

"You'll be asked the question down town," said the man. "They won't let you be more than a Casual there. They'll pass you on to your settlement, Missis, with all speed. You're not in a state to be let come upon strange parishes 'ceptin as a Casual."

"'Twas the deadness again!" murmured Betty Higden, with her hand to her head.

"It was the deadness, there's not a doubt about it," returned the man. "I should have thought the deadness was a mild word for it, if it had been named to me when we brought you in. Have you got any friends, Missis?"

"The best of friends, Master."

"I should recommend your looking 'em up if you consider 'em game to do anything for you," said the Deputy Lock. "Have you got any money?"

"Just a morsel of money, sir."

"Do you want to keep it?"

"Sure I do!"

"Well, you know," said the Deputy Lock, shrugging his shoulders with his hands in his pockets, and shaking his head in a sulkily ominous manner, "the parish authorities down town will have it out of you, if you go on, you may take your Alfred David." [10]

"Then I'll not go on."

---

10 Affidavit.

"They'll make you pay, as fur as your money will go," pursued the Deputy, "for your relief as a Casual and for your being passed to your Parish."

"Thank ye kindly, Master, for your warning, thank ye for your shelter, and good-night."

"Stop a bit," said the Deputy, striking in between her and the door. "Why are you all of a shake, and what's your hurry, Missis?"

"Oh, Master, Master," returned Betty Higden, "I've fought against the Parish and fled from it, all my life, and I want to die free of it!"

"I don't know," said the Deputy, with deliberation, "as I ought to let you go. I'm a honest man as gets my living by the sweat of my brow, and I may fall into trouble by letting you go. I've fell into trouble afore now, by George, and I know what it is, and it's made me careful. You might be took with your deadness again, half a mile off—or half of half a quarter for the matter of that—and then it would be asked, Why did that there honest Deputy Lock, let her go, instead of putting her safe with the Parish? That's what a man of his character ought to have done, it would be argueyfied," said the Deputy Lock, cunningly harping on the strong string of her terror; "he ought to have handed her over safe to the Parish. That was to be expected of a man of his merits."

As he stood in the doorway, the poor old, careworn, wayworn woman burst into tears, and clasped her hands, as if in a very agony she prayed to him.

"As I've told you, Master, I've the best of friends. This letter will show how true I spoke, and they will be thankful for me."

The Deputy Lock opened the letter with a grave face, which underwent no change as he eyed its contents. But it might have done, if he could have read them.

"What amount of small change, Missis," he said with an abstracted air, after a little meditation, "might you call a morsel of money?"

Hurriedly emptying her pocket, old Betty laid down on the table, a shilling and two sixpenny pieces, and a few pence.

"If I was to let you go instead of handing you over safe to the Parish," said the Deputy, counting the money with his eyes, "might it be your own free wish to leave that there behind you?"

"Take it, Master, take it, and welcome and thankful!"

"I'm a man," said the Deputy, giving her back the letter, and pocketing the coins, one by one, "as earns his living by the sweat of his brow;" here he drew his sleeve across his forehead, as if this particular portion of his humble gains were the result of sheer hard labour and virtuous industry; "and I won't stand in your way. Go where you like."

She was gone out of the Lock-house as soon as he gave her this permission, and her tottering steps were on the road again. But, afraid to go back and afraid to go forward; seeing what she fled from, in the sky-glare of the lights of the little town before her, and leaving a confused horror of it everywhere behind her, as if she had escaped it in every stone of every market-place; she struck off by side ways, among which she got bewildered and lost. That night she took refuge from the Samaritan in his latest accredited form, under a farmer's rick; and if—worth thinking of, perhaps, my fellow-Christians—the Samaritan had in the lonely night, "passed by on the other side," she would have most devoutly thanked High Heaven for her escape from him.

Book the Third: "A Long Lane," Chapter 8: "The End of a Long Journey"

12. These Epidemics

Little Dorrit

As previous excerpts have shown, Dickens was concerned with the effects of both individual sin and societal sin, and often shows them intertwined with and inseparable from each other. Little Dorrit, *which ruthlessly satirizes the byzantine workings of bureaucracy and the con artists who scam thousands out of their money, is one of the best examples of this. The book was originally titled* Nobody's Fault, *signaling that the causes of material and spiritual poverty are so widespread that no one person can be singled out for blame for it all.*

While the crook Mr. Merdle successfully convinces poor and rich alike to invest their money with him, Dickens suggests that he could never have gained such influence were it not for the all-too-human tendency to be fooled into believing in "get rich quick" schemes. Such tendencies are so natural to us, and so easily spread among us, that even good people like the novel's hero, Arthur Clennam, and his friend Mr. Pancks can fall prey to them. The fact that Arthur invests with Merdle out of altruism—wanting to help his business partner and his mother—makes little difference in the end.

"Do you mean, my good Pancks," asked Clennam, emphatically, "that you would put that thousand pounds of yours, let us say, for instance, out at this kind of interest?"

"Certainly," said Pancks. "Already done it, sir."

Mr. Pancks took another long inhalation, another long exhalation, another long sagacious look at Clennam.

"I tell you, Mr. Clennam, I've gone into it," said Pancks. "He's a man of immense resources—enormous capital—government influence. They're the best schemes afloat. They're safe. They're certain."

"Well!" returned Clennam, looking first at him gravely, and then at the fire gravely. "You surprise me!"

"Bah!" Pancks retorted. "Don't say that, sir. It's what you ought to do yourself! Why don't you do as I do?"

Of whom Mr. Pancks had taken the prevalent disease, he could no more have told than if he had unconsciously taken a fever. Bred at first, as many physical diseases are, in the wickedness of men, and then disseminated in their ignorance, these epidemics, after a period, get communicated to many sufferers who are neither ignorant nor wicked. Mr. Pancks might, or might not, have caught the illness himself from a subject of this class; but, in this category he appeared before Clennam, and the infection he threw off was all the more virulent.

"And you have really invested," Clennam had already passed to that word, "your thousand pounds, Pancks?"

"To be sure, sir!" replied Pancks, boldly, with a puff of smoke. "And only wish it ten!"

Now, Clennam had two subjects lying heavy on his lonely mind that night; the one, his partner's long-deferred hope; the other, what he had seen and heard at his mother's. In the relief of having this companion, and of feeling that he could trust him, he passed on to both, and both brought him round again, with an increase and acceleration of force, to his point of departure.

It came about in the simplest manner. Quitting the investment subject, after an interval of silent looking at the fire through the smoke of his pipe, he told Pancks how and why he was occupied with the great National Department. "A hard case it has been, and a hard case it is on Doyce," he finished by saying, with all the honest feeling the topic roused in him.

"Hard indeed," Pancks acquiesced. "But you manage for him, Mr. Clennam?"

"How do you mean?"

"Manage the money part of the business?"

"Yes. As well as I can."

"Manage it better, sir," said Pancks. "Recompense him for his toils and disappointments. Give him the chances of the time. He'll never benefit himself in that way, patient and pre-occupied workman. He looks to you, sir."

"I do my best, Pancks," returned Clennam, uneasily. "As to duly weighing and considering these new enterprises, of which I have had no experience, I doubt if I am fit for it, I am growing old."

"Growing old?" cried Pancks. "Ha, ha!"

There was something so indubitably genuine in the wonderful laugh, and series of snorts and puffs, engendered in Mr. Pancks's astonishment at, and utter rejection of, the idea, that his being quite in earnest could not be questioned.

"Growing old?" cried Pancks. "Hear, hear, hear! Old? Hear him, hear him!"

The positive refusal expressed in Mr. Pancks's continued snorts, no less than in these exclamations, to entertain the sentiment for a single instant, drove Arthur away from it. Indeed, he was fearful of something happening to Mr. Pancks in the violent conflict that took place between the breath he jerked out of himself and the smoke he jerked into himself. This abandonment of the second topic threw him on the third.

"Young, old, or middle-aged, Pancks," he said, when there was a favourable pause, "I am in a very anxious and uncertain state; a state that even leads me to doubt whether anything now seeming to belong to me, may be really mine. Shall I tell you how this is? Shall I put a great trust in you?"

"You shall, sir," said Pancks, "if you believe me worthy of it."

"I do."

"You may!" Mr. Pancks's short and sharp rejoinder, confirmed by the sudden outstretching of his coaly hand, was most expressive and convincing. Arthur shook the hand warmly.

He then, softening the nature of his old apprehensions as much as was possible consistently with their being made intelligible, and never alluding to his mother by name, but speaking vaguely of a relation of his, confided to Mr. Pancks a broad outline of the misgivings he entertained, and of the interview he had witnessed. Mr. Pancks listened with such interest that regardless of the charms of the Eastern pipe, he put it in the grate among the fire-irons, and occupied his hands during the whole recital in so erecting the loops and hooks of hair all over his head, that he looked, when it came to a conclusion, like a journeyman Hamlet in conversation with his father's spirit.

"Brings me back, sir," was his exclamation then, with a startling touch on Clennam's knee, "brings me back, sir, to the Investments! I don't say anything of your making yourself poor, to repair a wrong you never committed. That's you. A man must be himself. But, I say this. Fearing you may want money to save your own blood from exposure and disgrace—make as much as you can!"

Arthur shook his head, but looked at him thoughtfully too.

"Be as rich as you can, sir," Pancks adjured him with a powerful concentration of all his energies on the advice. "Be as rich as you honestly can. It's your duty. Not for your sake, but for the sake of others. Take time by the forelock. Poor Mr. Doyce (who really is growing old) depends upon you. Your relative depends upon you. You don't know what depends upon you."

"Well, well, well!" returned Arthur. "Enough for to-night."

"One word more, Mr. Clennam," retorted Pancks, "and then enough for to-night. Why should you leave all the gains to the gluttons, knaves, and impostors? Why should you leave all the gains that are to be got, to my proprietor and the like of him? Yet you're always doing it. When I say you, I mean such men as you. You know you are. Why, I see it every day of my life. I see nothing else. It's my business to see it. Therefore I say," urged Pancks, "Go in and win!"

"But what of Go in and lose?" said Arthur.

"Can't be done, sir," returned Pancks. "I have looked into it. Name up, everywhere—immense resources—enormous capital—great position—high connection—government influence. Can't be done!"

Gradually, after this closing exposition, Mr. Pancks subsided; allowed his hair to droop as much as it ever would droop on the utmost persuasion; reclaimed the pipe from the fire-irons, filled it anew, and smoked it out. They said little more; but were company to one another in silently pursuing the same subjects, and did not part until midnight. On taking his leave, Mr. Pancks, when he had shaken hands with Clennam, worked completely round him before he steamed out at the door. This, Arthur received as an assurance that he might implicitly rely on Pancks, if he ever should come to need assistance; either in any of the matters of which they had spoken that night, or any other subject that could in any way affect himself.

At intervals all next day, and even while his attention was fixed on other things, he thought of Mr. Pancks's investment of his thousand pounds, and of his having "looked into it." He thought of Mr. Pancks's being so sanguine in this matter, and of his not being usually of a sanguine character. He thought of the great National Department, and of the delight it would be to him to see Doyce better off. He thought of the darkly threatening place that went by the name of Home in his remembrance, and of the gathering shadows which made it yet more darkly threatening than of old. He observed anew that wherever he went, he saw, or heard, or touched, the celebrated name of Merdle; he found it difficult even to remain at his desk a couple of hours, without having it presented to one of his bodily senses through some agency or other. He began to think it was curious, too, that it should be everywhere, and that nobody but he should seem to have any mistrust of it. Though indeed he began to remember, when he got to this, even *he* did not mistrust it; he had only happened to keep aloof from it.

Such symptoms, when a disease of the kind is rife, are usually the signs of sickening.

Book the Second: "Riches," Chapter 13: "The Progress of an Epidemic"

When Mr. Merdle eventually goes bankrupt—dragging many, including Arthur Clennam, into bankruptcy with him—and commits suicide at a public bathhouse, note the religious language that Dickens uses to pronounce judgment on him.

Before parting, at Physician's door, [Merdle's doctor and lawyer] both looked up at the sunny morning sky, into which the smoke of a few early fires and the breath and voices of a few early stirrers were peacefully rising, and then looked round upon the immense city, and said, If all those hundreds and thousands of beggared people who were yet asleep could only know, as they two spoke, the ruin that impended over them, what a fearful cry against one miserable soul would go up to Heaven!

. . . Appalling whispers [began] to circulate, east, west, north, and south. At first, they were faint, and went no further than a doubt whether Mr. Merdle's wealth would be found to be as vast as had been supposed; whether there might not be a temporary difficulty in "realising it"; whether there might not even be a temporary suspension (say a month or so), on the part of the wonderful Bank. As the whispers became louder, which they did from that time every minute, they became more threatening. He had sprung from nothing, by no natural growth or process that any one could account for; he had been, after all, a low, ignorant fellow; he had been a down-looking man, and no one had ever been able to catch his eye; he had been taken up by all sorts of people in quite an unaccountable manner; he had never had any money of his own, his ventures had been utterly reckless, and his expenditure had been most enormous. In steady progression, as the day declined, the talk rose in sound and purpose. He had left a letter at the Baths addressed to his physician, and his physician had got the letter, and the letter would be produced at the Inquest on the morrow, and it would fall like a thunderbolt upon the multitude he had deluded. Numbers of men in every profession and trade would be blighted by his insolvency; old people who had been in easy circumstances all their lives would have no place of repentance for their trust in him but the workhouse; legions of women and children would have their whole future desolated by the hand of this mighty scoundrel. Every partaker of his magnificent feasts would be seen to have been a sharer in the plunder of innumerable homes; every servile worshipper of riches who had helped to set him on his pedestal, would have done better to worship the Devil point-blank. So, the talk, lashed louder and higher by confirmation on confirmation, and by edition after edition of the evening papers, swelled into such a roar when night came, as might have brought one to believe that a solitary watcher on the gallery above the Dome of St Paul's would have perceived the night air to be laden with a heavy muttering of the name of Merdle, coupled with every form of execration.

For by that time it was known that the late Mr. Merdle's complaint had been, simply, Forgery and Robbery. He, the uncouth object of such widespread adulation, the sitter at great men's feasts, the roc's egg[11] of great ladies' assemblies, the subduer of exclusiveness, the leveller of pride, the patron of patrons, the bargain-driver with a Minister for Lordships of the Circumlocution Office, the recipient of more acknowledgment within some ten or fifteen years, at most, than had been bestowed in England upon all peaceful public benefactors, and upon all the leaders of all the Arts and Sciences, with all their works to testify for them, during two centuries at least—he, the shining wonder, the new constellation to be followed by the wise men bringing gifts, until it stopped over certain carrion at the bottom of a bath and disappeared—was simply the greatest Forger and the greatest Thief that ever cheated the gallows.

Book the Second: "Riches," Chapter 25: "The Chief Butler Resigns the Seals of Office"

---

11 Something valuable and much sought after; from Middle Eastern mythology.

13. That Rotten Reed

Bleak House

Though Arthur Clennam and Mr. Pancks both make the mistake of buying into Mr. Merdle's fraudulent schemes, they at least manage to avoid becoming mentally and spiritually tainted by the experience. Such is not always the case in Dickens's works. In Bleak House, *when young Richard "Rick" Carstone thinks he sees a chance of gaining a fortune through Jarndyce and Jarndyce, an ongoing family lawsuit, it poisons his mind against John Jarndyce, the kindly relative who has been like a second father to him and his cousin Ada. Again, Dickens writes of this process as a sort of infection or disease. Here John Jarndyce is speaking with the narrator, Esther Summerson.*

". . . Well, dearest little woman, we must look forbearingly on it. He is not to blame. Jarndyce and Jarndyce has warped him out of himself, and perverted me in his eyes. I have known it do as bad deeds, and worse, many a time. If two angels could be concerned in it, I believe it would change their nature."

"It has not changed yours, Guardian."

"Oh yes, it has, my dear," he said, laughingly. "It has made the south wind easterly, I don't know how often. Rick mistrusts and suspects me—goes to lawyers, and is taught to mistrust and suspect me. Hears I have conflicting interests; claims clashing against his, and what not. Whereas, Heaven knows that if I could get out of the mountains of Wiglomeration on which my unfortunate name has been so long bestowed (which I can't), or could level them by the extinction of my own original right (which I can't either, and no human power ever can, anyhow, I believe, to such a pass have we got), I would do it this hour. I would rather restore to poor Rick his proper nature, than be endowed with all the money that dead suitors, broken, heart and soul, upon the wheel of Chancery[12], have left unclaimed with the Accountant-General—and that's money enough, my dear, to be cast into a pyramid, in memory of Chancery's transcendent wickedness."

"Is it possible, Guardian," I asked, amazed, "that Richard can be suspicious of you?"

"Ah, my love, my love," he said, "it is in the subtle poison of such abuses to breed such diseases. His blood is infected, and objects lose their natural aspects in his sight. It is not *his* fault."

"But it is a terrible misfortune, guardian."

"It is a terrible misfortune, little woman, to be ever drawn within the influences of Jarndyce and Jarndyce. I know none greater. By little and little he has been induced to trust in that rotten reed, and it communicates some portion of its rottenness to everything around him. But again, I say, with all my soul, we must be patient with poor Rick, and not blame him. What a troop of fine fresh hearts, like his, have I seen in my time turned by the same means!"

I could not help expressing something of my wonder and regret that his benevolent disinterested intentions had prospered so little.

"We must not say so, Dame Durden[13]," he cheerfully replied; "Ada is the happier, I hope; and that is much. I did think that I and both these young creatures might be friends, instead of distrustful foes, and that we might so far counteract the suit, and prove too strong for it. But it was too much to expect. Jarndyce and Jarndyce was the curtain of Rick's cradle."

"But, Guardian, may we not hope that a little experience will teach him what a false and wretched thing it is?"

---

12 The Court of Chancery handled property disputes.

13 One of Esther's nicknames.

"We *will* hope so, my Esther," said Mr. Jarndyce, "and that it may not teach him so too late. In any case we must not be hard on him. There are not many grown and matured men living while we speak, good men too, who, if they were thrown into this same court as suitors, would not be vitally changed and depreciated within three years—within two—within one. How can we stand amazed at poor Rick? A young man so unfortunate," here he fell into a lower tone, as if he were thinking aloud, "cannot at first believe (who could?) that Chancery is what it is. He looks to it, flushed and fitfully, to do something with his interests, and bring them to some settlement. It procrastinates, disappoints, tries, tortures him; wears out his sanguine hopes and patience, thread by thread; but he still looks to it, and hankers after it, and finds his whole world treacherous and hollow. Well, well, well! Enough of this, my dear!"

Chapter 35: "Esther's Narrative"

14. Absolutely without Pity

A Tale of Two Cities

Perhaps nowhere else does Dickens so expertly weave together personal and corporate sin as in this story of the French Revolution. The entwined history of the Manette, Defarge, and Evremonde families plays out against—and represents in miniature—the massive societal struggle taking place. On both the small and the large scale, cycles of cruelty and revenge crush generation after generation, fueling hatred that appears unstoppable. We catch a glimpse of the roots of the conflict in this early passage about the heartless behavior of the Marquis St. Evremonde.

With a wild rattle and clatter, and an inhuman abandonment of consideration not easy to be understood in these days, the carriage dashed through streets and swept round corners, with women screaming before it, and men clutching each other and clutching children out of its way. At last, swooping at a street corner by a fountain, one of its wheels came to a sickening little jolt, and there was a loud cry from a number of voices, and the horses reared and plunged.

But for the latter inconvenience, the carriage probably would not have stopped; carriages were often known to drive on, and leave their wounded behind, and why not? But the frightened valet had got down in a hurry, and there were twenty hands at the horses' bridles.

"What has gone wrong?" said Monsieur, calmly looking out.

A tall man in a nightcap had caught up a bundle from among the feet of the horses, and had laid it on the basement of the fountain, and was down in the mud and wet, howling over it like a wild animal.

"Pardon, Monsieur the Marquis!" said a ragged and submissive man, "it is a child."

"Why does he make that abominable noise? Is it his child?"

"Excuse me, Monsieur the Marquis—it is a pity—yes."

The fountain was a little removed; for the street opened, where it was, into a space some ten or twelve yards square. As the tall man suddenly got up from the ground, and came running at the carriage, Monsieur the Marquis clapped his hand for an instant on his sword-hilt.

"Killed!" shrieked the man, in wild desperation, extending both arms at their length above his head, and staring at him. "Dead!"

The people closed round, and looked at Monsieur the Marquis. There was nothing revealed by the many eyes that looked at him but watchfulness and eagerness; there was no visible menacing or anger. Neither did the people say anything; after the first cry, they had been silent, and they remained so. The voice of the submissive man who had spoken, was flat and tame in its extreme submission. Monsieur the Marquis ran his eyes over them all, as if they had been mere rats come out of their holes.

He took out his purse.

"It is extraordinary to me," said he, "that you people cannot take care of yourselves and your children. One or the other of you is for ever in the way. How do I know what injury you have done my horses. See! Give him that."

He threw out a gold coin for the valet to pick up, and all the heads craned forward that all the eyes might look down at it as it fell. The tall man called out again with a most unearthly cry, "Dead!"

He was arrested by the quick arrival of another man, for whom the rest made way. On seeing him, the miserable creature fell upon his shoulder, sobbing and crying, and pointing to the fountain, where some women were stooping over the motionless bundle, and moving gently about it. They were as silent, however, as the men.

"I know all, I know all," said the last comer. "Be a brave man, my Gaspard! It is better for the poor little plaything to die so, than to live. It has died in a moment without pain. Could it have lived an hour as happily?"

"You are a philosopher, you there," said the Marquis, smiling. "How do they call you?"

"They call me Defarge."

"Of what trade?"

"Monsieur the Marquis, vendor of wine."

"Pick up that, philosopher and vendor of wine," said the Marquis, throwing him another gold coin, "and spend it as you will. The horses there; are they right?"

Without deigning to look at the assemblage a second time, Monsieur the Marquis leaned back in his seat, and was just being driven away with the air of a gentleman who had accidentally broke some common thing, and had paid for it, and could afford to pay for it; when his ease was suddenly disturbed by a coin flying into his carriage, and ringing on its floor.

"Hold!" said Monsieur the Marquis. "Hold the horses! Who threw that?"

He looked to the spot where Defarge the vendor of wine had stood, a moment before; but the wretched father was grovelling on his face on the pavement in that spot, and the figure that stood beside him was the figure of a dark stout woman, knitting.

"You dogs!" said the Marquis, but smoothly, and with an unchanged front, except as to the spots on his nose: "I would ride over any of you very willingly, and exterminate you from the earth. If I knew which rascal threw at the carriage, and if that brigand were sufficiently near it, he should be crushed under the wheels."

So cowed was their condition, and so long and hard their experience of what such a man could do to them, within the law and beyond it, that not a voice, or a hand, or even an eye, was raised. Among the men, not one. But the woman who stood knitting looked up steadily, and looked the Marquis in the face. It was not for his dignity to notice it; his contemptuous eyes passed over her, and over all the other rats; and he leaned back in his seat again, and gave the word "Go on!"

Book the Second: "The Golden Thread," Chapter 7: "Monseigneur in Town"

As we eventually learn, the knitting woman, Madame Defarge, has very personal reasons to wreak revenge on the Marquis St. Evremonde. The Evremondes (the Marquis included) once raped, tortured, pillaged, and killed members of her family, until Madame Defarge is the only one left who remembers firsthand what happened to them. Dickens portrays her and her husband as being at the forefront of the revolution when it comes, gaining immense power—enough power to pose a serious threat to the Marquis's nephew, Charles Darnay, and his wife and daughter (both named Lucie). But at first, the Defarges feign a willingness to be helpful to Lucie, for the sake of her father, a former prisoner and Defarge's former employer.

"Is that his child?" said Madame Defarge, stopping in her work for the first time, and pointing her knitting-needle at little Lucie as if it were the finger of Fate.

"Yes, madame," answered Mr. Lorry; "this is our poor prisoner's darling daughter, and only child."

The shadow attendant on Madame Defarge and her party seemed to fall so threatening and dark on the child, that her mother instinctively kneeled on the ground beside her, and held her to her breast. The shadow attendant on Madame Defarge and her party seemed then to fall, threatening and dark, on both the mother and the child.

"It is enough, my husband," said Madame Defarge. "I have seen them. We may go."

But, the suppressed manner had enough of menace in it—not visible and presented, but indistinct and withheld—to alarm Lucie into saying, as she laid her appealing hand on Madame Defarge's dress:

"You will be good to my poor husband. You will do him no harm. You will help me to see him if you can?"

"Your husband is not my business here," returned Madame Defarge, looking down at her with perfect composure. "It is the daughter of your father who is my business here."

"For my sake, then, be merciful to my husband. For my child's sake! She will put her hands together and pray you to be merciful. We are more afraid of you than of these others."

Madame Defarge received it as a compliment, and looked at her husband. Defarge, who had been uneasily biting his thumb-nail and looking at her, collected his face into a sterner expression.

"What is it that your husband says in that little letter?" asked Madame Defarge, with a lowering smile. "Influence; he says something touching influence?"

"That my father," said Lucie, hurriedly taking the paper from her breast, but with her alarmed eyes on her questioner and not on it, "has much influence around him."

"Surely it will release him!" said Madame Defarge. "Let it do so."

"As a wife and mother," cried Lucie, most earnestly, "I implore you to have pity on me and not to exercise any power that you possess, against my innocent husband, but to use it in his behalf. O sister-woman, think of me. As a wife and mother!"

Madame Defarge looked, coldly as ever, at the suppliant, and said, turning to her friend The Vengeance:

"The wives and mothers we have been used to see, since we were as little as this child, and much less, have not been greatly considered? We have known *their* husbands and fathers laid in prison and kept from them, often enough? All our lives, we have seen our sister-women suffer, in themselves and in their children, poverty, nakedness, hunger, thirst, sickness, misery, oppression and neglect of all kinds?"

"We have seen nothing else," returned The Vengeance.

"We have borne this a long time," said Madame Defarge, turning her eyes again upon Lucie. "Judge you! Is it likely that the trouble of one wife and mother would be much to us now?"

She resumed her knitting and went out. The Vengeance followed. Defarge went last, and closed the door.

Book the Third: "The Track of a Storm," Chapter 3: "The Shadow"

There were many women at that time, upon whom the time laid a dreadfully disfiguring hand; but, there was not one among them more to be dreaded than this ruthless woman, now taking her way along the streets. Of a strong and fearless character, of shrewd sense and readiness, of great determination, of that kind of beauty which not only seems to impart to its possessor firmness and animosity, but to strike into others an instinctive recognition of those qualities; the troubled time would have heaved her up, under any circumstances. But, imbued from her childhood with a brooding sense of wrong, and an inveterate hatred of a class, opportunity had developed her into a tigress. She was absolutely without pity. If she had ever had the virtue in her, it had quite gone out of her.

It was nothing to her, that an innocent man was to die for the sins of his forefathers; she saw, not him, but them. It was nothing to her, that his wife was to be made a widow and his daughter an orphan; that was insufficient punishment, because they were her natural enemies and her prey, and as such had no right to live. To appeal to her, was made hopeless by her having no sense of pity, even for herself. If she had been laid low in the streets, in any of the many encounters in which she had been engaged, she would not have pitied herself; nor, if she had been ordered to the axe to-morrow, would she have gone to it with any softer feeling than a fierce desire to change places with the man who sent her there.

Such a heart Madame Defarge carried under her rough robe. Carelessly worn, it was a becoming robe enough, in a certain weird way, and her dark hair looked rich under her coarse red cap. Lying hidden in her bosom, was a loaded pistol. Lying hidden at her waist, was a sharpened dagger. Thus accoutred, and walking with the confident tread of such a character, and with the supple freedom of a woman who had habitually walked in her girlhood, bare-foot and bare-legged, on the brown sea-sand, Madame Defarge took her way along the streets.

Book the Third: "The Track of a Storm," Chapter 14: "The Knitting Done"

15. Destroying Angels

David Copperfield

In Dickens's world, it does not always take greed or vengeance to warp a mind and soul; even love can do it, if that love is tyrannical and domineering. Dickens's own domestic attitudes and actions left a great deal to be desired. But in his writings, he communicates a vision of family in which each person is loved, valued, and respected.

Mr. Murdstone in David Copperfield *is the flip side of that vision, and perhaps a case of Dickens being aware, on some level, of his own darkest impulses. For Mr. Murdstone, to love means to exercise absolute control (with help from his equally controlling sister). That insistence on power and control destroys young David's family after Mr. Murdstone marries David's mother. In particular, from his interaction with the Murdstones, David gains some new fears about the Christian faith.*

My mother did not suffer her authority to pass from her without a shadow of protest. One night when Miss Murdstone had been developing certain household plans to her brother, of which he signified his approbation, my mother suddenly began to cry, and said she thought she might have been consulted.

"Clara!" said Mr. Murdstone sternly. "Clara! I wonder at you."

"Oh, it's very well to say you wonder, Edward!" cried my mother, "and it's very well for you to talk about firmness, but you wouldn't like it yourself."

Firmness, I may observe, was the grand quality on which both Mr. and Miss Murdstone took their stand. However I might have expressed my comprehension of it at that time, if I had been called upon, I nevertheless did clearly comprehend in my own way, that it was another name for tyranny; and for a certain gloomy, arrogant, devil's humour, that was in them both. The creed, as I should state it now, was this. Mr. Murdstone was firm; nobody in his world was to be so firm as Mr. Murdstone; nobody else in his world was to be firm at all, for everybody was to be bent to his firmness. Miss Murdstone was an exception. She might be firm, but only by relationship, and in an inferior and tributary degree. My mother was another exception. She might be firm, and must be; but only in bearing their firmness, and firmly believing there was no other firmness upon earth.

"It's very hard," said my mother, "that in my own house—"

"*My* own house?" repeated Mr. Murdstone. "Clara!"

"*Our* own house, I mean," faltered my mother, evidently frightened—"I hope you must know what I mean, Edward—it's very hard that in *your* own house I may not have a word to say about domestic matters. I am sure I managed very well before we were married. There's evidence," said my mother, sobbing; "ask Peggotty if I didn't do very well when I wasn't interfered with!"

"Edward," said Miss Murdstone, "let there be an end of this. I go tomorrow."

"Jane Murdstone," said her brother, "be silent! How dare you to insinuate that you don't know my character better than your words imply?"

"I am sure," my poor mother went on, at a grievous disadvantage, and with many tears, "I don't want anybody to go. I should be very miserable and unhappy if anybody was to go. I don't ask much. I am not unreasonable. I only want to be consulted sometimes. I am very much obliged to anybody who assists me, and I only want to be consulted as a mere form, sometimes. I thought you were pleased, once, with my being a little inexperienced and girlish, Edward—I am sure you said so—but you seem to hate me for it now, you are so severe."

"Edward," said Miss Murdstone, again, "let there be an end of this. I go tomorrow."

"Jane Murdstone," thundered Mr. Murdstone. "Will you be silent? How dare you?"

Miss Murdstone made a jail-delivery of her pocket-handkerchief, and held it before her eyes.

"Clara," he continued, looking at my mother, "you surprise me! You astound me! Yes, I had a satisfaction in the thought of marrying an inexperienced and artless person, and forming her character, and infusing into it some amount of that firmness and decision of which it stood in need. But when Jane Murdstone is kind enough to come to my assistance in this endeavour, and to assume, for my sake, a condition something like a housekeeper's, and when she meets with a base return—"

"Oh, pray, pray, Edward," cried my mother, "don't accuse me of being ungrateful. I am sure I am not ungrateful. No one ever said I was before. I have many faults, but not that. Oh, don't, my dear!"

"When Jane Murdstone meets, I say," he went on, after waiting until my mother was silent, "with a base return, that feeling of mine is chilled and altered."

"Don't, my love, say that!" implored my mother very piteously. "Oh, don't, Edward! I can't bear to hear it. Whatever I am, I am affectionate. I know I am affectionate. I wouldn't say it, if I wasn't certain that I am. Ask Peggotty. I am sure she'll tell you I'm affectionate."

"There is no extent of mere weakness, Clara," said Mr. Murdstone in reply, "that can have the least weight with me. You lose breath."

"Pray let us be friends," said my mother, "I couldn't live under coldness or unkindness. I am so sorry. I have a great many defects, I know, and it's very good of you, Edward, with your strength of mind, to endeavour to correct them for me. Jane, I don't object to anything. I should be quite broken-hearted if you thought of leaving—" My mother was too much overcome to go on.

"Jane Murdstone," said Mr. Murdstone to his sister, "any harsh words between us are, I hope, uncommon. It is not my fault that so unusual an occurrence has taken place to-night. I was betrayed into it by another. Nor is it your fault. You were betrayed into it by another. Let us both try to forget it. And as this," he added, after these magnanimous words, "is not a fit scene for the boy—David, go to bed!"

I could hardly find the door, through the tears that stood in my eyes. I was so sorry for my mother's distress; but I groped my way out, and groped my way up to my room in the dark, without even having the heart to say good night to Peggotty, or to get a candle from her. When her coming up to look for me, an hour or so afterwards, awoke me, she said that my mother had gone to bed poorly, and that Mr. and Miss Murdstone were sitting alone.

Going down next morning rather earlier than usual, I paused outside the parlour-door, on hearing my mother's voice. She was very earnestly and humbly entreating Miss Murdstone's pardon, which that lady granted, and a perfect reconciliation took place. I never knew my mother afterwards to give an opinion on any matter, without first appealing to Miss Murdstone, or without having first ascertained by some sure means, what Miss Murdstone's opinion was; and I never saw Miss Murdstone, when out of temper (she was infirm that way), move her hand towards her bag as if she were going to take out the keys and offer to resign them to my mother, without seeing that my mother was in a terrible fright.

The gloomy taint that was in the Murdstone blood, darkened the Murdstone religion, which was austere and wrathful. I have thought, since, that its assuming that character was a necessary consequence of Mr. Murdstone's firmness, which wouldn't allow him to let anybody off from the utmost weight of the severest penalties he could find any excuse for. Be this as it may, I well remember the tremendous visages with which we used to go to church, and the changed air of the place. Again, the dreaded Sunday comes round, and I file into the old pew first, like a guarded captive brought to a condemned service. Again, Miss Murdstone, in a black velvet gown, that looks as if it had been made out of a pall, follows close upon me; then my mother; then her husband. There is no Peggotty now, as in the old time. Again, I listen to Miss Murdstone mumbling the responses, and emphasizing all the dread words with a cruel relish. Again, I see her dark eyes roll round the church when she says "miserable sinners," as if she were calling all the congregation names. Again, I catch rare glimpses of my mother, moving her lips timidly between the two, with one of them muttering at each ear like low thunder. Again, I wonder with a sudden fear whether it is likely that our good old clergyman can be wrong, and Mr. and Miss Murdstone right, and that all the angels in Heaven can be destroying angels. Again, if I move a finger or relax a muscle of my face, Miss Murdstone pokes me with her prayer-book, and makes my side ache.

Yes, and again, as we walk home, I note some neighbours looking at my mother and at me, and whispering. Again, as the three go on arm-in-arm, and I linger behind alone, I follow some of those looks, and wonder if my mother's step be really not so light as I have seen it, and if the gaiety of her beauty be really almost worried away. Again, I wonder whether any of the neighbours call to mind, as I do, how we used to walk home together, she and I; and I wonder stupidly about that, all the dreary, dismal day.

Chapter 4: "I Fall into Disgrace"

16. A Matter of Business

Nicholas Nickleby

Along with tyranny, a twisted and self-centered love can also lead to exploitation. The villainous Ralph Nickleby has a soft spot for his niece, Kate, but that does not keep him from letting his rich and powerful friends take advantage of her at a dinner party.

All this while, Kate had sat as silently as she could, scarcely daring to raise her eyes, lest they should encounter the admiring gaze of Lord Frederick Verisopht, or, what was still more embarrassing, the bold looks of his friend Sir Mulberry. The latter gentleman was obliging enough to direct general attention towards her.

"Here is Miss Nickleby," observed Sir Mulberry, "wondering why the deuce somebody doesn't make love to her."

"No, indeed," said Kate, looking hastily up, "I—" and then she stopped, feeling it would have been better to have said nothing at all.

"I'll hold any man fifty pounds," said Sir Mulberry, "that Miss Nickleby can't look in my face, and tell me she wasn't thinking so."

"Done!" cried the noble gull. "Within ten minutes."

"Done!" responded Sir Mulberry. The money was produced on both sides, and the Honourable Mr. Snobb was elected to the double office of stake-holder and time-keeper.

"Pray," said Kate, in great confusion, while these preliminaries were in course of completion,—"Pray do not make me the subject of any bets. Uncle, I cannot really—"

"Why not, my dear?" replied Ralph, in whose grating voice, however, there was an unusual huskiness, as though he spoke unwillingly, and would rather that the proposition had not been broached. "It is done in a moment; there is nothing in it. If the gentlemen insist on it—"

"*I* don't insist on it," said Sir Mulberry, with a loud laugh. "That is, I by no means insist upon Miss Nickleby's making the denial, for if she does, I lose; but I shall be glad to see her bright eyes, especially as she favours the mahogany so much."

"So she does, and it's too ba-a-d of you, Miss Nickleby," said the noble youth.

"Quite cruel," said Mr. Pyke.

"Horrid cruel," said Mr. Pluck.

"I don't care if I do lose," said Sir Mulberry; "for one tolerable look at Miss Nickleby's eyes is worth double the money."

"More," said Mr. Pyke.

"Far more," said Mr. Pluck.

"How goes the enemy, Snobb?" asked Sir Mulberry Hawk.

"Four minutes gone."

"Bravo!"

"Won't you ma-ake one effort for me, Miss Nickleby?" asked Lord Frederick, after a short interval.

"You needn't trouble yourself to inquire, my buck," said Sir Mulberry; "Miss Nickleby and I understand each other; she declares on my side, and shows her taste. You haven't a chance, old fellow. Time, Snobb?"

"Eight minutes gone."

"Get the money ready," said Sir Mulberry; "you'll soon hand over."

"Ha, ha, ha!" laughed Mr. Pyke.

Mr. Pluck, who always came second, and topped his companion if he could, screamed outright.

The poor girl, who was so overwhelmed with confusion that she scarcely knew what she did, had determined to remain perfectly quiet; but fearing that by so doing she might seem to countenance Sir Mulberry's boast, which had been uttered with great coarseness and vulgarity of manner, raised her eyes, and looked him in the face. There was something so odious, so insolent, so repulsive in the look which met her, that, without the power to stammer forth a syllable, she rose and hurried from the room. She restrained her tears by a great effort until she was alone up stairs, and then gave them vent.

"Capital!" said Sir Mulberry Hawk, putting the stakes in his pocket. "That's a girl of spirit, and we'll drink her health."

It is needless to say, that Pyke and Co. responded, with great warmth of manner, to this proposal, or that the toast was drunk with many little insinuations from the firm, relative to the completeness of Sir Mulberry's conquest. Ralph, who, while the attention of the other guests was attracted to the principals in the preceding scene, had eyed them like a wolf, appeared to breathe more freely now his niece was gone; the decanters passing quickly round, he leaned back in his chair, and turned his eyes from speaker to speaker, as they warmed with wine, with looks that seemed to search their hearts, and lay bare, for his distempered sport, every idle thought within them.

Meanwhile Kate, left wholly to herself, had, in some degree, recovered her composure. She had learnt, from a female attendant, that her uncle wished to see her before she left, and had also gleaned the satisfactory intelligence, that the gentlemen would take coffee at table. The prospect of seeing them no more contributed greatly to calm her agitation, and, taking up a book, she composed herself to read.

She started sometimes when the sudden opening of the dining-room door let loose a wild shout of noisy revelry, and more than once rose in great alarm, as a fancied footstep on the staircase impressed her with the fear that some stray member of the party was returning alone. Nothing occurring, however, to realise her apprehensions, she endeavoured to fix her attention more closely on her book, in which by degrees she became so much interested, that she had read on through several chapters without heed of time or place, when she was terrified by suddenly hearing her name pronounced by a man's voice close at her ear.

The book fell from her hand. Lounging on an ottoman close beside her, was Sir Mulberry Hawk, evidently the worse—if a man be a ruffian at heart, he is never the better—for wine.

"What a delightful studiousness!" said this accomplished gentleman. "Was it real, now, or only to display the eyelashes?"

Kate, looking anxiously towards the door, made no reply.

"I have looked at 'em for five minutes," said Sir Mulberry. "Upon my soul, they're perfect. Why did I speak and destroy such a pretty little picture!"

"Do me the favour to be silent now, sir," replied Kate.

"No, don't," said Sir Mulberry, folding his crush hat to lay his elbow on, and bringing himself still closer to the young lady. "Upon my life, you oughtn't to. Such a devoted slave of yours, Miss Nickleby—it's an infernal thing to treat him so harshly, upon my soul it is."

"I wish you to understand, sir," said Kate, trembling in spite of herself, but speaking with great indignation, "that your behaviour offends and disgusts me. If you have a spark of gentlemanly feeling remaining, you will leave me."

"Now why," said Sir Mulberry, "why will you keep up this appearance of excessive rigour, my sweet creature? Now be more natural—my dear Miss Nickleby, be more natural—do."

Kate hastily rose; but as she rose, Sir Mulberry caught her dress, and forcibly detained her.

"Let me go, sir," she cried, her heart swelling with anger. "Do you hear? Instantly—this moment."

"Sit down, sit down," said Sir Mulberry; "I want to talk to you."

"Unhand me, sir, this instant," cried Kate.

"Not for the world," rejoined Sir Mulberry. Thus speaking, he leaned over, as if to replace her in her chair; but the young lady, making a violent effort to disengage herself, he lost his balance, and measured his length upon the ground. As Kate sprung forward to leave the room, Mr. Ralph Nickleby appeared in the doorway, and confronted her.

"What is this?" said Ralph.

"It is this, sir," replied Kate, violently agitated: "that beneath the roof where I, a helpless girl, your dead brother's child, should most have found protection, I have been exposed to insult which should make you shrink to look upon me. Let me pass you."

Ralph *did* shrink, as the indignant girl fixed her kindling eye upon him; but he did not comply with her injunction, nevertheless; for he led her to a distant seat, and returning, and approaching Sir Mulberry Hawk, who had by this time risen, motioned towards the door.

"Your way lies there, sir," said Ralph, in a suppressed voice, that some devil might have owned with pride.

"What do you mean by that?" demanded his friend, fiercely.

The swollen veins stood out like sinews on Ralph's wrinkled forehead, and the nerves about his mouth worked as though some unendurable emotion wrung them; but he smiled disdainfully, and again pointed to the door.

"Do you know me, you old madman?" asked Sir Mulberry.

"Well," said Ralph. The fashionable vagabond for the moment quite quailed under the steady look of the older sinner, and walked towards the door, muttering as he went.

"You wanted the lord, did you?" he said, stopping short when he reached the door, as if a new light had broken in upon him, and confronting Ralph again. "Damme, I was in the way, was I?"

Ralph smiled again, but made no answer.

"Who brought him to you first?" pursued Sir Mulberry: "and how, without me, could you ever have wound him in your net as you have?"

"The net is a large one, and rather full," said Ralph. "Take care that it chokes nobody in the meshes."

"You would sell your flesh and blood for money; yourself, if you have not already made a bargain with the Devil," retorted the other. "Do you mean to tell me that your pretty niece was not brought here, as a decoy for the drunken boy downstairs?"

Although this hurried dialogue was carried on in a suppressed tone on both sides, Ralph looked involuntarily round to ascertain that Kate had not moved her position so as to be within hearing. His adversary saw the advantage he had gained, and followed it up.

"Do you mean to tell me," he asked again, "that it is not so? Do you mean to say that if he had found his way up here instead of me, you wouldn't have been a little more blind, and a little more deaf, and a little less flourishing, than you have been? Come, Nickleby, answer me that."

"I tell you this," replied Ralph, "that if I brought her here, as a matter of business—"

"Ay, that's the word," interposed Sir Mulberry, with a laugh. "You're coming to yourself again now."

"—As a matter of business," pursued Ralph, speaking slowly and firmly, as a man who has made up his mind to say no more, "because I thought she might make some impression on the silly youth you have taken in hand and are lending good help to ruin, I knew—knowing him—that it would be long before he outraged her girl's feelings, and that, unless he offended by mere puppyism and emptiness, he would, with a little management, respect the sex and conduct even of his usurer's niece. But if I thought to draw him on more gently by this device, I did not think of subjecting the girl to the licentiousness and brutality of so old a hand as you. And now we understand each other."

"Especially as there was nothing to be got by it—eh?" sneered Sir Mulberry.

"Exactly so," said Ralph. He had turned away, and looked over his shoulder to make this last reply. The eyes of the two worthies met, with an expression as if each rascal felt that there was no disguising himself from the other; and Sir Mulberry Hawk shrugged his shoulders and walked slowly out.

His friend closed the door, and looked restlessly towards the spot where his niece still remained in the attitude in which he had left her. She had flung herself heavily upon the couch, and with her head drooping over the cushion, and her face hidden in her hands, seemed to be still weeping in an agony of shame and grief.

Ralph would have walked into any poverty-stricken debtor's house, and pointed him out to a bailiff, though in attendance upon a young child's death-bed, without the smallest concern, because it would have been a matter quite in the ordinary course of business, and the man would have been an offender against his only code of morality. But here was a young girl, who had done no wrong save that of coming into the world alive; who had patiently yielded to all his wishes; who had tried hard to please him; above all, who didn't owe him money; and he felt awkward and nervous.

Ralph took a chair at some distance; then, another chair a little nearer; then, moved a little nearer still; then, nearer again, and finally sat himself on the same sofa, and laid his hand on Kate's arm.

"Hush, my dear!" he said, as she drew it back, and her sobs burst out afresh. "Hush, hush! Don't mind it now; don't think of it."

"O, for pity's sake, let me go home," cried Kate. "Let me leave this house, and go home."

"Yes, yes," said Ralph. "You shall. But you must dry your eyes first, and compose yourself. Let me raise your head. There—there."

"Oh, uncle!" exclaimed Kate, clasping her hands. "What have I done—what have I done—that you should subject me to this? If I had wronged you in thought, or word, or deed, it would have been most cruel to me, and the memory of one you must have loved in some old time; but—"

"Only listen to me for a moment," interrupted Ralph, seriously alarmed by the violence of her emotions. "I didn't know it would be so; it was impossible for me to foresee it. I did all I could.—Come, let us walk about. You are faint with the closeness of the room, and the heat of these lamps. You will be better now, if you make the slightest effort."

"I will do anything," replied Kate, "if you will only send me home."

"Well, well, I will," said Ralph; "but you must get back your own looks; for those you have, will frighten them, and nobody must know of this but you and I. Now let us walk the other way. There. You look better even now."

With such encouragements as these, Ralph Nickleby walked to and fro, with his niece leaning on his arm; actually trembling beneath her touch.

In the same manner, when he judged it prudent to allow her to depart, he supported her down stairs, after adjusting her shawl and performing such little offices, most probably for the first time in his life. Across the hall, and down the steps, Ralph led her too; nor did he withdraw his hand, until she was seated in the coach.

As the door of the vehicle was roughly closed, a comb fell from Kate's hair, close at her uncle's feet; and as he picked it up, and returned it into her hand, the light from a neighbouring lamp shone upon her face. The lock of hair that had escaped and curled loosely over her brow, the traces of tears yet scarcely dry, the flushed cheek, the look of sorrow, all fired some dormant train of recollection in the old man's breast; and the face of his dead brother seemed present before him, with the very look it bore on some occasion of boyish grief, of which every minutest circumstance flashed upon his mind, with the distinctness of a scene of yesterday.

Ralph Nickleby, who was proof against all appeals of blood and kindred—who was steeled against every tale of sorrow and distress—staggered while he looked, and went back into his house, as a man who had seen a spirit from some world beyond the grave.

Chapter 19: "Descriptive of a Dinner at Mr. Ralph Nickleby's, and of the Manner in Which the Company Entertained Themselves, before Dinner, at Dinner, and after Dinner"

II

Repentance and Grace

17. One Prayer for Mercy

Oliver Twist

One of Dickens's most famous characters—and in his own day, one of his most infamous—is Nancy, the prostitute who gives her life to save innocent young Oliver Twist from her own thieving associates. In a preface he wrote to a later edition of Oliver Twist, *Dickens responded as follows to those who had criticized him for portraying such a degraded character:*

> It is useless to discuss whether the conduct and character of the girl seems natural or unnatural, probable or improbable, right or wrong. IT IS TRUE. Every man who has watched these melancholy shades of life, must know it to be so. From the first introduction of that poor wretch, to her laying her blood-stained head upon the robber's breast, there is not one word exaggerated or over-wrought. It is emphatically God's truth, for it is the truth He leaves in such depraved and miserable breasts; the hope yet lingering there; the last fair drop of water at the bottom of the weed-choked well. It involves the best and worst shades of our nature; much of its ugliest hues, and something of its most beautiful; it is a contradiction, an anomaly, an apparent impossibility; but it is a truth. I am glad to have had it doubted, for in that circumstance I should find a sufficient assurance (if I wanted any) that it needed to be told.[1]

In the following passage, Nancy comes to warn Rose Maylie, a member of the family that is trying to help Oliver, of the dangers threatening the boy.

---

1 Charles Dickens, "Preface to the Charles Dickens Edition," *Oliver Twist*, 1867. An earlier version of this preface was written for the third edition in 1841.

The girl's life had been squandered in the streets, and among the most noisome of the stews and dens of London, but there was something of the woman's original nature left in her still; and when she heard a light step approaching the door opposite to that by which she had entered, and thought of the wide contrast which the small room would in another moment contain, she felt burdened with the sense of her own deep shame, and shrunk as though she could scarcely bear the presence of her with whom she had sought this interview.

But struggling with these better feelings was pride,—the vice of the lowest and most debased creatures no less than of the high and self-assured. The miserable companion of thieves and ruffians, the fallen outcast of low haunts, the associate of the scourings of the jails and hulks, living within the shadow of the gallows itself,—even this degraded being felt too proud to betray a feeble gleam of the womanly feeling which she thought a weakness, but which alone connected her with that humanity, of which her wasting life had obliterated so many, many traces when a very child.

She raised her eyes sufficiently to observe that the figure which presented itself was that of a slight and beautiful girl; then, bending them on the ground, she tossed her head with affected carelessness as she said:

"It's a hard matter to get to see you, lady. If I had taken offence, and gone away, as many would have done, you'd have been sorry for it one day, and not without reason either."

"I am very sorry if any one has behaved harshly to you," replied Rose. "Do not think of that. Tell me why you wished to see me. I am the person you inquired for."

The kind tone of this answer, the sweet voice, the gentle manner, the absence of any accent of haughtiness or displeasure, took the girl completely by surprise, and she burst into tears.

"Oh, lady, lady!" she said, clasping her hands passionately before her face, "if there was more like you, there would be fewer like me,—there would—there would!"

"Sit down," said Rose, earnestly. "If you are in poverty or affliction I shall be truly glad to relieve you if I can,—I shall indeed. Sit down."

"Let me stand, lady," said the girl, still weeping, "and do not speak to me so kindly till you know me better. It is growing late. Is—is—that door shut?"

"Yes," said Rose, recoiling a few steps, as if to be nearer assistance in case she should require it. "Why?"

"Because," said the girl, "I am about to put my life, and the lives of others in your hands. I am the girl that dragged little Oliver back to old Fagin's, on the night he went out from the house in Pentonville."

"You!" said Rose Maylie.

"I, lady!" replied the girl. "I am the infamous creature you have heard of, that lives among the thieves, and that never from the first moment I can recollect my eyes and senses opening on London streets have known any better life, or kinder words than they have given me, so help me God! Do not mind shrinking openly from me, lady. I am younger than you would think, to look at me, but I am well used to it. The poorest women fall back, as I make my way along the crowded pavement."

"What dreadful things are these!" said Rose, involuntarily falling from her strange companion.

"Thank Heaven upon your knees, dear lady," cried the girl, "that you had friends to care for and keep you in your childhood, and that you were never in the midst of cold and hunger, and riot and drunkenness, and—and—something worse than all—as I have been from my cradle. I may use the word, for the alley and the gutter were mine, as they will be my deathbed."

"I pity you!" said Rose, in a broken voice. "It wrings my heart to hear you!"

"Heaven bless you for your goodness!" rejoined the girl. "If you knew what I am sometimes, you would pity me, indeed. But I have stolen away from those who would surely murder me, if they knew I had been here, to tell you what I have overheard. Do you know a man named Monks?"

"No," said Rose.

"He knows you," replied the girl; "and knew you were here, for it was by hearing him tell the place that I found you out."

"I never heard the name," said Rose.

"Then he goes by some other amongst us," rejoined the girl, "which I more than thought before. Some time ago, and soon after Oliver was put into your house on the night of the robbery, I—suspecting this man—listened to a conversation held between him and Fagin in the dark. I found out, from what I heard, that Monks—the man I asked you about, you know—"

"Yes," said Rose, "I understand."

"—That Monks," pursued the girl, "had seen him accidentally with two of our boys on the day we first lost him, and had known him directly to be the same child that he was watching for, though I couldn't make out why. A bargain was struck with Fagin, that if Oliver was got back he should have a certain sum; and he was to have more for making him a thief, which this Monks wanted for some purpose of his own."

"For what purpose?" asked Rose.

"He caught sight of my shadow on the wall as I listened, in the hope of finding out," said the girl; "and there are not many people besides me that could have got out of their way in time to escape discovery. But I did; and I saw him no more till last night."

"And what occurred then?"

"I'll tell you, lady. Last night he came again. Again they went up-stairs, and I, wrapping myself up so that my shadow should not betray me, again listened at the door. The first words I heard Monks say were these: 'So the only proofs of the boy's identity lie at the bottom of the river, and the old hag that received them from the mother is rotting in her coffin.' They laughed, and talked of his success in doing this; and Monks, talking on about the boy, and getting very wild, said that though he had got the young devil's money safely now, he'd rather have had it the other way; for, what a game it would have been to have brought down the boast of the father's will, by driving him through every jail in town, and then hauling him up for some capital felony which Fagin could easily manage, after having made a good profit of him besides."

"What is all this!" said Rose.

"The truth, lady, though it comes from my lips," replied the girl. "Then, he said, with oaths common enough in my ears, but strange to yours, that if he could gratify his hatred by taking the boy's life without bringing his own neck in danger, he would; but, as he couldn't, he'd be upon the watch to meet him at every turn in life; and if he took advantage of his birth and history, he might harm him yet. 'In short, Fagin,' he says, 'Jew as you are,[2] you never laid such snares as I'll contrive for my young brother, Oliver.'"

"His brother!" exclaimed Rose.

"Those were his words," said Nancy, glancing uneasily round, as she had scarcely ceased to do, since she began to speak, for a vision of Sikes haunted her perpetually. "And more. When he spoke of you and the other lady, and said it seemed contrived by Heaven, or the devil, against him, that Oliver should come into your hands, he laughed, and said there was some comfort in

2 Dickens's stereotyped portrayal of Fagin's Jewishness caused complaints even in his own time. He protested that he meant no disrespect to the Jewish community, but in later editions he attempted to tone down the stereotypes somewhat.

that too, for how many thousands and hundreds of thousands of pounds would you not give, if you had them, to know who your two-legged spaniel was."

"You do not mean," said Rose, turning very pale, "to tell me that this was said in earnest?"

"He spoke in hard and angry earnest, if a man ever did," replied the girl, shaking her head. "He is an earnest man when his hatred is up. I know many who do worse things; but I'd rather listen to them all a dozen times, than to that Monks once. It is growing late, and I have to reach home without suspicion of having been on such an errand as this. I must get back quickly."

"But what can I do?" said Rose. "To what use can I turn this communication without you? Back! Why do you wish to return to companions you paint in such terrible colours? If you repeat this information to a gentleman whom I can summon in an instant from the next room, you can be consigned to some place of safety without half an hour's delay."

"I wish to go back," said the girl. "I must go back, because—how can I tell such things to an innocent lady like you?—because among the men I have told you of, there is one: the most desperate among them all: that I can't leave; no, not even to be saved from the life I am leading now."

"Your having interfered in this dear boy's behalf before," said Rose; "your coming here, at so great a risk, to tell me what you have heard; your manner, which convinces me of the truth of what you say; your evident contrition, and sense of shame; all lead me to believe that you might yet be reclaimed. Oh!" said the earnest girl, folding her hands as the tears coursed down her face, "do not turn a deaf ear to the entreaties of one of your own sex; the first—the first, I do believe, who ever appealed to you in the voice of pity and compassion. Do hear my words, and let me save you yet, for better things."

"Lady," cried the girl, sinking on her knees, "dear, sweet, angel lady, you *are* the first that ever blessed me with such words as these, and if I had heard them years ago, they might have turned me from a life of sin and sorrow; but it is too late, it is too late!"

"It is never too late," said Rose, "for penitence and atonement."

"It is," cried the girl, writhing in the agony of her mind; "I cannot leave him now! I could not be his death."

"Why should you be?" asked Rose.

"Nothing could save him," cried the girl. "If I told others what I have told you, and led to their being taken, he would be sure to die. He is the boldest, and has been so cruel!"

"Is it possible," cried Rose, "that for such a man as this, you can resign every future hope, and the certainty of immediate rescue? It is madness."

"I don't know what it is," answered the girl; "I only know that it is so, and not with me alone, but with hundreds of others as bad and wretched as myself. I must go back. Whether it is God's wrath for the wrong I have done, I do not know; but I am drawn back to him through every suffering and ill usage; and I should be, I believe, if I knew that I was to die by his hand at last."

"What am I to do?" said Rose. "I should not let you depart from me thus."

"You should, lady, and I know you will," rejoined the girl, rising. "You will not stop my going because I have trusted in your goodness, and forced no promise from you, as I might have done."

"Of what use, then, is the communication you have made?" said Rose. "This mystery must be investigated, or how will its disclosure to me, benefit Oliver, whom you are anxious to serve?"

"You must have some kind gentleman about you that will hear it as a secret, and advise you what to do," rejoined the girl.

"But where can I find you again when it is necessary?" asked Rose. "I do not seek to know where these dreadful people live, but where will you be walking or passing at any settled period from this time?"

"Will you promise me that you will have my secret strictly kept, and come alone, or with the only other person that knows it; and that I shall not be watched or followed?" asked the girl.

"I promise you solemnly," answered Rose.

"Every Sunday night, from eleven until the clock strikes twelve," said the girl without hesitation, "I will walk on London Bridge if I am alive."

"Stay another moment," interposed Rose, as the girl moved hurriedly towards the door. "Think once again on your own condition, and the opportunity you have of escaping from it. You have a claim on me: not only as the voluntary bearer of this intelligence, but as a woman lost almost beyond redemption. Will you return to this gang of robbers, and to this man, when a word can save you? What fascination is it that can take you back, and make you cling to wickedness and misery? Oh! is there no chord in your heart that I can touch! Is there nothing left, to which I can appeal against this terrible infatuation!"

"When ladies as young, and good, and beautiful as you are," replied the girl steadily, "give away your hearts, love will carry you all lengths—even such as you, who have home, friends, other admirers, everything, to fill them. When such as I, who have no certain roof but the coffin-lid, and no friend in sickness or death but the hospital nurse, set our rotten hearts on any man, and let him fill the place that has been a blank through all our wretched lives, who can hope to cure us? Pity us, lady—pity us for having only one feeling of the woman left, and for having that turned, by a heavy judgment, from a comfort and a pride, into a new means of violence and suffering."

"You will," said Rose, after a pause, "take some money from me, which may enable you to live without dishonesty—at all events until we meet again?"

"Not a penny," replied the girl, waving her hand.

"Do not close your heart against all my efforts to help you," said Rose, stepping gently forward. "I wish to serve you indeed."

"You would serve me best, lady," replied the girl, wringing her hands, "if you could take my life at once; for I have felt more grief to think of what I am, to-night, than I ever did before, and it would be something not to die in the hell in which I have lived. God bless you, sweet lady, and send as much happiness on your head as I have brought shame on mine!"

Thus speaking, and sobbing aloud, the unhappy creature turned away; while Rose Maylie, overpowered by this extraordinary interview, which had more the semblance of a rapid dream than an actual occurence, sank into a chair, and endeavoured to collect her wandering thoughts.

Chapter 40: "A Strange Interview, Which Is a Sequel to the Last Chapter"

When she can, Nancy shares Monks's location with Rose and Mr. Brownlow, another benefactor of Oliver's. Though Nancy has done everything possible to protect her lover, Bill Sikes, through all this, he still is infuriated to discover it.

Without one pause, or moment's consideration; without once turning his head to the right or left, or raising his eyes to the sky, or lowering them to the ground, but looking straight before him with savage resolution: his teeth so tightly compressed that the strained jaw seemed starting through his skin; the robber held on his headlong course, nor muttered a word, nor relaxed a muscle, until he reached his own door. He opened it, softly, with a key; strode lightly up the stairs; and entering his own room, double-locked the door, and lifting a heavy table against it, drew back the curtain of the bed.

The girl was lying, half-dressed, upon it. He had roused her from her sleep, for she raised herself with a hurried and startled look.

"Get up!" said the man.

"It *is* you, Bill!" said the girl, with an expression of pleasure at his return.

"It is," was the reply. "Get up."

There was a candle burning, but the man hastily drew it from the candlestick, and hurled it under the grate. Seeing the faint light of early day without, the girl rose to undraw the curtain.

"Let it be," said Sikes, thrusting his hand before her. "There's enough light for wot I've got to do."

"Bill," said the girl, in the low voice of alarm, "why do you look like that at me!"

The robber sat regarding her, for a few seconds, with dilated nostrils and heaving breast; and then, grasping her by the head and throat, dragged her into the middle of the room, and looking once towards the door, placed his heavy hand upon her mouth.

"Bill, Bill!" gasped the girl, wrestling with the strength of mortal fear,—"I—I won't scream or cry—not once—hear me—speak to me—tell me what I have done!"

"You know, you she devil!" returned the robber, suppressing his breath. "You were watched to-night; every word you said was heard."

"Then spare my life for the love of Heaven, as I spared yours," rejoined the girl, clinging to him. "Bill, dear Bill, you cannot have the heart to kill me. Oh! think of all I have given up, only this one night, for you. You *shall* have time to think, and save yourself this crime; I will not loose my hold, you cannot throw me off. Bill, Bill, for dear God's sake, for your own, for mine, stop before you spill my blood! I have been true to you, upon my guilty soul I have!"

The man struggled violently, to release his arms; but those of the girl were clasped round his, and tear her as he would, he could not tear them away.

"Bill," cried the girl, striving to lay her head upon his breast, "the gentleman and that dear lady, told me to-night of a home in some foreign country where I could end my days in solitude and peace. Let me see them again, and beg them, on my knees, to show the same mercy and goodness to you; and let us both leave this dreadful place, and far apart lead better lives, and forget how we have lived, except in prayers, and never see each other more. It is never too late to repent. They told me so—I feel it now—but we must have time—a little, little time!"

The house-breaker freed one arm, and grasped his pistol. The certainty of immediate detection if he fired, flashed across his mind even in the midst of his fury; and he beat it twice with all the force he could summon, upon the upturned face that almost touched his own.

She staggered and fell: nearly blinded with the blood that rained down from a deep gash in her forehead; but raising herself, with difficulty, on her knees, drew from her bosom a white handkerchief—Rose Maylie's own—and holding it up, in her folded hands, as high towards Heaven as her feeble strength would allow, breathed one prayer for mercy to her Maker.

It was a ghastly figure to look upon. The murderer staggering backward to the wall, and shutting out the sight with his hand, seized a heavy club and struck her down.

Chapter 47: "Fatal Consequences"

18. The Resurrection and the Life

A Tale of Two Cities

Like many other authors before and since, Dickens sometimes used a "Christ figure"—a character whose sacrificial attitude and actions mirror those of Jesus—in his works. But in creating the Christ figure of Sydney Carton, who ultimately acts heroically to save the Darnay family from the brutality of the French Revolution, Dickens gave the formula a twist: He created a Christ figure who was himself desperately in need of redemption. Before he saves others, Carton must himself be saved.

If Sydney Carton ever shone anywhere, he certainly never shone in the house of Doctor Manette. He had been there often, during a whole year, and had always been the same moody and morose lounger there. When he cared to talk, he talked well; but, the cloud of caring for nothing, which overshadowed him with such a fatal darkness, was very rarely pierced by the light within him.

And yet he did care something for the streets that environed that house, and for the senseless stones that made their pavements. Many a night he vaguely and unhappily wandered there, when wine had brought no transitory gladness to him; many a dreary daybreak revealed his solitary figure lingering there, and still lingering there when the first beams of the sun brought into strong relief, removed beauties of architecture in spires of churches and lofty buildings, as perhaps the quiet time brought some sense of better things, else forgotten and unattainable, into his mind. Of late, the neglected bed in the Temple Court had known him more scantily than ever; and often when he had thrown himself upon it no longer than a few minutes, he had got up again, and haunted that neighbourhood.

On a day in August . . . when the sight and scent of flowers in the City streets had some waifs of goodness in them for the worst, of health for the sickliest, and of youth for the oldest, Sydney's feet still trod those stones. From being irresolute and purposeless, his feet became animated by an intention, and, in the working out of that intention, they took him to the Doctor's door.

He was shown up-stairs, and found Lucie at her work, alone. She had never been quite at her ease with him, and received him with some little embarrassment as he seated himself near her table. But, looking up at his face in the interchange of the first few common-places, she observed a change in it.

"I fear you are not well, Mr. Carton!"

"No. But the life I lead, Miss Manette, is not conducive to health. What is to be expected of, or by, such profligates?"

"Is it not—forgive me; I have begun the question on my lips—a pity to live no better life?"

"God knows it is a shame!"

"Then why not change it?"

Looking gently at him again, she was surprised and saddened to see that there were tears in his eyes. There were tears in his voice too, as he answered:

"It is too late for that. I shall never be better than I am. I shall sink lower, and be worse."

He leaned an elbow on her table, and covered his eyes with his hand. The table trembled in the silence that followed.

She had never seen him softened, and was much distressed. He knew her to be so, without looking at her, and said:

"Pray forgive me, Miss Manette. I break down before the knowledge of what I want to say to you. Will you hear me?"

"If it will do you any good, Mr. Carton, if it would make you happier, it would make me very glad!"

"God bless you for your sweet compassion!"

He unshaded his face after a little while, and spoke steadily.

"Don't be afraid to hear me. Don't shrink from anything I say. I am like one who died young. All my life might have been."

"No, Mr. Carton. I am sure that the best part of it might still be; I am sure that you might be much, much worthier of yourself."

"Say of you, Miss Manette, and although I know better—although in the mystery of my own wretched heart I know better—I shall never forget it!"

She was pale and trembling. He came to her relief with a fixed despair of himself which made the interview unlike any other that could have been holden.

"If it had been possible, Miss Manette, that you could have returned the love of the man you see before you—flung away, wasted, drunken, poor creature of misuse as you know him to be—he would have been conscious this day and hour, in spite of his happiness, that he would bring you to misery, bring you to sorrow and repentance, blight you, disgrace you, pull you down with him. I know very well that you can have no tenderness for me; I ask for none; I am even thankful that it cannot be."

"Without it, can I not save you, Mr. Carton? Can I not recall you—forgive me again!—to a better course? Can I in no way repay your confidence? I know this is a confidence," she modestly said, after a little hesitation, and in earnest tears, "I know you would say this to no one else. Can I turn it to no good account for yourself, Mr. Carton?"

He shook his head.

"To none. No, Miss Manette, to none. If you will hear me through a very little more, all you can ever do for me is done. I wish you to know that you have been the last dream of my soul. In my degradation I have not been so degraded but that the sight of you with your father, and of this home made such a home by you, has stirred old shadows that I thought had died out of me. Since I knew you, I have been troubled by a remorse that I thought would never reproach me again, and have heard whispers from old voices impelling me upward, that I thought were silent for ever. I have had unformed ideas of striving afresh, beginning anew, shaking off sloth and sensuality, and fighting out the abandoned fight. A dream, all a dream, that ends in nothing, and leaves the sleeper where he lay down, but I wish you to know that you inspired it. . . . It is useless to say it, I know, but it rises out of my soul. For you, and for any dear to you, I would do anything. . . . Think now and then that there is a man who would give his life, to keep a life you love beside you!"

Book the Second: "The Golden Thread," Chapter 13: "The Fellow of No Delicacy"

Several years later, in Paris at the height of the revolution, Carton sees a chance to fulfill that old vow to Lucie. The knowledge of what he must do inspires a night of remembrance and reflection.

Long ago, when he had been famous among his earliest competitors as a youth of great promise, he had followed his father to the grave. His mother had died, years before. These solemn words, which had been read at his father's grave, arose in his mind as he went down the dark streets, among the heavy shadows, with the moon and the clouds sailing on high above him. "I am the resurrection and the life, saith the Lord: he that believeth in me, though he were dead, yet shall he live: and whosoever liveth and believeth in me, shall never die."

In a city dominated by the axe, alone at night, with natural sorrow rising in him for the sixty-three who had been that day put to death, and for to-morrow's victims then awaiting their doom in the prisons, and still of to-morrow's and to-morrow's, the chain of association that brought the words home, like a rusty old ship's anchor from the deep, might have been easily found. He did not seek it, but repeated them and went on.

With a solemn interest in the lighted windows where the people were going to rest, forgetful through a few calm hours of the horrors surrounding them; in the towers of the churches, where no prayers were said, for the popular revulsion had even travelled that length of self-destruction from years of priestly impostors, plunderers, and profligates; in the distant burial-places, reserved, as they wrote upon the gates, for Eternal Sleep; in the abounding jails; and in the streets along which the sixties rolled to a death which had become so common and material, that no sorrowful story of a haunting Spirit ever arose among the people out of all the working of the Guillotine; with a solemn interest in the whole life and death of the city settling down to its short nightly pause in fury; Sydney Carton crossed the Seine again for the lighter streets.

Few coaches were abroad, for riders in coaches were liable to be suspected, and gentility hid its head in red nightcaps, and put on heavy shoes, and trudged. But, the theatres were all well filled, and the people poured cheerfully out as he passed, and went chatting home. At one of the theatre doors, there was a little girl with a mother, looking for a way across the street through the mud. He carried the child over, and before the timid arm was loosed from his neck asked her for a kiss.

"I am the resurrection and the life, saith the Lord: he that believeth in me, though he were dead, yet shall he live: and whosoever liveth and believeth in me, shall never die."

Now, that the streets were quiet, and the night wore on, the words were in the echoes of his feet, and were in the air. Perfectly calm and steady, he sometimes repeated them to himself as he walked; but, he heard them always.

The night wore out, and, as he stood upon the bridge listening to the water as it splashed the river-walls of the Island of Paris, where the picturesque confusion of houses and cathedral shone bright in the light of the moon, the day came coldly, looking like a dead face out of the sky. Then, the night, with the moon and the stars, turned pale and died, and for a little while it seemed as if Creation were delivered over to Death's dominion.

But, the glorious sun, rising, seemed to strike those words, that burden of the night, straight and warm to his heart in its long bright rays. And looking along them, with reverently shaded eyes, a bridge of light appeared to span the air between him and the sun, while the river sparkled under it.

The strong tide, so swift, so deep, and certain, was like a congenial friend, in the morning stillness. He walked by the stream, far from the houses, and in the light and warmth of the sun fell asleep on the bank. When he awoke and was afoot again, he lingered there yet a little longer, watching an eddy that turned and turned purposeless, until the stream absorbed it, and carried it on to the sea.—"Like me!"

A trading-boat, with a sail of the softened colour of a dead leaf, then glided into his view, floated by him, and died away. As its silent track in the water disappeared, the prayer that had broken up out of his heart for a merciful consideration of all his poor blindnesses and errors, ended in the words, "I am the resurrection and the life."

Book the Third: "The Track of a Storm," Chapter 9: "The Game Made"

19. What Have I Done

Great Expectations

We saw in a previous excerpt how Miss Havisham had trained her adopted daughter, Estella, to feel no love of any kind for anyone. It is only after Miss Havisham sees how badly Estella's coldness has wounded Pip, the story's protagonist and narrator, that she realizes and repents of the evil she has done them both. When Pip asks her to help him do a favor for a friend, she seizes the opportunity to express her remorse.

As I brought another of the ragged chairs to the hearth and sat down, I remarked a new expression on her face, as if she were afraid of me.

"I want," she said, "to pursue that subject you mentioned to me when you were last here, and to show you that I am not all stone. But perhaps you can never believe, now, that there is anything human in my heart?"

When I said some reassuring words, she stretched out her tremulous right hand, as though she was going to touch me; but she recalled it again before I understood the action, or knew how to receive it.

"You said, speaking for your friend, that you could tell me how to do something useful and good. Something that you would like done, is it not?"

"Something that I would like done very very much."

"What is it?"

I began explaining to her that secret history of the partnership. I had not got far into it, when I judged from her looks that she was thinking in a discursive way of me, rather than of what I said. It seemed to be so, for, when I stopped speaking, many moments passed before she showed that she was conscious of the fact.

"Do you break off," she asked then, with her former air of being afraid of me, "because you hate me too much to bear to speak to me?"

"No, no," I answered, "how can you think so, Miss Havisham! I stopped because I thought you were not following what I said."

"Perhaps I was not," she answered, putting a hand to her head. "Begin again, and let me look at something else. Stay! Now tell me."

She set her hand upon her stick, in the resolute way that sometimes was habitual to her, and looked at the fire with a strong expression of forcing herself to attend. I went on with my explanation, and told her how I had hoped to complete the transaction out of my means, but how in this I was disappointed. That part of the subject (I reminded her) involved matters which could form no part of my explanation, for they were the weighty secrets of another.

"So!" said she, assenting with her head, but not looking at me. "And how much money is wanting to complete the purchase?"

I was rather afraid of stating it, for it sounded a large sum. "Nine hundred pounds."

"If I give you the money for this purpose, will you keep my secret as you have kept your own?"

"Quite as faithfully."

"And your mind will be more at rest?"

"Much more at rest."

"Are you very unhappy now?"

She asked this question, still without looking at me, but in an unwonted tone of sympathy. I could not reply at the moment, for my voice failed me. She put her left arm across the head of her stick, and softly laid her forehead on it.

"I am far from happy, Miss Havisham; but I have other causes of disquiet than any you know of. They are the secrets I have mentioned."

After a little while, she raised her head, and looked at the fire again.

"'Tis noble in you to tell me that you have other causes of unhappiness, Is it true?"

"Too true."

"Can I only serve you, Pip, by serving your friend? Regarding that as done, is there nothing I can do for you yourself?"

"Nothing. I thank you for the question. I thank you even more for the tone of the question. But, there is nothing."

She presently rose from her seat, and looked about the blighted room for the means of writing. There were none there, and she took from her pocket a yellow set of ivory tablets, mounted in tarnished gold, and wrote upon them with a pencil in a case of tarnished gold that hung from her neck.

"You are still on friendly terms with Mr. Jaggers?"

"Quite. I dined with him yesterday."

"This is an authority to him to pay you that money, to lay out at your irresponsible discretion for your friend. I keep no money here; but if you would rather Mr. Jaggers knew nothing of the matter, I will send it to you."

"Thank you, Miss Havisham; I have not the least objection to receiving it from him."

She read me what she had written, and it was direct and clear, and evidently intended to absolve me from any suspicion of profiting by the receipt of the money. I took the tablets from her hand, and it trembled again, and it trembled more as she took off the chain to which the pencil was attached, and put it in mine. All this she did, without looking at me.

"My name is on the first leaf. If you can ever write under my name, 'I forgive her,' though ever so long after my broken heart is dust—pray do it!"

"O Miss Havisham," said I, "I can do it now. There have been sore mistakes; and my life has been a blind and thankless one; and I want forgiveness and direction far too much, to be bitter with you."

She turned her face to me for the first time since she had averted it, and to my amazement, I may even add to my terror, dropped on her knees at my feet; with her folded hands raised to me in the manner in which, when her poor heart was young and fresh and whole, they must often have been raised to Heaven from her mother's side.

To see her with her white hair and her worn face, kneeling at my feet, gave me a shock through all my frame. I entreated her to rise, and got my arms about her to help her up; but she only pressed that hand of mine which was nearest to her grasp, and hung her head over it and wept. I had never seen her shed a tear before, and in the hope that the relief might do her good, I bent over her without speaking. She was not kneeling now, but was down upon the ground.

"O!" she cried, despairingly. "What have I done! What have I done!"

"If you mean, Miss Havisham, what have you done to injure me, let me answer. Very little. I should have loved her under any circumstances.—Is she married?"

"Yes!"

It was a needless question, for a new desolation in the desolate house had told me so.

"What have I done! What have I done!" She wrung her hands, and crushed her white hair, and returned to this cry over and over again. "What have I done!"

I knew not how to answer, or how to comfort her. That she had done a grievous thing in taking an impressionable child to mould into the form that her wild resentment, spurned affection, and wounded pride, found vengeance in, I knew full well. But that, in shutting out the light of day, she had shut out infinitely more; that, in seclusion, she had secluded herself from a thousand natural and healing influences; that, her mind, brooding solitary, had grown diseased, as all minds do and must and will that reverse the appointed order of their Maker; I knew equally well. And could I look upon her without compassion, seeing her punishment in the ruin she was, in her profound unfitness for this earth on which she was placed, in the vanity of sorrow which had become a master mania, like the vanity of penitence, the vanity of remorse, the vanity of unworthiness, and other monstrous vanities that have been curses in this world?

"Until you spoke to her the other day, and until I saw in you a looking-glass that showed me what I once felt myself, I did not know what I had done. What have I done! What have I done!" And so again, twenty, fifty times over, What had she done!

"Miss Havisham," I said, when her cry had died away, "you may dismiss me from your mind and conscience. But Estella is a different case, and if you can ever undo any scrap of what you have done amiss in keeping a part of her right nature away from her, it will be better to do that, than to bemoan the past through a hundred years."

"Yes, yes, I know it. But, Pip—my dear!" There was an earnest womanly compassion for me in her new affection. "My dear! Believe this: when she first came to me, I meant to save her from misery like my own. At first I meant no more."

"Well, well!" said I. "I hope so."

"But as she grew, and promised to be very beautiful, I gradually did worse, and with my praises, and with my jewels, and with my teachings, and with this figure of myself always before her a warning to back and point my lessons, I stole her heart away and put ice in its place."

"Better," I could not help saying, "to have left her a natural heart, even to be bruised or broken."

With that, Miss Havisham looked distractedly at me for a while, and then burst out again, What had she done!

Chapter 49

20. To Take You Home

David Copperfield

Sacrificial Christ figures are not the only biblical archetypes to appear in Dickens's work. Daniel Peggotty assumes the role of shepherd pursuing the lost sheep, after his niece, Emily, is seduced by the wealthy and dissolute Steerforth (an old school friend of David Copperfield), and leaves her family and her fiancé, Ham, to run away with Steerforth.

I remember a great wail and cry, and the women hanging about him, and we all standing in the room; I with a paper in my hand, which Ham had given me; Mr. Peggotty, with his vest torn open, his hair wild, his face and lips quite white, and blood trickling down his bosom (it had sprung from his mouth, I think), looking fixedly at me.

"Read it, sir," he said, in a low shivering voice. "Slow, please. I doen't know as I can understand."

In the midst of the silence of death, I read thus, from a blotted letter:

> When you, who love me so much better than I ever have deserved, even when my mind was innocent, see this, I shall be far away.

"I shall be fur away," he repeated slowly. "Stop! Em'ly fur away. Well!"

> When I leave my dear home—my dear home—oh, my dear home!—in the morning,

the letter bore date on the previous night:

> —it will be never to come back, unless he brings me back a lady. This will be found at night, many hours after, instead of

> me. Oh, if you knew how my heart is torn. If even you, that I have wronged so much, that never can forgive me, could only know what I suffer! I am too wicked to write about myself. Oh, take comfort in thinking that I am so bad. Oh, for mercy's sake, tell uncle that I never loved him half so dear as now. Oh, don't remember how affectionate and kind you have all been to me—don't remember we were ever to be married—but try to think as if I died when I was little, and was buried somewhere. Pray Heaven that I am going away from, have compassion on my uncle! Tell him that I never loved him half so dear. Be his comfort. Love some good girl that will be what I was once to uncle, and be true to you, and worthy of you, and know no shame but me. God bless all! I'll pray for all, often, on my knees. If he don't bring me back a lady, and I don't pray for my own self, I'll pray for all. My parting love to uncle. My last tears, and my last thanks, for uncle!

That was all.

He stood, long after I had ceased to read, still looking at me. At length I ventured to take his hand, and to entreat him, as well as I could, to endeavour to get some command of himself. He replied, "I thankee, sir, I thankee!" without moving.

Ham spoke to him. Mr. Peggotty was so far sensible of *his* affliction, that he wrung his hand; but, otherwise, he remained in the same state, and no one dared to disturb him.

Slowly, at last, he moved his eyes from my face, as if he were waking from a vision, and cast them round the room. Then he said, in a low voice:

"Who's the man? I want to know his name."

Ham glanced at me, and suddenly I felt a shock that struck me back.

"There's a man suspected," said Mr. Peggotty. "Who is it?"

"Mas'r Davy!" implored Ham. "Go out a bit, and let me tell him what I must. You doen't ought to hear it, sir."

I felt the shock again. I sank down in a chair, and tried to utter some reply; but my tongue was fettered, and my sight was weak.

"I want to know his name!" I heard said, once more.

"For some time past," Ham faltered, "there's been a servant about here, at odd times. There's been a gen'lm'n too. Both of 'em belonged to one another."

Mr. Peggotty stood fixed as before, but now looking at him.

"The servant," pursued Ham, "was seen along with—our poor girl—last night. He's been in hiding about here, this week or over. He was thought to have gone, but he was hiding. Doen't stay, Mas'r Davy, doen't!"

I felt Peggotty's[3] arm round my neck, but I could not have moved if the house had been about to fall upon me.

"A strange chay and hosses was outside town, this morning, on the Norwich road, a'most afore the day broke," Ham went on. "The servant went to it, and come from it, and went to it again. When he went to it again, Em'ly was nigh him. The t'other was inside. He's the man."

"For the Lord's love," said Mr. Peggotty, falling back, and putting out his hand, as if to keep off what he dreaded. "Doen't tell me his name's Steerforth!"

"Mas'r Davy," exclaimed Ham, in a broken voice, "it ain't no fault of yourn—and I am far from laying of it to you—but his name is Steerforth, and he's a damned villain!"

Mr. Peggotty uttered no cry, and shed no tear, and moved no more, until he seemed to wake again, all at once, and pulled down his rough coat from its peg in a corner.

---

3 Mr. Peggotty's sister, once a servant to David's mother.

"Bear a hand with this! I'm struck of a heap, and can't do it," he said, impatiently. "Bear a hand and help me. Well!" when somebody had done so. "Now give me that theer hat!"

Ham asked him whither he was going.

"I'm a going to seek my niece. I'm a going to seek my Em'ly. I'm a going, first, to stave in that theer boat, and sink it where I would have drownded *him*, as I'm a livin' soul, if I had had one thought of what was in him! As he sat afore me," he said, wildly, holding out his clenched right hand, "as he sat afore me, face to face, strike me down dead, but I'd have drownded him, and thought it right!—I'm a going to seek my niece."

"Where?" cried Ham, interposing himself before the door.

"Anywhere! I'm a going to seek my niece through the wureld. I'm a going to find my poor niece in her shame, and bring her back. No one stop me! I tell you I'm a going to seek my niece!"

"No, no!" cried Mrs. Gummidge, coming between them, in a fit of crying. "No, no, Dan'l, not as you are now. Seek her in a little while, my lone lorn Dan'l, and that'll be but right; but not as you are now. Sit ye down, and give me your forgiveness for having ever been a worrit to you, Dan'l—what have *my* contraries ever been to this!—and let us speak a word about them times when she was first an orphan, and when Ham was too, and when I was a poor widder woman, and you took me in. It'll soften your poor heart, Dan'l," laying her head upon his shoulder, "and you'll bear your sorrow better; for you know the promise, Dan'l, 'As you have done it unto one of the least of these, you have done it unto me';—and that can never fail under this roof, that's been our shelter for so many, many year!"

He was quite passive now; and when I heard him crying, the impulse that had been upon me to go down upon my knees, and ask their pardon for the desolation I had caused, and curse

Steerforth, yielded to a better feeling. My overcharged heart found the same relief, and I cried too.

Chapter 31: "A Greater Loss"

Later, David encounters Mr. Peggotty on his journey to find Emily. By now he has given up all vengeful sentiments against Steerforth, and thinks only of bringing his niece home.

On the steps of the church, there was the stooping figure of a man, who had put down some burden on the smooth snow, to adjust it. . . . I don't think I had stopped in my surprise; but, in any case, as I went on, he rose, turned, and came down towards me. I stood face to face with Mr. Peggotty! . . .

We shook hands heartily. At first, neither of us could speak a word.

"Mas'r Davy!" he said, gripping me tight, "it do my art good to see you, sir. Well met, well met!"

"Well met, my dear old friend!" said I.

"I had my thowts o' coming to make inquiration for you, sir, to-night," he said, "but knowing as your aunt was living along wi' you—fur I've been down yonder—Yarmouth way—I was afeerd it was too late. I should have come early in the morning, sir, afore going away."

"Again?" said I.

"Yes, sir," he replied, patiently shaking his head, "I'm away to-morrow."

"Where were you going now?" I asked.

"Well!" he replied, shaking the snow out of his long hair, "I was a-going to turn in somewheers."

In those days there was a side-entrance to the stable-yard of the Golden Cross, the inn so memorable to me in connexion with his misfortune, nearly opposite to where we stood. I pointed out the gateway, put my arm through his, and we went across. Two or three public-rooms opened out of the stable-yard; and looking into one of them, and finding it empty, and a good fire burning, I took him in there.

When I saw him in the light, I observed, not only that his hair was long and ragged, but that his face was burnt dark by the sun. He was greyer, the lines in his face and forehead were deeper, and he had every appearance of having toiled and wandered through all varieties of weather; but he looked very strong, and like a man upheld by steadfastness of purpose, whom nothing could tire out. He shook the snow from his hat and clothes, and brushed it away from his face, while I was inwardly making these remarks. As he sat down opposite to me at a table, with his back to the door by which we had entered, he put out his rough hand again, and grasped mine warmly.

"I'll tell you, Mas'r Davy," he said,—"wheer all I've been, and what-all we've heerd. I've been fur, and we've heerd little; but I'll tell you!"

I rang the bell for something hot to drink. He would have nothing stronger than ale; and while it was being brought, and being warmed at the fire, he sat thinking. There was a fine massive gravity in his face, I did not venture to disturb.

"When she was a child," he said, lifting up his head soon after we were left alone, "she used to talk to me a deal about the sea, and about them coasts where the sea got to be dark blue, and to lay a-shining and a-shining in the sun. I thowt, odd times, as her father being drownded made her think on it so much. I doen't know, you see, but maybe she believed—or hoped—he had drifted out to them parts, where the flowers is always a blowing, and the country bright."

"It is likely to have been a childish fancy," I replied.

"When she was—lost," said Mr. Peggotty, "I know'd in my mind, as he would take her to them countries. I know'd in my mind, as he'd have told her wonders of 'em, and how she was to be a lady theer, and how he got her to listen to him fust, along o' sech like. When we see his mother, I know'd quite well as I was right. I went across-channel to France, and landed theer, as if I'd fell down from the sky. . . .

"I found out an English gen'leman as was in authority," said Mr. Peggotty, "and told him I was a-going to seek my niece. He got me them papers as I wanted fur to carry me through—I doen't rightly know how they're called—and he would have give me money, but that I was thankful to have no need on. I thank him kind, for all he done, I'm sure! 'I've wrote afore you,' he says to me, 'and I shall speak to many as will come that way, and many will know you, fur distant from here, when you're a travelling alone.' I told him, best as I was able, what my gratitoode was, and went away through France."

"Alone, and on foot?" said I.

"Mostly a-foot," he rejoined; "sometimes in carts along with people going to market; sometimes in empty coaches. Many mile a day a-foot, and often with some poor soldier or another, travelling to see his friends. I couldn't talk to him," said Mr. Peggotty, "nor he to me; but we was company for one another, too, along the dusty roads."

I should have known that by his friendly tone.

"When I come to any town," he pursued, "I found the inn, and waited about the yard till someone turned up (someone mostly did) as know'd English. Then I told how that I was on my way to seek my niece, and they told me what manner of gentlefolks was in the house, and I waited to see any as seemed like her, going in or out. When it warn't Em'ly, I went on agen. By little and little, when I come to a new village or that, among the poor people, I found they know'd about me. They would set me down at their cottage doors, and give me what-not fur to eat and drink, and show me where to sleep; and many a woman, Mas'r Davy, as has had a daughter of about Em'ly's age, I've found a-waiting fur me, at Our Saviour's Cross outside the village, fur to do me sim'lar kindnesses. Some has had daughters as was dead. And God only knows how good them mothers was to me! . . .

"They would often put their children—partic'lar their little girls," said Mr. Peggotty, "upon my knee; and many a time you might have seen me sitting at their doors, when night was coming in, a'most as if they'd been my Darling's children. Oh, my Darling!"

Overpowered by sudden grief, he sobbed aloud. I laid my trembling hand upon the hand he put before his face. "Thankee, sir," he said, "doen't take no notice."

In a very little while he took his hand away and put it on his breast, and went on with his story. "They often walked with me," he said, "in the morning, maybe a mile or two upon my road; and when we parted, and I said, 'I'm very thankful to you! God bless you!' they always seemed to understand, and answered pleasant. At last I come to the sea. It warn't hard, you may suppose, for a seafaring man like me to work his way over to Italy. When I got theer, I wandered on as I had done afore. The people was just as good to me, and I should have gone from town to town, maybe the country through, but that I got news of her being seen among them Swiss mountains yonder. One as know'd his sarvant see 'em there, all three, and told me how they travelled, and where they was. I made fur them mountains, Mas'r Davy, day and night. Ever so fur as I went, ever so fur the mountains seemed to shift away from me. But I come up with 'em, and I crossed 'em. When I got nigh the place as I had been told of, I began to think within my own self, 'What shall I do when I see her?' . . .

"I never doubted her," said Mr. Peggotty. "No! Not a bit! On'y let her see my face—on'y let her heer my voice—on'y let my stanning still afore her bring to her thoughts the home she had fled away from, and the child she had been—and if she had growed to be a royal lady, she'd have fell down at my feet! I know'd it well! Many a time in my sleep had I heerd her cry out, 'Uncle!' and seen her fall like death afore me. Many a time in my sleep had I raised her up, and whispered to her, 'Em'ly, my dear, I am come fur to bring forgiveness, and to take you home!'"

He stopped and shook his head, and went on with a sigh.

"*He* was nowt to me now. Em'ly was all. I bought a country dress to put upon her; and I know'd that, once found, she would walk beside me over them stony roads, go where I would, and never, never, leave me more. To put that dress upon her, and to cast off what she wore—to take her on my arm again, and wander towards home—to stop sometimes upon the road, and heal her bruised feet and her worse-bruised heart—was all that I thowt of now. I doen't believe I should have done so much as look at him. But, Mas'r Davy, it warn't to be—not yet! I was too late, and they was gone. Wheer, I couldn't learn. Some said heer, some said theer. I travelled heer, some said theer. I travelled heer, and I travelled theer, but I found no Em'ly, and I travelled home."

Chapter 40: "The Wanderer"

When Emily finally leaves Steerforth, an old friend takes her in and tells Mr. Peggotty where she is. David is present for their reconciliation.

I heard a distant foot upon the stairs. I knew it, I was certain. It was his, thank God! . . .

The foot upon the stairs came nearer—nearer . . . rushed into the room!

"Uncle!"

Hablot K. Browne, *Mr. Peggoty's Dream Comes True*

A fearful cry followed the word. I paused a moment, and looking in, saw him supporting her insensible figure in his arms. He gazed for a few seconds in the face; then stooped to kiss it—oh, how tenderly!—and drew a handkerchief before it.

"Mas'r Davy," he said, in a low tremulous voice, when it was covered, "I thank my Heav'nly Father as my dream's come true! I thank Him hearty for having guided of me, in His own ways, to my darling!"

With those words he took her up in his arms; and, with the veiled face lying on his bosom, and addressed towards his own, carried her, motionless and unconscious, down the stairs.

Chapter 50: "Mr. Peggoty's Dream Comes True"

21. In Remembrance of Him

Little Dorrit

Like many other believers before and since, Dickens struggled with Old Testament depictions of God's wrath, as can be seen in this exchange between Mrs. Clennam, who has spent her life punishing those around her in God's name for their failures, and Amy Dorrit, who clings to the example of Christ in the Gospels.

"I have done," said Mrs. Clennam, "what it was given to me to do. I have set myself against evil; not against good. I have been an instrument of severity against sin. Have not mere sinners like myself been commissioned to lay it low in all time?"

"In all time?" repeated Little Dorrit.

"Even if my own wrong had prevailed with me, and my own vengeance had moved me, could I have found no justification? None in the old days when the innocent perished with the guilty, a thousand to one? When the wrath of the hater of the unrighteous was not slaked even in blood, and yet found favour?"

"O, Mrs. Clennam, Mrs. Clennam," said Little Dorrit, "angry feelings and unforgiving deeds are no comfort and no guide to you and me. My life has been passed in this poor prison, and my teaching has been very defective; but, let me implore you to remember later and better days. Be guided only by the healer of the sick, the raiser of the dead, the friend of all who were afflicted and forlorn, the patient Master who shed tears of compassion for our infirmities. We cannot but be right if we put all the rest away, and do everything in remembrance of Him. There is no vengeance and no infliction of suffering in His life, I am sure. There can be no confusion in following Him, and seeking for no other footsteps, I am certain!"

Book the Second: "Riches," Chapter 31: "Closed"

22. I Revoke No Disposition

Bleak House

When Lady Dedlock's scandalous past is revealed and she flees her home, her husband, Sir Leicester, becomes ill from the shock. But then he displays one of the most surprising examples of forgiveness in all of Dickens. Because he had been portrayed as a hidebound, self-absorbed old man who cared only for the family name and estate, his expression of love for his wife is, as Rowan Williams puts it in his book Luminaries, *"one of the strangest, most startling images that [Dickens] ever gives us of compassion and mercy." He quotes Sir Leicester's formal-sounding "I revoke no dispositions I have made in her favour," and adds, "In that appallingly stiff phrase we hear something of the hope of mercy."*[4]

They lay him down upon his bed, and chafe, and rub, and fan, and put ice to his head, and try every means of restoration. Howbeit, the day has ebbed away, and it is night in his room, before his stertorous breathing lulls, or his fixed eyes show any consciousness of the candle that is occasionally passed before them. But when this change begins, it goes on; and by-and-by he nods, or moves his eyes, or even his hand, in token that he hears and comprehends.

He fell down, this morning, a handsome stately gentleman; somewhat infirm, but of a fine presence, and with a well-filled face. He lies upon his bed, an aged man with sunken cheeks, the decrepit shadow of himself. His voice was rich and mellow; and he had so long been thoroughly persuaded of the weight and import to mankind of any word he said, that his words really

4 Rowan Williams, "Charles Dickens," reprinted in *Luminaries: Twenty Lives That Illuminate the Christian Way* (London: Society for Promoting Christian Knowledge, 2019), 93.

had come to sound as if there were something in them. But now he can only whisper, and what he whispers sounds like what it is—mere jumble and jargon.

His favourite and faithful housekeeper stands at his bedside. It is the first act he notices, and he clearly derives pleasure from it. After vainly trying to make himself understood in speech, he makes signs for a pencil. So inexpressively, that they cannot at first understand him; it is his old housekeeper who makes out what he wants, and brings in a slate.

After pausing for some time, he slowly scrawls upon it, in a hand that is not his, "Chesney Wold?"

No, she tells him; he is in London. He was taken ill in the library, this morning. Right thankful she is that she happened to come to London, and is able to attend upon him.

"It is not an illness of any serious consequence, Sir Leicester. You will be much better to-morrow, Sir Leicester. All the gentlemen say so." This, with the tears coursing down her fair old face.

After making a survey of the room, and looking with particular attention all round the bed where the doctors stand, he writes, "My Lady."

"My Lady went out, Sir Leicester, before you were taken ill, and don't know of your illness yet."

He points again, in great agitation, at the two words. They all try to quiet him, but he points again with increased agitation. On their looking at one another, not knowing what to say, he takes the slate once more, and writes "My Lady. For God's sake, where?" And makes an imploring moan.

It is thought better that his old housekeeper should give him Lady Dedlock's letter, the contents of which no one knows or can surmise. She opens it for him, and puts it out for his perusal. Having read it twice by a great effort, he turns it down so that it shall not be seen, and lies moaning. He passes into a kind of relapse, or into a swoon; and it is an hour before he opens his eyes, reclining on his faithful and attached old servant's arm. The doctors know that he is best with her; and, when not actively engaged about him, stand aloof.

The slate comes into requisition again; but the word he wants to write, he cannot remember. His anxiety, his eagerness, and affliction at this pass, are pitiable to behold. It seems as if he must go mad, in the necessity he feels for haste, and the inability under which he labours of expressing to do what, or to fetch whom. He has written the letter B, and there stopped. Of a sudden, in the height of his misery, he puts Mr. before it. The old housekeeper suggests Bucket.[5] Thank Heaven! That's his meaning.

Mr. Bucket is found to be down-stairs, by appointment. Shall he come up?

There is no possibility of misconstruing Sir Leicester's burning wish to see him, or the desire he signifies to have the room cleared of every one but the housekeeper. It is speedily done; and Mr. Bucket appears. Of all men upon earth, Sir Leicester seems fallen from his high estate to place his sole trust and reliance upon this man.

"Sir Leicester Dedlock, Baronet, I'm sorry to see you like this. I hope you'll cheer up. I'm sure you will, on account of the family credit."

Sir Leicester puts her letter in his hands, and looks intently in his face while he reads it. A new intelligence comes into Mr. Bucket's eye as he reads on; with one hook of his finger, while that eye is still glancing over the words, he indicates, "Sir Leicester Dedlock, Baronet, I understand you."

Sir Leicester writes upon the slate. "Full forgiveness. Find——" Mr. Bucket stops his hand.

---

5 A police detective who plays a key role in the story.

"Sir Leicester Dedlock, Baronet, I'll find her. But my search after her must be begun out of hand. Not a minute must be lost."

With the quickness of thought, he follows Sir Leicester Dedlock's look towards a little box upon a table.

"Bring it here, Sir Leicester Dedlock, Baronet? Certainly. Open it with one of these here keys? Certainly. The littlest key? To be sure. Take the notes out? So I will. Count 'em? That's soon done. Twenty and thirty's fifty, and twenty's seventy, and fifty's one twenty, and forty's one sixty. Take 'em for expenses? That I'll do, and render an account of course. Don't spare money? No, I won't."

The velocity and certainty of Mr. Bucket's interpretation on all these heads is little short of miraculous. Mrs. Rouncewell, who holds the light, is giddy with the swiftness of his eyes and hands as he starts up, furnished for his journey.

Chapter 56: "Pursuit"

Sir Leicester, evidently with a great determination to say, in his own manner, something that is on his mind before relapsing into silence, tries to raise himself among his pillows a little more. George, observant of the action, takes him in his arms again and places him as he desires to be. "Thank you, George. You are another self to me. You have often carried my spare gun at Chesney Wold, George. You are familiar to me in these strange circumstances, very familiar." He has put Sir Leicester's sounder arm over his shoulder in lifting him up, and Sir Leicester is slow in drawing it away again as he says these words.

"I was about to add," he presently goes on, "I was about to add, respecting this attack, that it was unfortunately simultaneous with a slight misunderstanding between my Lady and myself. I do not mean that there was any difference between us (for there has been none), but that there was a misunderstanding of certain circumstances important only to ourselves, which deprives me, for a little while, of my Lady's society. She has found it necessary to make a journey,—I trust will shortly return. Volumnia, do I make myself intelligible? The words are not quite under my command, in the manner of pronouncing them."

Volumnia understands him perfectly; and in truth he delivers himself with far greater plainness than could have been supposed possible a minute ago. The effort by which he does so, is written in the anxious and labouring expression of his face. Nothing but the strength of his purpose enables him to make it.

"Therefore, Volumnia, I desire to say in your presence—and in the presence of my old retainer and friend, Mrs. Rouncewell, whose truth and fidelity no one can question, and in the presence of her son George, who comes back like a familiar recollection of my youth in the home of my ancestors at Chesney Wold—in case I should relapse, in case I should not recover, in case I should lose both my speech and the power of writing, though I hope for better things—"

The old housekeeper weeping silently; Volumnia in the greatest agitation, with the freshest bloom on her cheeks; the trooper with his arms folded and his head a little bent, respectfully attentive.

"Therefore I desire to say, and to call you all to witness—beginning, Volumnia, with yourself, most solemnly—that I am on unaltered terms with Lady Dedlock. That I assert no cause whatever of complaint against her. That I have ever had the strongest affection for her, and that I retain it undiminished. Say this to herself, and to every one. If you ever say less than this, you will be guilty of deliberate falsehood to me."

Volumnia tremblingly protests that she will observe his injunctions to the letter.

"My Lady is too high in position, too handsome, too accomplished, too superior in most respects to the best of those by whom she is surrounded, not to have her enemies and traducers, I dare say. Let it be known to them, as I make it known to you, that being of sound mind, memory, and understanding, I revoke no disposition I have made in her favour. I abridge nothing I have ever bestowed upon her. I am on unaltered terms with her, and I recall—having the full power to do it if I were so disposed, as you see—no act I have done for her advantage and happiness."

His formal array of words might have at any other time, as it has often had, something ludicrous in it; but at this time it is serious and affecting. His noble earnestness, his fidelity, his gallant shielding of her, his generous conquest of his own wrong and his own pride for her sake, are simply honourable, manly, and true. Nothing less worthy can be seen through the lustre of such qualities in the commonest mechanic, nothing less worthy can be seen in the best-born gentleman. In such a light both aspire alike, both rise alike, both children of the dust shine equally.

Chapter 58: "A Wintry Day and Night"

23. God Forgive Us All

David Copperfield

David's great-aunt, Betsey Trotwood, was treated so badly by her husband that she had to separate from him, but this does not prevent her from showing him kindness and grace at the end of his life.

We went back next day to my aunt's house—not to mine; and when she and I sat alone, as of old, before going to bed, she said:

"Trot, do you really wish to know what I have had upon my mind lately?"

"Indeed I do, aunt. If there ever was a time when I felt unwilling that you should have a sorrow or anxiety which I could not share, it is now."

"You have had sorrow enough, child," said my aunt, affectionately, "without the addition of my little miseries. I could have no other motive, Trot, in keeping anything from you."

"I know that well," said I. "But tell me now."

"Would you ride with me a little way to-morrow morning?" asked my aunt.

"Of course."

"At nine," said she. "I'll tell you then, my dear."

At nine, accordingly, we went out in a little chariot, and drove to London. We drove a long way through the streets until we came to one of the large hospitals. Standing hard by the building was a plain hearse. The driver recognised my aunt, and in obedience to a motion of her hand at the window, drove slowly off; we following.

"You understand it now, Trot," said my aunt. "He is gone!"

"Did he die in the hospital?"

"Yes."

She sat immovable beside me; but, again I saw the stray tears on her face.

"He was there once before," said my aunt presently. "He was ailing a long time—a shattered, broken man, these many years. When he knew his state in this last illness, he asked them to send for me. He was sorry then. Very sorry."

"You went, I know, aunt."

"I went. I was with him a good deal afterwards."

"He died the night before we went to Canterbury?" said I.

My aunt nodded. "No one can harm him now," she said. "It was a vain threat."

We drove away, out of town, to the churchyard at Hornsey. "Better here than in the streets," said my aunt. "He was born here."

We alighted; and followed the plain coffin to a corner I remember well, where the service was read consigning it to the dust.

"Six-and-thirty years ago, this day, my dear," said my aunt, as we walked back to the chariot, "I was married. God forgive us all!"

We took our seats in silence; and so she sat beside me for a long time, holding my hand. At length she suddenly burst into tears, and said:

"He was a fine-looking man when I married him, Trot—and he was sadly changed!"

It did not last long. After the relief of tears, she soon became composed, and even cheerful. Her nerves were a little shaken, she said, or she would not have given way to it. God forgive us all!

Chapter 54: "Mr. Micawber's Transactions"

24. Ever the Best of Friends

Great Expectations

Many characters in this novel need both to give and to receive grace. Pip must overcome the revulsion he feels in the presence of the humble ex-convict Magwitch, and show him grace as he lies dying in prison. Later, Pip in turn receives grace from Joe, the loving brother-in-law who helped to raise him and whom he had treated with arrogance and contempt.

[Magwitch] lay in prison very ill, during the whole interval between his committal for trial, and the coming round of the Sessions. He had broken two ribs, they had wounded one of his lungs, and he breathed with great pain and difficulty, which increased daily. It was a consequence of his hurt, that he spoke so low as to be scarcely audible; therefore, he spoke very little. But, he was ever ready to listen to me, and it became the first duty of my life to say to him, and read to him, what I knew he ought to hear.

Being far too ill to remain in the common prison, he was removed, after the first day or so, into the infirmary. This gave me opportunities of being with him that I could not otherwise have had. And but for his illness he would have been put in irons, for he was regarded as a determined prison-breaker, and I know not what else.

Although I saw him every day, it was for only a short time; hence the regularly recurring spaces of our separation were long enough to record on his face any slight changes that occurred in his physical state. I do not recollect that I once saw any change in it for the better; he wasted, and became slowly weaker and worse, day by day from the day when the prison door closed upon him.

The kind of submission or resignation that he showed, was that of a man who was tired out. I sometimes derived an impression, from his manner or from a whispered word or two which escaped him, that he pondered over the question whether he might have been a better man under better circumstances. But, he never justified himself by a hint tending that way, or tried to bend the past out of its eternal shape.

It happened on two or three occasions in my presence, that his desperate reputation was alluded to by one or other of the people in attendance on him. A smile crossed his face then, and he turned his eyes on me with a trustful look, as if he were confident that I had seen some small redeeming touch in him, even so long ago as when I was a little child. As to all the rest, he was humble and contrite, and I never knew him complain.

When the Sessions came round, Mr. Jaggers caused an application to be made for the postponement of his trial until the following Sessions. It was obviously made with the assurance that he could not live so long, and was refused. The trial came on at once, and when he was put to the bar, he was seated in a chair. No objection was made to my getting close to the dock, on the outside of it, and holding the hand that he stretched forth to me.

The trial was very short and very clear. Such things as could be said for him, were said—how he had taken to industrious habits, and had thriven lawfully and reputably. But, nothing could unsay the fact that he had returned[6], and was there in presence of the Judge and Jury. It was impossible to try him for that, and do otherwise than find him guilty.

At that time, it was the custom (as I learnt from my terrible experience of that Sessions) to devote a concluding day to the passing of Sentences, and to make a finishing effect with the

6 Magwitch had been deported to New South Wales for previous crimes. Here he is being tried for sneaking back into England.

Sentence of Death. But for the indelible picture that my remembrance now holds before me, I could scarcely believe, even as I write these words, that I saw two-and-thirty men and women put before the Judge to receive that sentence together. Foremost among the two-and-thirty was he; seated, that he might get breath enough to keep life in him.

The whole scene starts out again in the vivid colours of the moment, down to the drops of April rain on the windows of the court, glittering in the rays of April sun. Penned in the dock, as I again stood outside it at the corner with his hand in mine, were the two-and-thirty men and women; some defiant, some stricken with terror, some sobbing and weeping, some covering their faces, some staring gloomily about. There had been shrieks from among the women convicts, but they had been stilled, and a hush had succeeded. The sheriffs with their great chains and nosegays, other civic gewgaws and monsters, criers, ushers, a great gallery full of people—a large theatrical audience—looked on, as the two-and-thirty and the Judge were solemnly confronted. Then, the Judge addressed them. Among the wretched creatures before him whom he must single out for special address, was one who almost from his infancy had been an offender against the laws; who, after repeated imprisonments and punishments, had been at length sentenced to exile for a term of years; and who, under circumstances of great violence and daring, had made his escape and been re-sentenced to exile for life. That miserable man would seem for a time to have become convinced of his errors, when far removed from the scenes of his old offences, and to have lived a peaceable and honest life. But in a fatal moment, yielding to those propensities and passions, the indulgence of which had so long rendered him a scourge to society, he had quitted his haven of rest and repentance, and had come back to the country where he was proscribed. Being here presently denounced, he had for a time succeeded in evading the officers of Justice, but being at length seized while in the act of flight, he had resisted them, and had—he best knew whether by express design, or in the blindness of his hardihood—caused the death of his denouncer, to whom his whole career was known. The appointed punishment for his return to the land that had cast him out being Death, and his case being this aggravated case, he must prepare himself to Die.

The sun was striking in at the great windows of the court, through the glittering drops of rain upon the glass, and it made a broad shaft of light between the two-and-thirty and the Judge, linking both together, and perhaps reminding some among the audience, how both were passing on, with absolute equality, to the greater Judgment that knoweth all things and cannot err. Rising for a moment, a distinct speck of face in this way of light, the prisoner said, "My Lord, I have received my sentence of Death from the Almighty, but I bow to yours," and sat down again. There was some hushing, and the Judge went on with what he had to say to the rest. Then, they were all formally doomed, and some of them were supported out, and some of them sauntered out with a haggard look of bravery, and a few nodded to the gallery, and two or three shook hands, and others went out chewing the fragments of herb they had taken from the sweet herbs lying about. He went last of all, because of having to be helped from his chair and to go very slowly; and he held my hand while all the others were removed, and while the audience got up (putting their dresses right, as they might at church or elsewhere) and pointed down at this criminal or at that, and most of all at him and me.

I earnestly hoped and prayed that he might die before the Recorder's Report was made, but, in the dread of his lingering on,

I began that night to write out a petition to the Home Secretary of State, setting forth my knowledge of him, and how it was that he had come back for my sake. I wrote it as fervently and pathetically as I could, and when I had finished it and sent it in, I wrote out other petitions to such men in authority as I hoped were the most merciful, and drew up one to the Crown itself. For several days and nights after he was sentenced I took no rest, except when I fell asleep in my chair, but was wholly absorbed in these appeals. And after I had sent them in, I could not keep away from the places where they were, but felt as if they were more hopeful and less desperate when I was near them. In this unreasonable restlessness and pain of mind, I would roam the streets of an evening, wandering by those offices and houses where I had left the petitions. To the present hour, the weary western streets of London on a cold dusty spring night, with their ranges of stern shut-up mansions and their long rows of lamps, are melancholy to me from this association.

The daily visits I could make him were shortened now, and he was more strictly kept. Seeing, or fancying, that I was suspected of an intention of carrying poison to him, I asked to be searched before I sat down at his bedside, and told the officer who was always there, that I was willing to do anything that would assure him of the singleness of my designs. Nobody was hard with him or with me. There was duty to be done, and it was done, but not harshly. The officer always gave me the assurance that he was worse, and some other sick prisoners in the room, and some other prisoners who attended on them as sick nurses (malefactors, but not incapable of kindness, GOD be thanked!), always joined in the same report.

As the days went on, I noticed more and more that he would lie placidly looking at the white ceiling, with an absence of light in his face, until some word of mine brightened it for an instant, and then it would subside again. Sometimes he was almost, or quite, unable to speak; then, he would answer me with slight pressures on my hand, and I grew to understand his meaning very well.

The number of the days had risen to ten, when I saw a greater change in him than I had seen yet. His eyes were turned towards the door, and lighted up as I entered.

"Dear boy," he said, as I sat down by his bed: "I thought you was late. But I knowed you couldn't be that."

"It is just the time," said I. "I waited for it at the gate."

"You always waits at the gate; don't you, dear boy?"

"Yes. Not to lose a moment of the time."

"Thank'ee, dear boy, thank'ee. God bless you! You've never deserted me, dear boy."

I pressed his hand in silence, for I could not forget that I had once meant to desert him.

"And what's the best of all," he said, "you've been more comfortable alonger me, since I was under a dark cloud, than when the sun shone. That's best of all."

He lay on his back, breathing with great difficulty. Do what he would, and love me though he did, the light left his face ever and again, and a film came over the placid look at the white ceiling.

"Are you in much pain to-day?"

"I don't complain of none, dear boy."

"You never do complain."

He had spoken his last words. He smiled, and I understood his touch to mean that he wished to lift my hand, and lay it on his breast. I laid it there, and he smiled again, and put both his hands upon it.

The allotted time ran out, while we were thus; but, looking round, I found the governor of the prison standing near me, and he whispered, "You needn't go yet." I thanked him gratefully, and asked, "Might I speak to him, if he can hear me?"

The governor stepped aside, and beckoned the officer away. The change, though it was made without noise, drew back the film from the placid look at the white ceiling, and he looked most affectionately at me.

"Dear Magwitch, I must tell you, now at last. You understand what I say?"

A gentle pressure on my hand.

"You had a child once, whom you loved and lost."

A stronger pressure on my hand.

"She lived and found powerful friends. She is living now. She is a lady and very beautiful. And I love her!"

With a last faint effort, which would have been powerless but for my yielding to it and assisting it, he raised my hand to his lips. Then, he gently let it sink upon his breast again, with his own hands lying on it. The placid look at the white ceiling came back, and passed away, and his head dropped quietly on his breast.

Mindful, then, of what we had read together, I thought of the two men who went up into the Temple to pray, and I knew there were no better words that I could say beside his bed, than "O Lord, be merciful to him, a sinner!"

Chapter 56

After his long vigil at Magwitch's deathbed, Pip himself becomes ill.

"What do you want?" I asked, starting; "I don't know you."

"Well, sir," returned one of them, bending down and touching me on the shoulder, "this is a matter that you'll soon arrange, I dare say, but you're arrested."

"What is the debt?"

"Hundred and twenty-three pound, fifteen, six. Jeweller's account, I think."

"What is to be done?"

"You had better come to my house," said the man. "I keep a very nice house."

I made some attempt to get up and dress myself. When I next attended to them, they were standing a little off from the bed, looking at me. I still lay there.

"You see my state," said I. "I would come with you if I could; but indeed I am quite unable. If you take me from here, I think I shall die by the way."

Perhaps they replied, or argued the point, or tried to encourage me to believe that I was better than I thought. Forasmuch as they hang in my memory by only this one slender thread, I don't know what they did, except that they forbore to remove me.

That I had a fever and was avoided, that I suffered greatly, that I often lost my reason, that the time seemed interminable, that I confounded impossible existences with my own identity; that I was a brick in the house wall, and yet entreating to be released from the giddy place where the builders had set me; that I was a steel beam of a vast engine, clashing and whirling over a gulf, and yet that I implored in my own person to have the engine stopped, and my part in it hammered off; that I passed through these phases of disease, I know of my own remembrance, and did in some sort know at the time. That I sometimes struggled with real people, in the belief that they were murderers, and that I would all at once comprehend that they meant to do me good, and would then sink exhausted in their arms, and suffer them to lay me down, I also knew at the time. But, above all, I knew that there was a constant tendency in all these people—who, when I was very ill, would present all kinds of extraordinary transformations of the human face, and would be much dilated in size—above all, I say, I knew that there was an extraordinary tendency in all these people, sooner or later to settle down into the likeness of Joe.

After I had turned the worse point of my illness, I began to notice that while all its other features changed, this one consistent feature did not change. Whoever came about me, still settled down into Joe. I opened my eyes in the night, and I saw in the great chair at the bedside, Joe. I opened my eyes in the day, and, sitting on the window-seat, smoking his pipe in the shaded open window, still I saw Joe. I asked for cooling drink, and the dear hand that gave it me was Joe's. I sank back on my pillow after drinking, and the face that looked so hopefully and tenderly upon me was the face of Joe.

At last, one day, I took courage, and said, "*Is* it Joe?"

And the dear old home-voice answered, "Which it air, old chap."

"O Joe, you break my heart! Look angry at me, Joe. Strike me, Joe. Tell me of my ingratitude. Don't be so good to me!"

For, Joe had actually laid his head down on the pillow at my side, and put his arm round my neck, in his joy that I knew him.

"Which dear old Pip, old chap," said Joe, "you and me was ever friends. And when you're well enough to go out for a ride—what larks!"

After which, Joe withdrew to the window, and stood with his back towards me, wiping his eyes. And as my extreme weakness prevented me from getting up and going to him, I lay there, penitently whispering, "O God bless him! O God bless this gentle Christian man!" . . .

I was slow to gain strength, but I did slowly and surely become less weak, and Joe stayed with me, and I fancied I was little Pip again.

For, the tenderness of Joe was so beautifully proportioned to my need, that I was like a child in his hands. He would sit and talk to me in the old confidence, and with the old simplicity, and in the old unassertive protecting way, so that I would half believe that all my life since the days of the old kitchen was one of the mental troubles of the fever that was gone. He did everything for me except the household work, for which he had engaged a very decent woman, after paying off the laundress on his first arrival. "Which I do assure you, Pip," he would often say, in explanation of that liberty; "I found her a tapping the spare bed, like a cask of beer, and drawing off the feathers in a bucket, for sale. Which she would have tapped yourn next, and draw'd it off with you a laying on it, and was then a carrying away the coals gradiwally in the soup-tureen and wegetable-dishes, and the wine and spirits in your Wellington boots."

We looked forward to the day when I should go out for a ride, as we had once looked forward to the day of my apprenticeship. And when the day came, and an open carriage was got into the Lane, Joe wrapped me up, took me in his arms, carried me down to it, and put me in, as if I were still the small helpless creature to whom he had so abundantly given of the wealth of his great nature.

And Joe got in beside me, and we drove away together into the country, where the rich summer growth was already on the trees and on the grass, and sweet summer scents filled all the air. The day happened to be Sunday, and when I looked on the loveliness around me, and thought how it had grown and changed, and how the little wild flowers had been forming, and the voices of the birds had been strengthening, by day and by night, under the sun and under the stars, while poor I lay burning and tossing on my bed, the mere remembrance of having burned and tossed there, came like a check upon my peace. But, when I heard the Sunday bells, and looked around a little more upon the outspread beauty, I felt that I was not nearly thankful enough—that I was too weak yet, to be even that—and I laid my head on Joe's shoulder, as I had laid it long ago when he had taken me to the Fair or where not, and it was too much for my young senses.

More composure came to me after a while, and we talked as we used to talk, lying on the grass at the old Battery. There was no change whatever in Joe. Exactly what he had been in my eyes then, he was in my eyes still; just as simply faithful, just as simply right.

When we got back again and he lifted me out, and carried me—so easily!—across the court and up the stairs, I thought of that eventful Christmas Day when he had carried me over the marshes. We had not yet made any allusion to my change of fortune, nor did I know how much of my late history he was acquainted with. I was so doubtful of myself now, and put so much trust in him, that I could not satisfy myself whether I ought to refer to it when he did not.

"Have you heard, Joe," I asked him that evening, upon further consideration, as he smoked his pipe at the window, "who my patron was?"

"I heerd," returned Joe, "as it were not Miss Havisham, old chap."

"Did you hear who it was, Joe?"

"Well! I heerd as it were a person what sent the person what giv' you the bank-notes at the Jolly Bargemen, Pip."

"So it was."

"Astonishing!" said Joe, in the placidest way.

"Did you hear that he was dead, Joe?" I presently asked, with increasing diffidence.

"Which? Him as sent the bank-notes, Pip?"

"Yes."

"I think," said Joe, after meditating a long time, and looking rather evasively at the window-seat, "as I *did* hear tell that how he were something or another in a general way in that direction."

"Did you hear anything of his circumstances, Joe?"

"Not partickler, Pip."

"If you would like to hear, Joe—" I was beginning, when Joe got up and came to my sofa.

"Lookee here, old chap," said Joe, bending over me. "Ever the best of friends; ain't us, Pip?"

I was ashamed to answer him.

"Wery good, then," said Joe, as if I *had* answered; "that's all right, that's agreed upon. Then why go into subjects, old chap, which as betwixt two sech must be for ever onnecessary? There's subjects enough as betwixt two sech, without onnecessary ones. Lord! To think of your poor sister and her Rampages! And don't you remember Tickler?"[7]

"I do indeed, Joe."

"Lookee here, old chap," said Joe. "I done what I could to keep you and Tickler in sunders, but my power were not always fully equal to my inclinations. For when your poor sister had a mind to drop into you, it were not so much," said Joe, in his favourite argumentative way, "that she dropped into me too, if I put myself in opposition to her, but that she dropped into you always heavier for it. I noticed that. It ain't a grab at a man's whisker, not yet a shake or two of a man (to which your sister was quite welcome), that 'ud put a man off from getting a little child out of punishment. But when that little child is dropped into, heavier, for that grab of whisker or shaking, then that man naterally up

7 The cane with which Pip's sister used to beat Pip.

and says to himself, 'Where is the good as you are a doing? I grant you I see the 'arm,' says the man, 'but I don't see the good. I call upon you, sir, therefore, to pint out the good.'"

"The man says?" I observed, as Joe waited for me to speak.

"The man says," Joe assented. "Is he right, that man?"

"Dear Joe, he is always right."

"Well, old chap," said Joe, "then abide by your words. If he's always right (which in general he's more likely wrong), he's right when he says this: —Supposing ever you kep any little matter to yourself, when you was a little child, you kep it mostly because you know'd as J. Gargery's power to part you and Tickler in sunders, were not fully equal to his inclinations. Therefore, think no more of it as betwixt two sech, and do not let us pass remarks upon onnecessary subjects. Biddy giv' herself a deal o' trouble with me afore I left (for I am most awful dull), as I should view it in this light, and, viewing it in this light, as I should ser put it. Both of which," said Joe, quite charmed with his logical arrangement, "being done, now this to you a true friend, say. Namely. You mustn't go a over-doing on it, but you must have your supper and your wine-and-water, and you must be put betwixt the sheets."

The delicacy with which Joe dismissed this theme, and the sweet tact and kindness with which Biddy—who with her woman's wit had found me out so soon—had prepared him for it, made a deep impression on my mind. But whether Joe knew how poor I was, and how my great expectations had all dissolved, like our own marsh mists before the sun, I could not understand.

Another thing in Joe that I could not understand when it first began to develop itself, but which I soon arrived at a sorrowful comprehension of, was this: As I became stronger and better,

Joe became a little less easy with me. In my weakness and entire dependence on him, the dear fellow had fallen into the old tone, and called me by the old names, the dear "old Pip, old chap," that now were music in my ears. I too had fallen into the old ways, only happy and thankful that he let me. But, imperceptibly, though I held by them fast, Joe's hold upon them began to slacken; and whereas I wondered at this, at first, I soon began to understand that the cause of it was in me, and that the fault of it was all mine.

Ah! Had I given Joe no reason to doubt my constancy, and to think that in prosperity I should grow cold to him and cast him off? Had I given Joe's innocent heart no cause to feel instinctively that as I got stronger, his hold upon me would be weaker, and that he had better loosen it in time and let me go, before I plucked myself away?

It was on the third or fourth occasion of my going out walking in the Temple Gardens, leaning on Joe's arm, that I saw this change in him very plainly. We had been sitting in the bright warm sunlight, looking at the river, and I chanced to say as we got up:

"See, Joe! I can walk quite strongly. Now, you shall see me walk back by myself."

"Which do not over-do it, Pip," said Joe; "but I shall be happy fur to see you able, sir."

The last word grated on me; but how could I remonstrate! I walked no further than the gate of the gardens, and then pretended to be weaker than I was, and asked Joe for his arm. Joe gave it me, but was thoughtful.

I, for my part, was thoughtful too; for, how best to check this growing change in Joe, was a great perplexity to my remorseful thoughts. That I was ashamed to tell him exactly how I was placed, and what I had come down to, I do not seek to conceal; but, I hope my reluctance was not quite an unworthy one. He would want to help me out of his little savings, I knew, and I knew that he ought not to help me, and that I must not suffer him to do it.

It was a thoughtful evening with both of us. But, before we went to bed, I had resolved that I would wait over to-morrow, to-morrow being Sunday, and would begin my new course with the new week. . . . As I cleared, Joe cleared, and it seemed as though he had sympathetically arrived at a resolution too.

We had a quiet day on the Sunday, and we rode out into the country, and then walked in the fields.

"I feel thankful that I have been ill, Joe," I said.

"Dear old Pip, old chap, you're a'most come round, sir."

"It has been a memorable time for me, Joe."

"Likeways for myself, sir," Joe returned.

"We have had a time together, Joe, that I can never forget. There were days once, I know, that I did for a while forget; but I never shall forget these."

"Pip," said Joe, appearing a little hurried and troubled, "there has been larks. And, dear sir, what have been betwixt us—have been."

At night, when I had gone to bed, Joe came into my room, as he had done all through my recovery. He asked me if I felt sure that I was as well as in the morning?

"Yes, dear Joe, quite."

"And are always a getting stronger, old chap?"

"Yes, dear Joe, steadily."

Joe patted the coverlet on my shoulder with his great good hand, and said, in what I thought a husky voice, "Good night!"

When I got up in the morning, refreshed and stronger yet, I was full of my resolution to tell Joe all, without delay. I would tell him before breakfast. I would dress at once and go to his room and surprise him; for, it was the first day I had been up early. I went to his room, and he was not there. Not only was he not there, but his box was gone.

I hurried then to the breakfast-table, and on it found a letter. These were its brief contents.

"Not wishful to intrude I have departured fur you are well again dear Pip and will do better without Jo.

"P.S. Ever the best of friends."

Enclosed in the letter, was a receipt for the debt and costs on which I had been arrested. Down to that moment I had vainly supposed that my creditor had withdrawn or suspended proceedings until I should be quite recovered. I had never dreamed of Joe's having paid the money; but, Joe had paid it, and the receipt was in his name.

Chapter 57

25. That We May Forgive

The Haunted Man and the Ghost's Bargain

In the last of his "Christmas Books," Dickens tells the story of Redlaw, a wronged and tormented chemist who makes a bargain to give up his memory, only to find that the loss brings even more torment to him and others. It takes a reminder of the Christian virtue of forgiveness, and the example of a compassionate servant named Milly, to restore him to himself.

"Do you know me?" asked the Chemist.

"I should be glad," returned the other, "and that is an unwonted word for me to use, if I could answer no."

The Chemist looked at the man, standing in self-abasement and degradation before him, and would have looked longer, in an ineffectual struggle for enlightenment, but that Milly resumed her late position by his side, and attracted his attentive gaze to her own face.

"See how low he is sunk, how lost he is!" she whispered, stretching out her arm towards him, without looking from the Chemist's face. "If you could remember all that is connected with him, do you not think it would move your pity to reflect that one you ever loved (do not let us mind how long ago, or in what belief that he has forfeited), should come to this?"

"I hope it would," he answered. "I believe it would."

His eyes wandered to the figure standing near the door, but came back speedily to her, on whom he gazed intently, as if he strove to learn some lesson from every tone of her voice, and every beam of her eyes.

"I have no learning, and you have much," said Milly; "I am not used to think, and you are always thinking. May I tell you why it seems to me a good thing for us to remember wrong that has been done us?"

"Yes."

"That we may forgive it."

"Pardon me, great Heaven!" said Redlaw, lifting up his eyes, "for having thrown away thine own high attribute!"

"And if," said Milly, "if your memory should one day be restored, as we will hope and pray it may be, would it not be a blessing to you to recall at once a wrong and its forgiveness?"

He looked at the figure by the door, and fastened his attentive eyes on her again; a ray of clearer light appeared to him to shine into his mind, from her bright face.

"He cannot go to his abandoned home. He does not seek to go there. He knows that he could only carry shame and trouble to those he has so cruelly neglected; and that the best reparation he can make them now, is to avoid them. A very little money carefully bestowed, would remove him to some distant place, where he might live and do no wrong, and make such atonement as is left within his power for the wrong he has done. To the unfortunate lady who is his wife, and to his son, this would be the best and kindest boon that their best friend could give them—one too that they need never know of; and to him, shattered in reputation, mind, and body, it might be salvation."

He took her head between his hands, and kissed it, and said: "It shall be done. I trust to you to do it for me, now and secretly; and to tell him that I would forgive him, if I were so happy as to know for what."

As she rose, and turned her beaming face towards the fallen man, implying that her mediation had been successful, he advanced a step, and without raising his eyes, addressed himself to Redlaw.

"You are so generous," he said, "—you ever were—that you will try to banish your rising sense of retribution in the spectacle that is before you. I do not try to banish it from myself, Redlaw. If you can, believe me."

The Chemist entreated Milly, by a gesture, to come nearer to him; and, as he listened, looked in her face, as if to find in it the clue to what he heard.

"I am too decayed a wretch to make professions; I recollect my own career too well, to array any such before you. But from the day on which I made my first step downward, in dealing falsely by you, I have gone down with a certain, steady, doomed progression. That, I say."

Redlaw, keeping her close at his side, turned his face towards the speaker, and there was sorrow in it. Something like mournful recognition too.

"I might have been another man, my life might have been another life, if I had avoided that first fatal step. I don't know that it would have been. I claim nothing for the possibility. Your sister is at rest, and better than she could have been with me, if I had continued even what you thought me: even what I once supposed myself to be."

Redlaw made a hasty motion with his hand, as if he would have put that subject on one side.

"I speak," the other went on, "like a man taken from the grave. I should have made my own grave, last night, had it not been for this blessed hand."

"Oh dear, he likes me too!" sobbed Milly, under her breath. "That's another!"

"I could not have put myself in your way, last night, even for bread. But to-day, my recollection of what has been is so strongly stirred, and is presented to me, I don't know how, so vividly, that I have dared to come at her suggestion, and to take your bounty, and to thank you for it, and to beg you, Redlaw, in your dying hour, to be as merciful to me in your thoughts, as you are in your deeds."

He turned towards the door, and stopped a moment on his way forth.

"I hope my son may interest you, for his mother's sake. I hope he may deserve to do so. Unless my life should be preserved a long time, and I should know that I have not misused your aid, I shall never look upon him more."

Going out, he raised his eyes to Redlaw for the first time. Redlaw, whose steadfast gaze was fixed upon him, dreamily held out his hand. He returned and touched it—little more—with both his own—and bending down his head, went slowly out.

In the few moments that elapsed, while Milly silently took him to the gate, the Chemist dropped into his chair, and covered his face with his hands. Seeing him thus, when she came back, accompanied by her husband and his father (who were both greatly concerned for him), she avoided disturbing him, or permitting him to be disturbed; and kneeled down near the chair to put some warm clothing on the boy.

"That's exactly where it is. That's what I always say, father!" exclaimed her admiring husband. "There's a motherly feeling in Mrs. William's breast that must and will have went!"

"Ay, ay," said the old man; "you're right. My son William's right!"

"It happens all for the best, Milly dear, no doubt," said Mr. William, tenderly, "that we have no children of our own; and yet I sometimes wish you had one to love and cherish. Our little dead child that you built such hopes upon, and that never breathed the breath of life—it has made you quiet-like, Milly."

"I am very happy in the recollection of it, William dear," she answered. "I think of it every day."

"I was afraid you thought of it a good deal."

"Don't say afraid; it is a comfort to me; it speaks to me in so many ways. The innocent thing that never lived on earth is like an angel to me, William."

"You are like an angel to father and me," said Mr. William, softly. "I know that."

"When I think of all those hopes I built upon it, and the many times I sat and pictured to myself the little smiling face upon my bosom that never lay there, and the sweet eyes turned up to mine that never opened to the light," said Milly, "I can feel a greater tenderness, I think, for all the disappointed hopes in which there is no harm. When I see a beautiful child in its fond mother's arms, I love it all the better, thinking that my child might have been like that, and might have made my heart as proud and happy."

Redlaw raised his head, and looked towards her.

"All through life, it seems by me," she continued, "to tell me something. For poor neglected children, my little child pleads as if it were alive, and had a voice I knew, with which to speak to me. When I hear of youth in suffering or shame, I think that my child might have come to that, perhaps, and that God took it from me in his mercy. Even in age and grey hair, such as father's, it is present: saying that it too might have lived to be old, long and long after you and I were gone, and to have needed the respect and love of younger people."

Her quiet voice was quieter than ever, as she took her husband's arm, and laid her head against it.

"Children love me so, that sometimes I half fancy—it's a silly fancy, William—they have some way I don't know of, of feeling for my little child, and me, and understanding why their love is precious to me. If I have been quiet since, I have been more happy, William, in a hundred ways. Not least happy, dear, in this—that even when my little child was born and dead but a few days and I was weak and sorrowful, and could not help grieving a little, the thought arose, that if I tried to lead a good life, I should meet in Heaven a bright creature, who would call me, Mother!"

Redlaw fell upon his knees, with a loud cry.

"O Thou," he said, "who through the teaching of pure love, hast graciously restored me to the memory which was the memory of Christ upon the Cross, and of all the good who perished in His cause, receive my thanks, and bless her!"

Chapter 3: "The Gift Reversed"

III

The Righteous Life

26. Merciful and Tender

The Life of Our Lord

It seems right to start this section with a few excerpts from the account of the life of Christ that Dickens put together for his children, to tell them about the man he understood to be the most righteous person who ever lived.

My dear children, I am very anxious that you should know something about the History of Jesus Christ. For everybody ought to know about Him. No one ever lived, who was so good, so kind, so gentle, and so sorry for all people who did wrong, or were in anyway ill or miserable, as he[1] was. And as he is now in Heaven, where we hope to go, and all to meet each other after we are dead, and there be happy always together, you never can think what a good place Heaven is, without knowing who he was and what he did.

Chapter the First

That there might be some good men to go about with Him, teaching the people, Jesus Christ chose Twelve poor men to be His companions. These twelve are called *The apostles* or *Disciples*, and he chose them from among Poor Men, in order that the Poor might know—always after that; in all years to come—that Heaven was made for them as well as for the rich, and that God makes no difference between those who wear good clothes and those who go barefoot and in rags. The most miserable, the most ugly, deformed, wretched creatures that live, will be bright Angels in Heaven if they are good here on earth.[2]

1 The inconsistency in the capitalization of "He" and "Him" appears in Dickens's original handwritten manuscript.

2 A bit of theology that Dickens owed more to his Victorian culture than to Scripture.

Never forget this, when you are grown up. Never be proud or unkind, my dears, to any poor man, woman, or child. If they are bad, think that they would have been better if they had had kind friends, and good homes, and had been better taught. So, always try to make them better by kind persuading words; and always try to teach them and relieve them if you can. And when people speak ill of the Poor and Miserable, think how Jesus Christ went among them, and taught them, and thought them worthy of His care. And always pity them yourselves, and think as well of them as you can. . . .

. . . He was always merciful and tender. And because he did such Good, and taught people how to love God and how to hope to go to Heaven after death, he was called *Our Saviour.*

Chapter the Third

27. I Will Not Stand By

Nicholas Nickleby

One characteristic of a Christian hero for Dickens is that he stands up for the weak. Dotheboys Hall, the boarding school run by the sadistic Wackford Squeers, is one of the most wretched places in all of Dickens's oeuvre, which is saying something. Nicholas establishes his heroism by confronting the headmaster over his brutal treatment of an orphaned, mentally challenged runaway named Smike.

Another day came, and Nicholas was scarcely awake when he heard the wheels of a chaise approaching the house. It stopped. The voice of Mrs. Squeers was heard, and in exultation, ordering a glass of spirits for somebody, which was in itself a sufficient sign that something extraordinary had happened. Nicholas hardly dared to look out of the window; but he did so, and the very first object that met his eyes was the wretched Smike, so bedabbled with mud and rain, so haggard and worn, and wild, that, but for his garments being such as no scarecrow was ever seen to wear, he might have been doubtful, even then, of his identity.

"Lift him out," said Squeers, after he had literally feasted his eyes, in silence, upon the culprit. "Bring him in; bring him in!"

"Take care," cried Mrs. Squeers, as her husband proffered his assistance. "We tied his legs under the apron and made 'em fast to the chaise, to prevent his giving us the slip again."

With hands trembling with delight, Squeers unloosened the cord; and Smike, to all appearance more dead than alive, was brought into the house and securely locked up in a cellar, until such time as Mr. Squeers should deem it expedient to operate upon him, in presence of the assembled school.

Upon a hasty consideration of the circumstances, it may be matter of surprise to some persons, that Mr. and Mrs. Squeers should have taken so much trouble to repossess themselves of an incumbrance of which it was their wont to complain so loudly; but their surprise will cease when they are informed that the manifold services of the drudge, if performed by anybody else, would have cost the establishment some ten or twelve shillings per week in the shape of wages; and furthermore, that all runaways were, as a matter of policy, made severe examples of, at Dotheboys Hall, inasmuch as, in consequence of the limited extent of its attractions, there was but little inducement, beyond the powerful impulse of fear, for any pupil, provided with the usual number of legs and the power of using them, to remain.

The news that Smike had been caught and brought back in triumph ran like wildfire through the hungry community, and expectation was on tiptoe all the morning. On tiptoe it was destined to remain, however, until afternoon; when Squeers, having refreshed himself with his dinner, and further strengthened himself by an extra libation or so, made his appearance (accompanied by his amiable partner) with a countenance of portentous import, and a fearful instrument of flagellation, strong, supple, wax-ended, and new,—in short, purchased that morning expressly for the occasion.

"Is every boy here?" asked Squeers, in a tremendous voice.

Every boy was there, but every boy was afraid to speak; so Squeers glared along the lines to assure himself; and every eye drooped, and every head cowered down, as he did so.

"Each boy keep his place," said Squeers, administering his favourite blow to the desk, and regarding with gloomy satisfaction the universal start which it never failed to occasion. "Nickleby! to your desk, sir."

It was remarked by more than one small observer, that there was a very curious and unusual expression in the usher's face; but he took his seat, without opening his lips in reply. Squeers, casting a triumphant glance at his assistant and a look of most comprehensive despotism on the boys, left the room, and shortly afterwards returned, dragging Smike by the collar,—or rather by that fragment of his jacket which was nearest the place where his collar would have been, had he boasted such a decoration.

In any other place, the appearance of the wretched, jaded, spiritless object would have occasioned a murmur of compassion and remonstrance. It had some effect, even there; for the lookers-on moved uneasily in their seats; and a few of the boldest ventured to steal looks at each other, expressive of indignation and pity.

They were lost on Squeers, however, whose gaze was fastened on the luckless Smike, as he inquired, according to custom in such cases, whether he had anything to say for himself.

"Nothing, I suppose?" said Squeers, with a diabolical grin.

Smike glanced round, and his eye rested, for an instant, on Nicholas, as if he had expected him to intercede; but his look was riveted on his desk.

"Have you anything to say?" demanded Squeers again, giving his right arm two or three flourishes to try its power and suppleness. "Stand a little out of the way, Mrs. Squeers, my dear; I've hardly got room enough."

"Spare me, sir!" cried Smike.

"O, that's all, is it?" said Squeers. "Yes, I'll flog you within an inch of your life, and spare you that."

"Ha, ha, ha!" laughed Mrs. Squeers, "that's a good 'un!"

"I was driven to do it," said Smike, faintly, and casting another imploring look about him.

"Driven to do it, were you?" said Squeers. "O, it wasn't your fault; it was mine, I suppose,—eh?"

"A nasty, ungrateful, pig-headed, brutish, obstinate, sneaking dog," exclaimed Mrs. Squeers, taking Smike's head under her arm, and administering a cuff at every epithet; "what does he mean by that?"

"Stand aside, my dear," replied Squeers. "We'll try and find out."

Mrs. Squeers, being out of breath with her exertions, complied. Squeers caught the boy firmly in his grip; one desperate cut had fallen on his body; he was wincing from the lash and uttering a scream of pain; it was raised again, and again about to fall, when Nicholas Nickleby, suddenly starting up, cried "Stop!" in a voice that made the rafters ring.

"Who cried stop?" said Squeers, turning savagely round.

"I," said Nicholas, stepping forward. "This must not go on."

"Must not go on!" cried Squeers, almost in a shriek.

"No!" thundered Nicholas.

Aghast and stupefied by the boldness of the interference, Squeers released his hold of Smike, and, falling back a pace or two, gazed upon Nicholas with looks that were positively frightful.

"I say must not," repeated Nicholas, nothing daunted,—"shall not. I will prevent it."

Squeers continued to gaze upon him, with his eyes starting out of his head; but astonishment had actually, for the moment, bereft him of speech.

"You have disregarded all my quiet interference in the miserable lad's behalf," said Nicholas; "you have returned no answer to the letter in which I begged forgiveness for him, and offered to be responsible that he would remain quietly here. Don't blame me for this public interference. You have brought it upon yourself; not I."

"Sit down, beggar!" screamed Squeers, almost beside himself with rage, and seizing Smike as he spoke.

Hablot K. Browne, *Nicholas's Vengeance on Squeers*

"Wretch," rejoined Nicholas, fiercely, "touch him at your peril! I will not stand by, and see it done. My blood is up, and I have the strength of ten such men as you. Look to yourself, for by Heaven I will not spare you, if you drive me on!"

"Stand back," cried Squeers, brandishing his weapon.

"I have a long series of insults to avenge," said Nicholas, flushed with passion; "and my indignation is aggravated by the dastardly cruelties practised on helpless infancy in this foul den. Have a care; for if you do raise the devil within me, the consequences shall fall heavily upon your own head!"

He had scarcely spoken, when Squeers, in a violent outbreak of wrath, and with a cry like the howl of a wild beast, spat upon him, and struck him a blow across the face with his instrument of torture, which raised up a bar of livid flesh as it was inflicted. Smarting with the agony of the blow, and concentrating into that one moment all his feelings of rage, scorn, and indignation, Nicholas sprang upon him, wrested the weapon from his hand, and pinning him by the throat, beat the ruffian till he roared for mercy.

The boys—with the exception of Master Squeers, who, coming to his father's assistance, harassed the enemy in the rear—moved not, hand or foot; but Mrs. Squeers, with many shrieks for aid, hung on to the tail of her partner's coat, and endeavoured to drag him from his infuriated adversary; while Miss Squeers, who had been peeping through the keyhole in expectation of a very different scene, darted in at the very beginning of the attack, and after launching a shower of inkstands at the usher's head, beat Nicholas to her heart's content, animating herself, at every blow, with the recollection of his having refused her proffered love, and thus imparting additional strength to an arm which (as she took after her mother in this respect) was, at no time, one of the weakest.

Nicholas, in the full torrent of his violence, felt the blows no more than if they had been dealt with feathers; but, becoming tired of the noise and uproar, and feeling that his arm grew weak besides, he threw all his remaining strength into half a dozen finishing cuts, and flung Squeers from him, with all the force he could muster. The violence of his fall precipitated Mrs. Squeers completely over an adjacent form; and Squeers, striking his head against it in his descent, lay at his full length on the ground, stunned and motionless.

Having brought affairs to this happy termination, and ascertained, to his thorough satisfaction, that Squeers was only stunned, and not dead (upon which point he had had some unpleasant doubts at first), Nicholas left his family to restore him, and retired to consider what course he had better adopt. He looked anxiously round for Smike, as he left the room, but he was nowhere to be seen.

After a brief consideration, he packed up a few clothes in a small leathern valise, and, finding that nobody offered to oppose his progress, marched boldly out by the front door, and shortly afterwards, struck into the road which led to Greta Bridge. . . .

He did not travel far, that afternoon, for by this time it was nearly dark, and there had been a heavy fall of snow, which not only rendered the way toilsome, but the track uncertain and difficult to find, after daylight, save by experienced wayfarers. He lay that night at a cottage, where beds were let at a cheap rate to the more humble class of travellers; and, rising betimes next morning, made his way before night to Boroughbridge. Passing through that town in search of some cheap resting-place, he stumbled upon an empty barn within a couple of hundred yards of the roadside; in a warm corner of which he stretched his weary limbs, and soon fell asleep.

When he awoke next morning, and tried to recollect his dreams, which had been all connected with his recent sojourn at Dotheboys Hall, he sat up, rubbed his eyes, and stared—not with the most composed countenance possible—at some motionless object which seemed to be stationed within a few yards in front of him.

"Strange!" cried Nicholas. "Can this be some lingering creation of the visions that have scarcely left me? It cannot be real—and yet I—I am awake! Smike!"

The form moved, rose, advanced, and dropped upon its knees at his feet. It was Smike indeed.

"Why do you kneel to me?" said Nicholas, hastily raising him.

"To go with you—anywhere—everywhere—to the world's end—to the churchyard grave," replied Smike, clinging to his hand. "Let me, O do let me! You are my home—my kind friend—take me with you, pray."

"I am a friend who can do little for you," said Nicholas, kindly. "How came you here?"

He had followed him, it seemed; had never lost sight of him all the way; had watched while he slept, and when he halted for refreshment; and had feared to appear before, lest he should be sent back. He had not intended to appear now, but Nicholas had awakened more suddenly than he looked for, and he had had no time to conceal himself.

"Poor fellow!" said Nicholas, "your hard fate denies you any friend but one, and he is nearly as poor and helpless as yourself."

"May I—may I go with you?" asked Smike, timidly. "I will be your faithful hard-working servant, I will, indeed. I want no clothes," added the poor creature, drawing his rags together; "these will do very well. I only want to be near you."

"And you shall," cried Nicholas. "And the world shall deal by you as it does by me, till one or both of us shall quit it for a better. Come!"

With these words, he strapped his burden on his shoulders, and, taking his stick in one hand, extended the other to his delighted charge; and so they passed out of the old barn, together.

Chapter 13: "Nicholas Varies the Monotony of Dothebys Hall by a Most Vigorous and Remarkable Proceeding, Which Leads to Consequences of Some Importance"

28. Little Mother

Little Dorrit

Meek Amy Dorrit is not the kind of person who could give a schoolmaster a thrashing, but in her own quiet way, she, too, heroically stands up for the weak. One example is the way she cares for Maggy, a brain-damaged young woman with no family to look after her.

They walked back through the miserable muddy streets, and among the poor, mean shops, and were jostled by the crowds of dirty hucksters usual to a poor neighbourhood. There was nothing, by the short way, that was pleasant to any of the five senses. Yet it was not a common passage through common rain, and mire, and noise, to Clennam, having this little, slender, careful creature on his arm. How young she seemed to him, or how old he to her; or what a secret either to the other, in that beginning of the destined interweaving of their stories, matters not here. He thought of her having been born and bred among these scenes, and shrinking through them now, familiar yet misplaced; he thought of her long acquaintance with the squalid needs of life, and of her innocence; of her old solicitude for others, and her few years, and her childish aspect.

They were come into the High Street, where the prison stood, when a voice cried, "Little mother, little mother!" Little Dorrit stopping and looking back, an excited figure of a strange kind bounced against them (still crying, "little mother"), fell down, and scattered the contents of a large basket, filled with potatoes, in the mud.

"Oh, Maggy," said Little Dorrit, "what a clumsy child you are!"

Maggy was not hurt, but picked herself up immediately, and then began to pick up the potatoes, in which both Little Dorrit and Arthur Clennam helped. Maggy picked up very few potatoes, and a great quantity of mud; but they were all recovered, and deposited in the basket. Maggy then smeared her muddy face with her shawl, and presenting it to Mr. Clennam as a type of purity, enabled him to see what she was like.

She was about eight-and-twenty, with large bones, large features, large feet and hands, large eyes and no hair. Her large eyes were limpid and almost colourless; they seemed to be very little affected by light, and to stand unnaturally still. There was also that attentive listening expression in her face, which is seen in the faces of the blind; but she was not blind, having one tolerably serviceable eye. Her face was not exceedingly ugly, though it was only redeemed from being so by a smile; a good-humoured smile, and pleasant in itself, but rendered pitiable by being constantly there. A great white cap, with a quantity of opaque frilling that was always flapping about, apologised for Maggy's baldness, and made it so very difficult for her old black bonnet to retain its place upon her head, that it held on round her neck like a gipsy's baby. A commission of haberdashers could alone have reported what the rest of her poor dress was made of, but it had a strong general resemblance to seaweed, with here and there a gigantic tea-leaf. Her shawl looked particularly like a tea-leaf, after long infusion.

Arthur Clennam looked at Little Dorrit, with the expression of one saying, "May I ask who this is?" Little Dorrit, whose hand this Maggy, still calling her little mother had begun to fondle, answered in words (they were under a gateway into which the majority of the potatoes had rolled).

"This is Maggy, sir."

"Maggy, sir," echoed the personage presented. "Little mother!"

"She is the grand-daughter—" said Little Dorrit.

"Grand-daughter," echoed Maggy.

Hablot K. Browne, *Little Mother*

"Of my old nurse, who has been dead a long time. Maggy, how old are you?"

"Ten, mother," said Maggy.

"You can't think how good she is, sir," said Little Dorrit, with infinite tenderness.

"Good *she* is," echoed Maggy, transferring the pronoun in a most expressive way from herself to her little mother.

"Or how clever," said Little Dorrit. "She goes on errands as well as any one." Maggy laughed. "And is as trustworthy as the Bank of England." Maggy laughed. "She earns her own living entirely. Entirely, sir!" said Little Dorrit, in a lower and triumphant tone. "Really does!"

"What is her history?" asked Clennam.

"Think of that, Maggy?" said Little Dorrit, taking her two large hands and clapping them together. "A gentleman from thousands of miles away, wanting to know your history!"

"*My* history?" cried Maggy. "Little mother."

"She means me," said Little Dorrit, rather confused; "she is very much attached to me. Her old grandmother was not so kind to her as she should have been; was she, Maggy?"

Maggy shook her head, made a drinking vessel of her clenched left hand, drank out of it, and said, "Gin." Then beat an imaginary child, and said, "Broom-handles and pokers."

"When Maggy was ten years old," said Little Dorrit, watching her face while she spoke, "she had a bad fever, sir, and she has never grown any older ever since."

"Ten years old," said Maggy, nodding her head. "But what a nice hospital! So comfortable, wasn't it? Oh so nice it was. Such a Ev'nly place!"

"She had never been at peace before, sir," said Little Dorrit, turning towards Arthur for an instant and speaking low, "and she always runs off upon that."

"Such beds there is there!" cried Maggy. "Such lemonades! Such oranges! Such d'licious broth and wine! Such Chicking! Oh, AIN'T it a delightful place to go and stop at!"

"So Maggy stopped there as long as she could," said Little Dorrit, in her former tone of telling a child's story; the tone designed for Maggy's ear, "and at last, when she could stop there no longer, she came out. Then because she was never to be more than ten years old, however long she lived—"

"However long she lived," echoed Maggy.

"And because she was very weak; indeed was so weak that when she began to laugh she couldn't stop herself—which was a great pity—"

(Maggy mighty grave of a sudden.)

"Her grandmother did not know what to do with her, and for some years was very unkind to her indeed. At length, in course of time, Maggy began to take pains to improve herself, and to be very attentive and very industrious; and by degrees was allowed to come in and out as often as she liked, and got enough to do to support herself, and does support herself. And that," said Little Dorrit, clapping the two great hands together again, "is Maggy's history, as Maggy knows!"

Ah! But Arthur would have known what was wanting to its completeness, though he had never heard of the words Little mother; though he had never seen the fondling of the small spare hand; though he had had no sight for the tears now standing in the colourless eyes; though he had had no hearing for the sob that checked the clumsy laugh. The dirty gateway with the wind and rain whistling through it, and the basket of muddy potatoes waiting to be spilt again or taken up, never seemed the common hole it really was, when he looked back to it by these lights. Never, never!

They were very near the end of their walk, and they now came out of the gateway to finish it. Nothing would serve Maggy but that they must stop at a grocer's window, short of their destination, for her to show her learning. She could read after a sort; and picked out the fat figures in the tickets of prices, for the most part correctly. She also stumbled, with a large balance of success against her failures, through various philanthropic recommendations to Try our Mixture, Try our Family Black, Try our Orange-flavoured Pekoe, challenging competition at the head of Flowery Teas; and various cautions to the public against spurious establishments and adulterated articles. When he saw how pleasure brought a rosy tint into Little Dorrit's face when Maggy made a hit, he felt that he could have stood there making a library of the grocer's window until the rain and wind were tired.

Book the First: "Poverty," Chapter 9: "Little Mother"

Arthur, too, is the kind of person who instinctively reaches out to help those in need, even when going through difficulties of his own.

"A fresh night!" said Arthur.

"Yes, it's pretty fresh," assented Pancks. "As a stranger you feel the climate more than I do, I dare say. Indeed I haven't got time to feel it."

"You lead such a busy life?"

"Yes, I have always some of 'em to look up, or something to look after. But I like business," said Pancks, getting on a little faster. "What's a man made for?"

"For nothing else?" said Clennam.

Pancks put the counter question, "What else?" It packed up, in the smallest compass, a weight that had rested on Clennam's life; and he made no answer.

"That's what I ask our weekly tenants," said Pancks. "Some of 'em will pull long faces to me, and say, Poor as you see us, master, we're always grinding, drudging, toiling, every minute we're awake. I say to them, What else are you made for? It shuts them up. They haven't a word to answer. What else are you made for? That clinches it."

"Ah dear, dear, dear!" sighed Clennam.

"Here am I," said Pancks, pursuing his argument with the weekly tenant. "What else do you suppose I think I am made for? Nothing. Rattle me out of bed early, set me going, give me as short a time as you like to bolt my meals in, and keep me at it. Keep me always at it, and I'll keep you always at it, you keep somebody else always at it. There you are with the Whole Duty of Man in a commercial country."

When they had walked a little further in silence, Clennam said: "Have you no taste for anything, Mr. Pancks?"

"What's taste?" drily retorted Pancks.

"Let us say inclination."

"I have an inclination to get money, sir," said Pancks, "if you will show me how." He blew off that sound again, and it occurred to his companion for the first time that it was his way of laughing. He was a singular man in all respects; he might not have been quite in earnest, but that the short, hard, rapid manner in which he shot out these cinders of principles, as if it were done by mechanical revolvency, seemed irreconcilable with banter.

"You are no great reader, I suppose?" said Clennam.

"Never read anything but letters and accounts. Never collect anything but advertisements relative to next of kin. If that's a taste, I have got that. You're not of the Clennams of Cornwall, Mr. Clennam?"

"Not that I ever heard of."

"I know you're not. I asked your mother, sir. She has too much character to let a chance escape her."

"Supposing I had been of the Clennams of Cornwall?"

"You'd have heard of something to your advantage."

"Indeed! I have heard of little enough to my advantage for some time."

"There's a Cornish property going a begging, sir, and not a Cornish Clennam to have it for the asking," said Pancks, taking his note-book from his breast pocket and putting it in again. "I turn off here. I wish you good-night."

"Good-night!" said Clennam. But the Tug, suddenly lightened, and untrammelled by having any weight in tow, was already puffing away into the distance.

They had crossed Smithfield together, and Clennam was left alone at the corner of Barbican. He had no intention of presenting himself in his mother's dismal room that night, and could not have felt more depressed and cast away if he had been in a wilderness. He turned slowly down Aldersgate Street, and was pondering his way along towards Saint Paul's, purposing to come into one of the great thoroughfares for the sake of their light and life, when a crowd of people flocked towards him on the same pavement, and he stood aside against a shop to let them pass. As they came up, he made out that they were gathered around a something that was carried on men's shoulders. He soon saw that it was a litter, hastily made of a shutter or some such thing; and a recumbent figure upon it, and the scraps of conversation in the crowd, and a muddy bundle carried by one man, and a muddy hat carried by another, informed him that an accident had occurred. The litter stopped under a lamp before it had passed him half a dozen paces, for some re-adjustment of the burden; and, the crowd stopping too, he found himself in the midst of the array.

"An accident going to the Hospital?" he asked an old man beside him, who stood shaking his head, inviting conversation.

"Yes," said the man, "along of them Mails. They ought to be prosecuted and fined, them Mails. They come a racing out of Lad Lane and Wood Street at twelve or fourteen mile a hour, them Mails do. The only wonder is, that people ain't killed oftener by them Mails."

"This person is not killed, I hope?"

"I don't know!" said the man, "it an't for the want of a will in them Mails, if he an't." The speaker having folded his arms, and set in comfortably to address his depreciation of them Mails to any of the bystanders who would listen, several voices, out of pure sympathy with the sufferer, confirmed him; one voice saying to Clennam, "They're a public nuisance, them Mails, sir"; another, "*I* see one on 'em pull up within half a inch of a boy, last night"; another, "*I* see one on 'em go over a cat, sir—and it might have been your own mother"; and all representing, by implication, that if he happened to possess any public influence, he could not use it better than against them Mails.

"Why, a native Englishman is put to it every night of his life, to save his life from them Mails," argued the first old man; "and *he* knows when they're a coming round the corner, to tear him limb from limb. What can you expect from a poor foreigner who don't know nothing about 'em!"

"Is this a foreigner?" said Clennam, leaning forward to look.

In the midst of such replies as "Frenchman, sir," "Porteghee, sir," "Dutchman, sir," "Prooshan, sir," and other conflicting testimony, he now heard a feeble voice asking, both in Italian and in French, for water. A general remark going round, in reply, of "Ah, poor fellow, he says he'll never get over it; and no wonder!" Clennam begged to be allowed to pass, as he understood the poor creature. He was immediately handed to the front, to speak to him.

"First, he wants some water," said he, looking round. (A dozen good fellows dispersed to get it.) "Are you badly hurt, my friend?" he asked the man on the litter, in Italian.

"Yes, sir; yes, yes, yes. It's my leg, it's my leg. But it pleases me to hear the old music, though I am very bad."

"You are a traveller! Stay! See, the water! Let me give you some."

They had rested the litter on a pile of paving stones. It was at a convenient height from the ground, and by stooping he could lightly raise the head with one hand, and hold the glass to his lips with the other. A little, muscular, brown man, with black hair and white teeth. A lively face, apparently. Ear-rings in his ears.

"That's well. You are a traveller?"

"Surely, sir."

"A stranger in this city?"

"Surely, surely, altogether. I am arrived this unhappy evening."

"From what country?"

"Marseilles."

"Why, see there! I also! Almost as much a stranger here as you, though born here, I came from Marseilles a little while ago. Don't be cast down." The face looked up at him imploringly, as he rose from wiping it, and gently replaced the coat that covered the writhing figure. "I won't leave you till you shall be well taken care of. Courage! You will be very much better, half an hour hence."

"Ah! Altro, Altro!" cried the poor little man, in a faintly incredulous tone; and as they took him up, hung out his right hand to give the forefinger a back-handed shake in the air.

Arthur Clennam turned; and walking beside the litter, and saying an encouraging word now and then, accompanied it to the neighbouring hospital of Saint Bartholomew. None of the crowd but the bearers and he being admitted, the disabled man was soon laid on a table in a cool, methodical way, and carefully examined by a surgeon: who was as near at hand, and as ready to appear, as Calamity herself. "He hardly knows an English word," said Clennam; "is he badly hurt?" "Let us know all about it first," said the surgeon, continuing his examination with a business-like delight in it, "before we pronounce."

After trying the leg with a finger and two fingers, and one hand and two hands, and over and under, and up and down, and in this direction and in that, and approvingly remarking on the points of interest to another gentleman who joined him, the surgeon at last clapped the patient on the shoulder, and said, "He won't hurt. He'll do very well. It's difficult enough, but we shall not want him to part with his leg this time." Which Clennam interpreted to the patient, who was full of gratitude, and, in his demonstrative way, kissed both the interpreter's hand and the surgeon's several times.

"It's a serious injury, I suppose?" said Clennam.

"Ye-es," replied the surgeon, with the thoughtful pleasure of an artist, contemplating the work upon his easel. "Yes, it's enough. There's a compound fracture above the knee, and a dislocation below. They are both of a beautiful kind." He gave the patient a friendly clap on the shoulder again, as if he really felt that he was a very good fellow indeed, and worthy of all commendation for having broken his leg in a manner interesting to science.

"He speaks French?" said the surgeon.

"Oh yes, he speaks French."

"He'll be at no loss here, then.—You have only to bear a little pain like a brave fellow, my friend, and to be thankful that all goes as well as it does," he added, in that tongue, "and you'll walk again to a marvel. Now, let us see whether there's anything else the matter, and how our ribs are?"

There was nothing else the matter, and our ribs were sound. Clennam remained until everything possible to be done had been skilfully and promptly done—the poor belated wanderer in a strange land movingly besought that favour of him—and lingered by the bed to which he was in due time removed, until he had fallen into a doze. Even then he wrote a few words for him on his card, with a promise to return to-morrow, and left it to be given to him when he should awake.

All these proceedings occupied so long, that it struck eleven o'clock at night as he came out at the Hospital Gate. He had hired a lodging for the present in Covent Garden, and he took the nearest way to that quarter, by Snow Hill and Holborn.

Left to himself again, after the solicitude and compassion of his last adventure, he was naturally in a thoughtful mood. As naturally, he could not walk on thinking for ten minutes, without recalling Flora. She necessarily recalled to him his life, with all its misdirection and little happiness.

When he got to his lodging, he sat down before the dying fire, as he had stood at the window of his old room looking out upon the blackened forest of chimneys, and turned his gaze back upon the gloomy vista by which he had come to that stage in his existence. So long, so bare, so blank. No childhood; no youth, except for one remembrance; that one remembrance proved, only that day, to be a piece of folly.

It was a misfortune to him, trifle as it might have been to another. For, while all that was hard and stern in his recollection, remained Reality on being proved—was obdurate to the sight and touch, and relaxed nothing of its old indomitable grimness—the one tender recollection of his experience would not bear the same test, and melted away. He had foreseen this, on the former night, when he had dreamed with waking eyes; but he had not felt it then; and he had now.

He was a dreamer in such wise, because he was a man who had, deep-rooted in his nature, a belief in all the gentle and good things his life had been without. Bred in meanness and hard dealing, this had rescued him to be a man of honourable mind and open hand. Bred in coldness and severity, this had rescued him to have a warm and sympathetic heart. Bred in a creed too darkly audacious to pursue, through its process of reversing the making of man in the image of his Creator to the making of his Creator in the image of an erring man, this had rescued him to judge not, and in humility to be merciful, and have hope and charity.

And this saved him still from the whimpering weakness and cruel selfishness of holding that because such a happiness or such a virtue had not come into his little path, or worked well for him, therefore it was not in the great scheme, but was reducible, when found in appearance, to the basest elements. A disappointed mind he had, but a mind too firm and healthy for such unwholesome air. Leaving himself in the dark, it could rise into the light, seeing it shine on others and hailing it.

Therefore, he sat before his dying fire, sorrowful to think upon the way by which he had come to that night, yet not strewing poison on the way by which other men had come to it. That he should have missed so much, and at his time of life should look so far about him for any staff to bear him company upon his downward journey and cheer it, was a just regret. He looked at the fire from which the blaze departed, from which the afterglow subsided, in which the ashes turned grey, from which they dropped to dust, and thought, "How soon I too shall pass through such changes, and be gone!"

Book the First: "Poverty," Chapter 13: "Patriarchal"

29. A Good Pair

The Mystery of Edwin Drood

Dickens uses the character of the Rev. Septimus Crisparkle to represent the popular trend of "muscular Christianity," which blended faith with an emphasis on health and manliness. Note, however, that Crisparkle is no mindlessly macho Christian, but one who treats his mother with gentleness and treats people in general with respect and kindness.

The Reverend Septimus Crisparkle (Septimus, because six little brother Crisparkles before him went out, one by one, as they were born, like six weak little rushlights, as they were lighted), having broken the thin morning ice near Cloisterham Weir with his amiable head, much to the invigoration of his frame, was now assisting his circulation by boxing at a looking-glass with great science and prowess. A fresh and healthy portrait the looking-glass presented of the Reverend Septimus, feinting and dodging with the utmost artfulness, and hitting out from the shoulder with the utmost straightness, while his radiant features teemed with innocence, and soft-hearted benevolence beamed from his boxing-gloves.

It was scarcely breakfast-time yet, for Mrs. Crisparkle—mother, not wife, of the Reverend Septimus—was only just down, and waiting for the urn. Indeed, the Reverend Septimus left off at this very moment to take the pretty old lady's entering face between his boxing-gloves and kiss it. Having done so with tenderness, the Reverend Septimus turned to again, countering with his left, and putting in his right, in a tremendous manner.

"I say, every morning of my life, that you'll do it at last, Sept," remarked the old lady, looking on; "and so you will."

"Do what, Ma dear?"

"Break the pier-glass, or burst a blood-vessel."

"Neither, please God, Ma dear. Here's wind, Ma. Look at this!"

In a concluding round of great severity, the Reverend Septimus administered and escaped all sorts of punishment, and wound up by getting the old lady's cap into Chancery—such is the technical term used in scientific circles by the learned in the Noble Art—with a lightness of touch that hardly stirred the lightest lavender or cherry riband on it. Magnanimously releasing the defeated, just in time to get his gloves into a drawer and feign to be looking out of window in a contemplative state of mind when a servant entered, the Reverend Septimus then gave place to the urn and other preparations for breakfast. These completed, and the two alone again, it was pleasant to see (or would have been, if there had been any one to see it, which there never was), the old lady standing to say the Lord's Prayer aloud, and her son, Minor Canon nevertheless, standing with bent head to hear it, he being within five years of forty: much as he had stood to hear the same words from the same lips when he was within five months of four.

What is prettier than an old lady—except a young lady—when her eyes are bright, when her figure is trim and compact, when her face is cheerful and calm, when her dress is as the dress of a china shepherdess: so dainty in its colours, so individually assorted to herself, so neatly moulded on her? Nothing is prettier, thought the good Minor Canon frequently, when taking his seat at table opposite his long-widowed mother. Her thought at such times may be condensed into the two words that oftenest did duty together in all her conversations: "My Sept!"

They were a good pair to sit breakfasting together in Minor Canon Corner, Cloisterham. For, Minor Canon Corner was a quiet place in the shadow of the Cathedral, which the cawing of the rooks, the echoing footsteps of rare passers, the sound of the Cathedral bell, or the roll of the Cathedral organ, seemed to render more quiet than absolute silence. Swaggering fighting men had had their centuries of ramping and raving about Minor Canon Corner, and beaten serfs had had their centuries of drudging and dying there, and powerful monks had had their centuries of being sometimes useful and sometimes harmful there, and behold they were all gone out of Minor Canon Corner, and so much the better. Perhaps one of the highest uses of their ever having been there, was, that there might be left behind, that blessed air of tranquillity which pervaded Minor Canon Corner, and that serenely romantic state of the mind—productive for the most part of pity and forbearance—which is engendered by a sorrowful story that is all told, or a pathetic play that is played out.

Red-brick walls harmoniously toned down in colour by time, strong-rooted ivy, latticed windows, panelled rooms, big oaken beams in little places, and stone-walled gardens where annual fruit yet ripened upon monkish trees, were the principal surroundings of pretty old Mrs. Crisparkle and the Reverend Septimus as they sat at breakfast.

Chapter 6: "Philanthropy in Minor Canon Corner"

30. Contented with the Time

A Christmas Carol

Despite his own failures in that area, Dickens had an appreciation for the ideal of a healthy Christian family life. His books are filled with appealing glimpses of such families, among them the Cratchits.

"Why, where's our Martha?" cried Bob Cratchit, looking round.

"Not coming," said Mrs. Cratchit.

"Not coming!" said Bob, with a sudden declension in his high spirits; for he had been Tim's blood horse all the way from church, and had come home rampant. "Not coming upon Christmas Day!"

Martha didn't like to see him disappointed, if it were only in joke; so she came out prematurely from behind the closet door, and ran into his arms, while the two young Cratchits hustled Tiny Tim, and bore him off into the wash-house, that he might hear the pudding singing in the copper.

"And how did little Tim behave?" asked Mrs. Cratchit, when she had rallied Bob on his credulity, and Bob had hugged his daughter to his heart's content.

"As good as gold," said Bob, "and better. Somehow he gets thoughtful, sitting by himself so much, and thinks the strangest things you ever heard. He told me, coming home, that he hoped the people saw him in the church, because he was a cripple, and it might be pleasant to them to remember upon Christmas Day, who made lame beggars walk, and blind men see."

Bob's voice was tremulous when he told them this, and trembled more when he said that Tiny Tim was growing strong and hearty.

His active little crutch was heard upon the floor, and back came Tiny Tim before another word was spoken, escorted by his brother and sister to his stool before the fire; and while Bob, turning up his cuffs—as if, poor fellow, they were capable of being made more shabby—compounded some hot mixture in a jug with gin and lemons, and stirred it round and round and put it on the hob to simmer; Master Peter, and the two ubiquitous young Cratchits went to fetch the goose, with which they soon returned in high procession.

Such a bustle ensued that you might have thought a goose the rarest of all birds; a feathered phenomenon, to which a black swan was a matter of course—and in truth it was something very like it in that house. Mrs. Cratchit made the gravy (ready beforehand in a little saucepan) hissing hot; Master Peter mashed the potatoes with incredible vigour; Miss Belinda sweetened up the apple-sauce; Martha dusted the hot plates; Bob took Tiny Tim beside him in a tiny corner at the table; the two young Cratchits set chairs for everybody, not forgetting themselves, and mounting guard upon their posts, crammed spoons into their mouths, lest they should shriek for goose before their turn came to be helped. At last the dishes were set on, and grace was said. It was succeeded by a breathless pause, as Mrs. Cratchit, looking slowly all along the carving-knife, prepared to plunge it in the breast; but when she did, and when the long expected gush of stuffing issued forth, one murmur of delight arose all round the board, and even Tiny Tim, excited by the two young Cratchits, beat on the table with the handle of his knife, and feebly cried Hurrah!

There never was such a goose. Bob said he didn't believe there ever was such a goose cooked. Its tenderness and flavour, size and cheapness, were the themes of universal admiration.

Eked out by apple-sauce and mashed potatoes, it was a sufficient dinner for the whole family; indeed, as Mrs. Cratchit said with great delight (surveying one small atom of a bone upon the dish), they hadn't ate it all at last! Yet every one had had enough, and the youngest Cratchits in particular, were steeped in sage and onion to the eyebrows! . . .

Bob Cratchit told them how he had a situation in his eye for Master Peter, which would bring in, if obtained, full five-and-sixpence weekly. The two young Cratchits laughed tremendously at the idea of Peter's being a man of business; and Peter himself looked thoughtfully at the fire from between his collars, as if he were deliberating what particular investments he should favour when he came into the receipt of that bewildering income. Martha, who was a poor apprentice at a milliner's, then told them what kind of work she had to do, and how many hours she worked at a stretch, and how she meant to lie abed to-morrow morning for a good long rest; to-morrow being a holiday she passed at home. Also how she had seen a countess and a lord some days before, and how the lord "was much about as tall as Peter"; at which Peter pulled up his collars so high that you couldn't have seen his head if you had been there. All this time the chestnuts and the jug went round and round; and by-and-bye they had a song, about a lost child travelling in the snow, from Tiny Tim, who had a plaintive little voice, and sang it very well indeed.

There was nothing of high mark in this. They were not a handsome family; they were not well dressed; their shoes were far from being water-proof; their clothes were scanty; and Peter might have known, and very likely did, the inside of a pawnbroker's. But, they were happy, grateful, pleased with one another, and contented with the time; and when they faded, and looked happier yet in the bright sprinklings of the Spirit's torch at parting, Scrooge had his eye upon them, and especially on Tiny Tim, until the last.

Stave Three: "The Second of the Three Spirits"

31. What Sunday Might Be

Sunday under Three Heads

Dickens released this pamphlet in 1836, in response to a bill that would have forced shops, bakeries, theaters, museums, and other places of business and recreation to close on Sundays. Dickens believed this measure would unfairly penalize the poor, who had few opportunities for shopping and leisure except on Sundays. (This is the source of his reference in A Christmas Carol *to those who desired to close "means of dining every seventh day.") As Keith Hooper puts it, Dickens in this pamphlet "express[es] the view that Christian observance and relaxation on a Sunday were not mutually exclusive, but complementary."*[3]

I was travelling in the west of England a summer or two back, and was induced by the beauty of the scenery, and the seclusion of the spot, to remain for the night in a small village, distant about seventy miles from London. The next morning was Sunday; and I walked out, towards the church. Groups of people—the whole population of the little hamlet apparently—were hastening in the same direction. Cheerful and good-humoured congratulations were heard on all sides, as neighbours overtook each other, and walked on in company. Occasionally I passed an aged couple, whose married daughter and her husband were loitering by the side of the old people, accommodating their rate of walking to their feeble pace, while a little knot of children hurried on before; stout young labourers in clean round frocks; and buxom girls with healthy, laughing faces, were plentifully sprinkled about in couples, and the whole scene was one of quiet and tranquil contentment, irresistibly captivating. The morning was bright and pleasant, the hedges were green and blooming,

3 Hooper, *Charles Dickens*, 99.

and a thousand delicious scents were wafted on the air, from the wild flowers which blossomed on either side of the footpath. The little church was one of those venerable simple buildings which abound in the English counties; half overgrown with moss and ivy, and standing in the centre of a little plot of ground, which, but for the green mounds with which it was studded, might have passed for a lovely meadow. I fancied that the old clanking bell which was now summoning the congregation together, would seem less terrible when it rung out the knell of a departed soul, than I had ever deemed possible before—that the sound would tell only of a welcome to calmness and rest, amidst the most peaceful and tranquil scene in nature.

I followed into the church—a low-roofed building with small arched windows, through which the sun's rays streamed upon a plain tablet on the opposite wall, which had once recorded names, now as undistinguishable on its worn surface, as were the bones beneath, from the dust into which they had resolved. The impressive service of the Church of England was spoken—not merely *read*—by a grey-headed minister, and the responses delivered by his auditors, with an air of sincere devotion as far removed from affectation or display, as from coldness or indifference. The psalms were accompanied by a few instrumental performers, who were stationed in a small gallery extending across the church at the lower end, over the door: and the voices were led by the clerk, who, it was evident, derived no slight pride and gratification from this portion of the service. The discourse was plain, unpretending, and well adapted to the comprehension of the hearers. At the conclusion of the service, the villagers waited in the churchyard, to salute the clergyman as he passed; and two or three, I observed, stepped aside, as if communicating some little difficulty, and asking his advice. This, to guess from the homely bows, and other rustic expressions of gratitude, the old gentleman readily conceded. He seemed intimately acquainted with the circumstances of all his parishioners; for I heard him inquire after one man's youngest child, another man's wife, and so forth; and that he was fond of his joke, I discovered from overhearing him ask a stout, fresh-coloured young fellow, with a very pretty bashful-looking girl on his arm, "when those banns were to be put up?"—an inquiry which made the young fellow more fresh-coloured, and the girl more bashful, and which, strange to say, caused a great many other girls who were standing round, to colour up also, and look anywhere but in the faces of their male companions.

As I approached this spot in the evening about half an hour before sunset, I was surprised to hear the hum of voices, and occasionally a shout of merriment from the meadow beyond the churchyard; which I found, when I reached the stile, to be occasioned by a very animated game of cricket, in which the boys and young men of the place were engaged, while the females and old people were scattered about: some seated on the grass watching the progress of the game, and others sauntering about in groups of two or three, gathering little nosegays of wild roses and hedge flowers. I could not but take notice of one old man in particular, with a bright-eyed grand-daughter by his side, who was giving a sunburnt young fellow some instructions in the game, which he received with an air of profound deference, but with an occasional glance at the girl, which induced me to think that his attention was rather distracted from the old gentleman's narration of the fruits of his experience. When it was his turn at the wicket, too, there was a glance towards the pair every now and then, which the old grandfather very complacently considered as an appeal to his judgment of a particular hit, but which a certain blush in the girl's face, and a downcast look of the bright eye, led me to believe was intended for somebody else than the old man,—and understood by somebody else, too, or I am much mistaken.

I was in the very height of the pleasure which the contemplation of this scene afforded me, when I saw the old clergyman making his way towards us. I trembled for an angry interruption to the sport, and was almost on the point of crying out, to warn the cricketers of his approach; he was so close upon me, however, that I could do nothing but remain still, and anticipate the reproof that was preparing. What was my agreeable surprise to see the old gentleman standing at the stile, with his hands in his pockets, surveying the whole scene with evident satisfaction! And how dull I must have been, not to have known till my friend the grandfather (who, by-the-bye, said he had been a wonderful cricketer in his time) told me, that it was the clergyman himself who had established the whole thing: that it was his field they played in; and that it was he who had purchased stumps, bats, ball, and all!

It is such scenes as this, I would see near London, on a Sunday evening. It is such men as this, who would do more in one year to make people properly religious, cheerful, and contented, than all the legislation of a century could ever accomplish.

It will be said—it has been very often—that it would be matter of perfect impossibility to make amusements and exercises succeed in large towns, which may be very well adapted to a country population. Here, again, we are called upon to yield to bare assertions on matters of belief and opinion, as if they were established and undoubted facts. That there is a wide difference between the two cases, no one will be prepared to dispute; that the difference is such as to prevent the application of the same principle to both, no reasonable man, I think, will be disposed to maintain. The great majority of the people who make holiday on Sunday now, are industrious, orderly, and well-behaved persons. It is not unreasonable to suppose that they would be no more inclined to an abuse of pleasures provided for them, than they are to an abuse of the pleasures they provide for themselves; and if any people, for want of something better to do, resort to criminal practices on the Sabbath as at present observed, no better remedy for the evil can be imagined, than giving them the opportunity of doing something which will amuse them, and hurt nobody else. . . .

This is what Sunday might be made, and what it might be made without impiety or profanation. The wise and beneficent Creator who places men upon earth, requires that they shall perform the duties of that station of life to which they are called, and He can never intend that the more a man strives to discharge those duties, the more he shall be debarred from happiness and enjoyment. Let those who have six days in the week for all the world's pleasures, appropriate the seventh to fasting and gloom, either for their own sins or those of other people, if they like to bewail them; but let those who employ their six days in a worthier manner, devote their seventh to a different purpose. Let divines set the example of true morality: preach it to their flocks in the morning, and dismiss them to enjoy true rest in the afternoon; and let them select for their text, and let Sunday legislators take for their motto, the words which fell from the lips of that Master, whose precepts they misconstrue, and whose lessons they pervert—"The Sabbath was made for man, and not man to serve the Sabbath."

Section III: "As It Might Be Made"

32. Peace and Perfect Happiness

The Old Curiosity Shop

Thousands of readers—and Dickens himself—were deeply affected by his portrayal of the death and burial of Little Nell, the innocent young heroine of this book. Later generations, by contrast, tended to find these scenes overly sentimental and the once-beloved Nell too saintly to be believed. Still, Dickens's words on her death, particularly the way he weaves in the faith of the person who died and of those left behind, are well worth reading and reflecting on.

She was dead. No sleep so beautiful and calm, so free from trace of pain, so fair to look upon. She seemed a creature fresh from the hand of God, and waiting for the breath of life; not one who had lived and suffered death.

Her couch was dressed with here and there some winter berries and green leaves, gathered in a spot she had been used to favour. "When I die, put near me something that has loved the light, and had the sky above it always." Those were her words.

She was dead. Dear, gentle, patient, noble Nell was dead. Her little bird—a poor slight thing the pressure of a finger would have crushed—was stirring nimbly in its cage; and the strong heart of its child mistress was mute and motionless for ever.

Where were the traces of her early cares, her sufferings, and fatigues? All gone. Sorrow was dead indeed in her, but peace and perfect happiness were born; imaged in her tranquil beauty and profound repose.

And still her former self lay there, unaltered in this change. Yes. The old fireside had smiled upon that same sweet face; it had passed, like a dream, through haunts of misery and care; at the door of the poor schoolmaster on the summer evening, before the furnace fire upon the cold wet night, at the still bedside of the dying boy, there had been the same mild lovely look. So shall we know the angels in their majesty, after death.

The old man held one languid arm in his, and had the small hand tight folded to his breast, for warmth. It was the hand she had stretched out to him with her last smile—the hand that had led him on, through all their wanderings. Ever and anon he pressed it to his lips; then hugged it to his breast again, murmuring that it was warmer now; and, as he said it, he looked, in agony, to those who stood around, as if imploring them to help her.

She was dead, and past all help, or need of it. The ancient rooms she had seemed to fill with life, even while her own was waning fast—the garden she had tended—the eyes she had gladdened—the noiseless haunts of many a thoughtful hour—the paths she had trodden as it were but yesterday—could know her never more.

"It is not," said the schoolmaster, as he bent down to kiss her on the cheek, and gave his tears free vent, "it is not on earth that Heaven's justice ends. Think what earth is, compared with the World to which her young spirit has winged its early flight; and say, if one deliberate wish expressed in solemn terms above this bed could call her back to life, which of us would utter it!"

Chapter 71

And now the bell—the bell she had so often heard, by night and day, and listened to with solemn pleasure almost as a living voice—rung its remorseless toll, for her, so young, so beautiful, so good. Decrepit age, and vigorous life, and blooming youth, and helpless infancy, poured forth—on crutches, in the pride of strength and health, in the full blush of promise, in the mere dawn of life—to gather round her tomb. Old men were there, whose eyes were dim and senses failing—grandmothers, who might have died ten years ago, and still been old—the deaf, the blind, the lame, the palsied, the living dead in many shapes and forms, to see the closing of that early grave. What was the death it would shut in, to that which still could crawl and creep above it!

Along the crowded path they bore her now; pure as the newly-fallen snow that covered it; whose day on earth had been as fleeting. Under the porch, where she had sat when Heaven in its mercy brought her to that peaceful spot, she passed again; and the old church received her in its quiet shade.

They carried her to one old nook, where she had many and many a time sat musing, and laid their burden softly on the pavement. The light streamed on it through the coloured window—a window, where the boughs of trees were ever rustling in the summer, and where the birds sang sweetly all day long. With every breath of air that stirred among those branches in the sunshine, some trembling, changing light, would fall upon her grave.

Earth to earth, ashes to ashes, dust to dust! Many a young hand dropped in its little wreath, many a stifled sob was heard. Some—and they were not a few—knelt down. All were sincere and truthful in their sorrow.

The service done, the mourners stood apart, and the villagers closed round to look into the grave before the pavement-stone should be replaced. One called to mind how he had seen her sitting on that very spot, and how her book had fallen on her lap, and she was gazing with a pensive face upon the sky. Another told, how he had wondered much that one so delicate as she, should be so bold; how she had never feared to enter the church alone at night, but had loved to linger there when all was quiet, and even to climb the tower stair, with no more light than that of the moon rays stealing through the loopholes in the thick old wall. A whisper went about among the oldest, that she had seen and talked with angels; and when they called to mind how she had looked, and spoken, and her early death, some thought it might be so, indeed. Thus, coming to the grave in little knots, and glancing down, and giving place to others, and falling off in whispering groups of three or four, the church was cleared in time, of all but the sexton and the mourning friends.

They saw the vault covered, and the stone fixed down. Then, when the dusk of evening had come on, and not a sound disturbed the sacred stillness of the place—when the bright moon poured in her light on tomb and monument, on pillar, wall, and arch, and most of all (it seemed to them) upon her quiet grave—in that calm time, when outward things and inward thoughts teem with assurances of immortality, and worldly hopes and fears are humbled in the dust before them—then, with tranquil and submissive hearts they turned away, and left the child with God.

Oh! it is hard to take to heart the lesson that such deaths will teach, but let no man reject it, for it is one that all must learn, and is a mighty, universal Truth. When Death strikes down the innocent and young, for every fragile form from which he lets the panting spirit free, a hundred virtues rise, in shapes of mercy, charity, and love, to walk the world, and bless it. Of every tear that sorrowing mortals shed on such green graves, some good is born, some gentler nature comes. In the Destroyer's steps there spring up bright creations that defy his power, and his dark path becomes a way of light to Heaven.

Chapter 72

33. A Modest Life

Little Dorrit

As Dickens grew older and more cynical about the state of society and its institutions, he still held on to hope for redemption at the level of the individual and the family. The wedding that ends Little Dorrit *shows his vision of the family in sharp relief against the vanity and emptiness of the world around it. Right before their wedding, Amy asks Arthur to destroy a codicil that, unbeknownst to him, represents the long division, injustice, and bitterness between their families.*

"My dear love," said Arthur. "Why does Maggy light the fire? We shall be gone directly."

"I asked her to do it. I have taken such an odd fancy. I want you to burn something for me."

"What?"

"Only this folded paper. If you will put it in the fire with your own hand, just as it is, my fancy will be gratified."

"Superstitious, darling Little Dorrit? Is it a charm?"

"It is anything you like best, my own," she answered, laughing with glistening eyes and standing on tiptoe to kiss him, "if you will only humour me when the fire burns up."

So they stood before the fire, waiting: Clennam with his arm about her waist, and the fire shining, as the fire in that same place had often shone, in Little Dorrit's eyes. "Is it bright enough now?" said Arthur. "Quite bright enough now," said Little Dorrit. "Does the charm want any words to be said?" asked Arthur, as he held the paper over the flame. "You can say (if you don't mind) 'I love you!'" answered Little Dorrit. So he said it, and the paper burned away.

They passed very quietly along the yard; for, no one was there, though many heads were stealthily peeping from the windows. Only one face, familiar of old, was in the Lodge. When they had both accosted it, and spoken many kind words, Little Dorrit turned back one last time with her hand stretched out, saying, "Good-bye, good John! I hope you will live very happy, dear!"

Then they went up the steps of the neighbouring Saint George's Church, and went up to the altar, where Daniel Doyce was waiting in his paternal character. And there, was Little Dorrit's old friend who had given her the Burial Register for a pillow;[4] full of admiration that she should come back to them to be married, after all.

And they were married, with the sun shining on them through the painted figure of Our Saviour on the window. And they went into the very room where Little Dorrit had slumbered after her party, to sign the Marriage Register. And there, Mr. Pancks (destined to be chief clerk to Doyce and Clennam, and afterwards partner in the house), sinking the Incendiary in the peaceful friend, looked in at the door to see it done, with Flora gallantly supported on one arm and Maggy on the other, and a back-ground of John Chivery and father and other turnkeys, who had run round for the moment, deserting the parent Marshalsea for its happy child. Nor had Flora the least signs of seclusion upon her, notwithstanding her recent declaration; but, on the contrary, was wonderfully smart, and enjoyed the ceremonies mightily, though in a fluttered way.

Little Dorrit's old friend held the inkstand as she signed her name, and the clerk paused in taking off the good clergyman's surplice, and all the witnesses looked on with special interest.

---

4 Little Dorrit had been forced to sleep in the church one night after getting home late and being locked out of the Marshalsea.

"For, you see," said Little Dorrit's old friend, "this young lady is one of our curiosities, and has come now to the third volume of our Registers. Her birth is in what I call the first volume; she lay asleep, on this very floor, with her pretty head on what I call the second volume; and she's now a-writing her little name as a bride, in what I call the third volume."

They all gave place when the signing was done, and Little Dorrit and her husband walked out of the church alone. They paused for a moment on the steps of the portico, looking at the fresh perspective of the street in the autumn morning sun's bright rays, and then went down.

Went down into a modest life of usefulness and happiness. Went down to give a mother's care, in the fulness of time, to Fanny's neglected children no less than to their own, and to leave that lady going into Society for ever and a day. Went down to give a tender nurse and friend to Tip for some few years, who was never vexed by the great exactions he made of her, in return for the riches he might have given her if he had ever had them, and who lovingly closed his eyes upon the Marshalsea and all its blighted fruits. They went quietly down into the roaring streets, inseparable and blessed; and as they passed along in sunshine and shade, the noisy and the eager, and the arrogant and the forward and the vain, fretted, and chafed, and made their usual uproar.

Book the Second: "Riches," Chapter 34: "Gone"

34. The Object of His Life

Dombey and Son

The merchant Paul Dombey cares only for his young son, also named Paul, as the one to whom he can pass on his family business; he cares nothing for his daughter, Florence. After his little boy dies and his second wife leaves him, he lashes out at and even strikes Florence, who runs away. At long last, he reaches out for God's forgiveness, and is reconciled with his daughter and her family. The passage below is Dickens's portrait of a once arrogant and cruel man redeemed and humbled, a once neglectful father turned into a loving grandfather.

Autumn days are shining, and on the sea-beach there are often a young lady, and a white-haired gentleman. With them, or near them, are two children: boy and girl. And an old dog is generally in their company.

The white-haired gentleman walks with the little boy, talks with him, helps him in his play, attends upon him, watches him, as if he were the object of his life. If he be thoughtful, the white-haired gentleman is thoughtful too; and sometimes when the child is sitting by his side, and looks up in his face, asking him questions, he takes the tiny hand in his, and holding it, forgets to answer. Then the child says:

"What, grandpapa! Am I so like my poor little uncle again?"

"Yes, Paul. But he was weak, and you are very strong."

"Oh yes, I am very strong."

"And he lay on a little bed beside the sea, and you can run about."

And so they range away again, busily, for the white-haired gentleman likes best to see the child free and stirring; and as they go about together, the story of the bond between them goes about, and follows them.

But no one, except Florence, knows the measure of the white-haired gentleman's affection for the girl. That story never goes about. The child herself almost wonders at a certain secrecy he keeps in it. He hoards her in his heart. He cannot bear to see a cloud upon her face. He cannot bear to see her sit apart. He fancies that she feels a slight, when there is none. He steals away to look at her, in her sleep. It pleases him to have her come, and wake him in the morning. He is fondest of her and most loving to her, when there is no creature by. The child says then, sometimes:

"Dear grandpapa, why do you cry when you kiss me?"

He only answers, "Little Florence! Little Florence!" and smooths away the curls that shade her earnest eyes.

Chapter 62: "Final"

35. A Far, Far Better Thing

A Tale of Two Cities

Just before sacrificing himself to save others, Sydney Carton has a more hopeful vision of the future, even as the scene all around him is one of horror and destruction.

They said of him, about the city that night, that it was the peacefullest man's face ever beheld there. Many added that he looked sublime and prophetic.

One of the most remarkable sufferers by the same axe—a woman—had asked at the foot of the same scaffold, not long before, to be allowed to write down the thoughts that were inspiring her. If he had given any utterance to his, and they were prophetic, they would have been these:

"I see Barsad, and Cly, Defarge, The Vengeance, the Juryman, the Judge, long ranks of the new oppressors who have risen on the destruction of the old, perishing by this retributive instrument, before it shall cease out of its present use. I see a beautiful city and a brilliant people rising from this abyss, and, in their struggles to be truly free, in their triumphs and defeats, through long years to come, I see the evil of this time and of the previous time of which this is the natural birth, gradually making expiation for itself and wearing out.

"I see the lives for which I lay down my life, peaceful, useful, prosperous and happy, in that England which I shall see no more. I see Her with a child upon her bosom, who bears my name. I see her father, aged and bent, but otherwise restored, and faithful to all men in his healing office, and at peace. I see the good old man, so long their friend, in ten years' time enriching them with all he has, and passing tranquilly to his reward.

Frederick Barnard, *Sydney Carton*

"I see that I hold a sanctuary in their hearts, and in the hearts of their descendants, generations hence. I see her, an old woman, weeping for me on the anniversary of this day. I see her and her husband, their course done, lying side by side in their last earthly bed, and I know that each was not more honoured and held sacred in the other's soul, than I was in the souls of both.

"I see that child who lay upon her bosom and who bore my name, a man winning his way up in that path of life which once was mine. I see him winning it so well, that my name is made illustrious there by the light of his. I see the blots I threw upon it, faded away. I see him, foremost of just judges and honoured men, bringing a boy of my name, with a forehead that I know and golden hair, to this place—then fair to look upon, with not a trace of this day's disfigurement—and I hear him tell the child my story, with a tender and a faltering voice.

"It is a far, far better thing that I do, than I have ever done; it is a far, far better rest that I go to than I have ever known."

Book the Third: "The Track of a Storm," Chapter 15: "The Footsteps Die Out For Ever"

36. God Bless Us, Every One

A Christmas Carol

It seems fitting to end this book with the redeemed Ebenezer Scrooge—not only because we started with the sinful Ebenezer Scrooge, but because his redemption is one of the most dramatic, most complete, and most joyous, not just in Dickens, but perhaps in all of English literature.

The Spirit stood among the graves, and pointed down to One. He advanced towards it trembling. The Phantom was exactly as it had been, but he dreaded that he saw new meaning in its solemn shape.

"Before I draw nearer to that stone to which you point," said Scrooge, "answer me one question. Are these the shadows of the things that Will be, or are they shadows of things that May be, only?"

Still the Ghost pointed downward to the grave by which it stood.

"Men's courses will foreshadow certain ends, to which, if persevered in, they must lead," said Scrooge. "But if the courses be departed from, the ends will change. Say it is thus with what you show me!"

The Spirit was immovable as ever.

Scrooge crept towards it, trembling as he went; and following the finger, read upon the stone of the neglected grave his own name, EBENEZER SCROOGE.

"Am *I* that man who lay upon the bed?" he cried, upon his knees.

The finger pointed from the grave to him, and back again.

"No, Spirit! Oh no, no!"

The finger still was there.

"Spirit!" he cried, tight clutching at its robe, "hear me! I am not the man I was. I will not be the man I must have been but for this intercourse. Why show me this, if I am past all hope!"

For the first time the hand appeared to shake.

"Good Spirit," he pursued, as down upon the ground he fell before it: "Your nature intercedes for me, and pities me. Assure me that I yet may change these shadows you have shown me, by an altered life!"

The kind hand trembled.

"I will honour Christmas in my heart, and try to keep it all the year. I will live in the Past, the Present, and the Future. The Spirits of all Three shall strive within me. I will not shut out the lessons that they teach. Oh, tell me I may sponge away the writing on this stone!"

In his agony, he caught the spectral hand. It sought to free itself, but he was strong in his entreaty, and detained it. The Spirit, stronger yet, repulsed him.

Holding up his hands in a last prayer to have his fate reversed, he saw an alteration in the Phantom's hood and dress. It shrunk, collapsed, and dwindled down into a bedpost.

Stave Four: "The Last of the Spirits"

Yes! and the bedpost was his own. The bed was his own, the room was his own. Best and happiest of all, the Time before him was his own, to make amends in!

"I will live in the Past, the Present, and the Future!" Scrooge repeated, as he scrambled out of bed. "The Spirits of all Three shall strive within me. Oh Jacob Marley! Heaven, and the Christmas Time be praised for this! I say it on my knees, old Jacob, on my knees!"

He was so fluttered and so glowing with his good intentions, that his broken voice would scarcely answer to his call. He had been sobbing violently in his conflict with the Spirit, and his face was wet with tears.

"They are not torn down," cried Scrooge, folding one of his bed-curtains in his arms, "they are not torn down, rings and all. They are here—I am here—the shadows of the things that would have been, may be dispelled. They will be. I know they will!"

His hands were busy with his garments all this time; turning them inside out, putting them on upside down, tearing them, mislaying them, making them parties to every kind of extravagance.

"I don't know what to do!" cried Scrooge, laughing and crying in the same breath; and making a perfect Laocoön[5] of himself with his stockings. "I am as light as a feather, I am as happy as an angel, I am as merry as a schoolboy. I am as giddy as a drunken man. A merry Christmas to everybody! A happy New Year to all the world. Hallo here! Whoop! Hallo!"

He had frisked into the sitting-room, and was now standing there: perfectly winded.

"There's the saucepan that the gruel was in!" cried Scrooge, starting off again, and going round the fireplace. "There's the door, by which the Ghost of Jacob Marley entered! There's the corner where the Ghost of Christmas Present, sat! There's the window where I saw the wandering Spirits! It's all right, it's all true, it all happened. Ha ha ha!"

Really, for a man who had been out of practice for so many years, it was a splendid laugh, a most illustrious laugh. The father of a long, long line of brilliant laughs!

---

5 A mythological Trojan priest who was strangled to death by snakes.

"I don't know what day of the month it is!" said Scrooge. "I don't know how long I've been among the Spirits. I don't know anything. I'm quite a baby. Never mind. I don't care. I'd rather be a baby. Hallo! Whoop! Hallo here!"

He was checked in his transports by the churches ringing out the lustiest peals he had ever heard. Clash, clang, hammer; ding, dong, bell. Bell, dong, ding; hammer, clang, clash! Oh, glorious, glorious!

Running to the window, he opened it, and put out his head. No fog, no mist; clear, bright, jovial, stirring, cold; cold, piping for the blood to dance to; Golden sunlight; Heavenly sky; sweet fresh air; merry bells. Oh, glorious! Glorious!

"What's to-day!" cried Scrooge, calling downward to a boy in Sunday clothes, who perhaps had loitered in to look about him.

"EH?" returned the boy, with all his might of wonder.

"What's to-day, my fine fellow?" said Scrooge.

"To-day!" replied the boy. "Why, CHRISTMAS DAY."

"It's Christmas Day!" said Scrooge to himself. "I haven't missed it. The Spirits have done it all in one night. They can do anything they like. Of course they can. Of course they can. Hallo, my fine fellow!"

"Hallo!" returned the boy.

"Do you know the Poulterer's, in the next street but one, at the corner?" Scrooge inquired.

"I should hope I did," replied the lad.

"An intelligent boy!" said Scrooge. "A remarkable boy! Do you know whether they've sold the prize Turkey that was hanging up there?— Not the little prize Turkey: the big one?"

"What, the one as big as me?" returned the boy.

"What a delightful boy!" said Scrooge. "It's a pleasure to talk to him. Yes, my buck."

"It's hanging there now," replied the boy.

"Is it?" said Scrooge. "Go and buy it."

"Walk-ER!"[6] exclaimed the boy.

"No, no," said Scrooge, "I am in earnest. Go and buy it, and tell 'em to bring it here, that I may give them the direction where to take it. Come back with the man, and I'll give you a shilling. Come back with him in less than five minutes and I'll give you half-a-crown!"

The boy was off like a shot. He must have had a steady hand at a trigger who could have got a shot off half so fast.

"I'll send it to Bob Cratchit's!" whispered Scrooge, rubbing his hands, and splitting with a laugh. "He shan't know who sends it. It's twice the size of Tiny Tim. Joe Miller never made such a joke as sending it to Bob's will be!"

The hand in which he wrote the address was not a steady one, but write it he did, somehow, and went down-stairs to open the street door, ready for the coming of the poulterer's man. As he stood there, waiting his arrival, the knocker caught his eye.

"I shall love it, as long as I live!" cried Scrooge, patting it with his hand. "I scarcely ever looked at it before. What an honest expression it has in its face! It's a wonderful knocker!—Here's the Turkey! Hallo! Whoop! How are you! Merry Christmas!"

It *was* a Turkey! He never could have stood upon his legs, that bird. He would have snapped 'em short off in a minute, like sticks of sealing-wax.

"Why, it's impossible to carry that to Camden Town," said Scrooge. "You must have a cab."

The chuckle with which he said this, and the chuckle with which he paid for the Turkey, and the chuckle with which he paid for the cab, and the chuckle with which he recompensed

---

6 An expression of disbelief.

the boy, were only to be exceeded by the chuckle with which he sat down breathless in his chair again, and chuckled till he cried.

Shaving was not an easy task, for his hand continued to shake very much; and shaving requires attention, even when you don't dance while you are at it. But if he had cut the end of his nose off, he would have put a piece of sticking-plaister over it, and been quite satisfied.

He dressed himself "all in his best," and at last got out into the streets. The people were by this time pouring forth, as he had seen them with the Ghost of Christmas Present; and walking with his hands behind him, Scrooge regarded every one with a delighted smile. He looked so irresistibly pleasant, in a word, that three or four good-humoured fellows said, "Good morning, sir! A merry Christmas to you!" And Scrooge said often afterwards, that of all the blithe sounds he had ever heard, those were the blithest in his ears.

He had not gone far, when coming on towards him he beheld the portly gentleman, who had walked into his counting-house the day before, and said, "Scrooge and Marley's, I believe?" It sent a pang across his heart to think how this old gentleman would look upon him when they met; but he knew what path lay straight before him, and he took it.

"My dear sir," said Scrooge, quickening his pace, and taking the old gentleman by both his hands. "How do you do? I hope you succeeded yesterday. It was very kind of you. A merry Christmas to you, sir!"

"Mr. Scrooge?"

"Yes," said Scrooge. "That is my name, and I fear it may not be pleasant to you. Allow me to ask your pardon. And will you have the goodness"—here Scrooge whispered in his ear.

"Lord bless me!" cried the gentleman, as if his breath were taken away. "My dear Mr. Scrooge, are you serious?"

"If you please," said Scrooge. "Not a farthing less. A great many back-payments are included in it, I assure you. Will you do me that favour?"

"My dear sir," said the other, shaking hands with him. "I don't know what to say to such munifi—"

"Don't say anything, please," retorted Scrooge. "Come and see me. Will you come and see me?"

"I will!" cried the old gentleman. And it was clear he meant to do it.

"Thank you," said Scrooge. "I am much obliged to you. I thank you fifty times. Bless you!"

He went to church, and walked about the streets, and watched the people hurrying to and fro, and patted children on the head, and questioned beggars, and looked down into the kitchens of houses, and up to the windows, and found that everything could yield him pleasure. He had never dreamed that any walk—that anything—could give him so much happiness. In the afternoon he turned his steps towards his nephew's house.

He passed the door a dozen times, before he had the courage to go up and knock. But he made a dash, and did it:

"Is your master at home, my dear?" said Scrooge to the girl. Nice girl! Very.

"Yes, sir."

"Where is he, my love?" said Scrooge.

"He's in the dining-room, sir, along with mistress. I'll show you up-stairs, if you please."

"Thank'ee. He knows me," said Scrooge, with his hand already on the dining-room lock. "I'll go in here, my dear."

He turned it gently, and sidled his face in, round the door. They were looking at the table (which was spread out in great array); for these young housekeepers are always nervous on such points, and like to see that everything is right.

"Fred!" said Scrooge.

Dear heart alive, how his niece by marriage started! Scrooge had forgotten, for the moment, about her sitting in the corner with the footstool,[7] or he wouldn't have done it, on any account.

"Why bless my soul!" cried Fred, "who's that?"

"It's I. Your uncle Scrooge. I have come to dinner. Will you let me in, Fred?"

Let him in! It is a mercy he didn't shake his arm off. He was at home in five minutes. Nothing could be heartier. His niece looked just the same. So did Topper when *he* came. So did the plump sister when *she* came. So did every one when *they* came. Wonderful party, wonderful games, wonderful unanimity, won-der-ful happiness!

But he was early at the office next morning. Oh, he was early there. If he could only be there first, and catch Bob Cratchit coming late! That was the thing he had set his heart upon.

And he did it; yes, he did! The clock struck nine. No Bob. A quarter past. No Bob. He was full eighteen minutes and a half behind his time. Scrooge sat with his door wide open, that he might see him come into the Tank.

His hat was off, before he opened the door; his comforter too. He was on his stool in a jiffy; driving away with his pen, as if he were trying to overtake nine o'clock.

"Hallo!" growled Scrooge, in his accustomed voice, as near as he could feign it. "What do you mean by coming here at this time of day?"

"I am very sorry, sir," said Bob. "I *am* behind my time."

"You are?" repeated Scrooge. "Yes. I think you are. Step this way, sir, if you please."

---

7 A reference to her being pregnant and having to sit out during rambunctious games.

"It's only once a year, sir," pleaded Bob, appearing from the Tank. "It shall not be repeated. I was making rather merry yesterday, sir."

"Now, I'll tell you what, my friend," said Scrooge, "I am not going to stand this sort of thing any longer. And therefore," he continued, leaping from his stool, and giving Bob such a dig in the waistcoat that he staggered back into the Tank again; "and therefore I am about to raise your salary!"

Bob trembled, and got a little nearer to the ruler. He had a momentary idea of knocking Scrooge down with it, holding him, and calling to the people in the court for help and a strait-waistcoat.

"A merry Christmas, Bob," said Scrooge, with an earnestness that could not be mistaken, as he clapped him on the back. "A merrier Christmas, Bob, my good fellow, than I have given you for many a year. I'll raise your salary, and endeavour to assist your struggling family, and we will discuss your affairs this very afternoon, over a Christmas bowl of smoking bishop, Bob! Make up the fires, and buy another coal-scuttle before you dot another i, Bob Cratchit!"

Scrooge was better than his word. He did it all, and infinitely more; and to Tiny Tim, who did NOT die, he was a second father. He became as good a friend, as good a master, and as good a man, as the good old city knew, or any other good old city, town, or borough, in the good old world. Some people laughed to see the alteration in him, but he let them laugh, and little heeded them; for he was wise enough to know that nothing ever happened on this globe, for good, at which some people did not have their fill of laughter in the outset; and knowing that such as these would be blind anyway, he thought it quite as well that they should wrinkle up their eyes in grins, as have the malady in less attractive forms. His own heart laughed: and that was quite enough for him.

He had no further intercourse with Spirits, but lived upon the Total Abstinence Principle, ever afterwards; and it was always said of him, that he knew how to keep Christmas well, if any man alive possessed the knowledge. May that be truly said of us, and all of us! And so, as Tiny Tim observed, God bless Us, Every One!

Stave Five: "The End of It"

Appendix

Two Letters

In the introduction, I quoted from a letter in which Dickens wrote about his faith. Here are two more such letters. The first was written to his son Edward "Plorn" Dickens, who was about to emigrate to Australia at the age of sixteen.

My Dearest Plorn,

I write this note to-day because your going away is much upon my mind, and because I want you to have a few parting words from me to think of now and then at quiet times. I need not tell you that I love you dearly, and am very, very sorry in my heart to part with you. But this life is half made up of partings, and these pains must be borne. It is my comfort and my sincere conviction that you are going to try the life for which you are best fitted. I think its freedom and wildness more suited to you than any experiment in a study or office would ever have been; and without that training, you could have followed no other suitable occupation.

What you have always wanted until now has been a set, steady, constant purpose. I therefore exhort you to persevere in a thorough determination to do whatever you have to do as well as you can do it. I was not so old as you are now when I first had to win my food, and do it out of this determination, and I have never slackened in it since.

Never take a mean advantage of anyone in any transaction, and never be hard upon people who are in your power. Try to do to others, as you would have them do to you, and do not be discouraged if they fail sometimes. It is much better for you that they should fail in obeying the greatest rule laid down by our Saviour, than that you should.

I put a New Testament among your books, for the very same reasons, and with the very same hopes that made me write an easy account of it for you, when you were a little child; because it is the best book that ever was or will be known in the world, and because it teaches you the best lessons by which any human creature who tries to be truthful and faithful to duty can possibly be guided. As your brothers have gone away, one by one, I have written to each such words as I am now writing to you, and have entreated them all to guide themselves by this book, putting aside the interpretations and inventions of man.

You will remember that you have never at home been wearied about religious observances or mere formalities. I have always been anxious not to weary my children with such things before they are old enough to form opinions respecting them. You will therefore understand the better that I now most solemnly impress upon you the truth and beauty of the Christian religion, as it came from Christ Himself, and the impossibility of your going far wrong if you humbly but heartily respect it.

Only one thing more on this head. The more we are in earnest as to feeling it, the less we are disposed to hold forth about it. Never abandon the wholesome practice of saying your own private prayers, night and morning. I have never abandoned it myself, and I know the comfort of it.

I hope you will always be able to say in after life, that you had a kind father. You cannot show your affection for him so well, or make him so happy, as by doing your duty.

Your affectionate Father[1]

The last letter Dickens ever wrote, the day before he died, was to John Makeham, a reader who had taken issue with a scriptural phrase ("lamb to the slaughter") that Dickens had adapted for use in The Mystery of Edwin Drood.

GAD'S HILL PLACE, HIGHAM BY ROCHESTER, KENT.
Wednesday Eighth June 1870

Dear Sir

It would be quite inconceivable to me—but for your letter—that any reasonable reader could possibly attach a scriptural reference to a passage in a book of mine, reproducing a much abused social figure of speech, impressed into all sorts of service, on all sorts of inappropriate occasions, without the faintest connexion of it with its original source. I am truly shocked to find that any reader can make the mistake.

I have always striven in my writings to express veneration for the life and lessons of Our Saviour; because I feel it; and because I re-wrote that history for my children—every one of whom knew it from having it repeated to them, long before they could read, and almost as soon as they could speak.

But I have never made proclamation of this from the house tops.

Faithfully yours
CHARLES DICKENS[2]

---

1 Dickens, letter to Edward Dickens, September 26, 1868, *Selected Letters.*

2 Dickens, letter to John Makeham, June 8, 1870, *Selected Letters.*

Acknowledgments

Thanks to my family and friends, who have patiently listened to me chatter on about Dickens for many, many years!

Thanks to the faithful readers of Dickensblog, and to my friends in the Dickens Fellowship and the Dickens Society. Thanks to all those—too many to name—whose writings on Dickens have inspired me. Thanks to Jonathan Cross and the rest of the Washington Philosophical Society for their encouragement and enthusiasm about this project.

Thanks to Sam Hine, Alina Meier, Trevor Wiser, and the rest of the team at Plough Publishing House—and especially Veery Huleatt, who first gave me the idea of writing for Plough. Thanks to my agent, Chris Park, of Foundry Literary + Media.

Thanks to Dr. Karen Swallow Prior for her wonderful foreword.

Thanks to Mrs. Danelo, the ninth-grade teacher who made the fateful introduction to *Great Expectations* that ultimately led to this project.

Thanks most of all to the novelist who has taught me and given me so much: the incomparable Charles Dickens.

A Note on the Text

All excerpts of Dickens's writings have been taken from editions based on the Charles Dickens Edition of 1867–8, which was edited by Dickens himself, with the following exceptions:

> *The Mystery of Edwin Drood*, which was left unfinished at Dickens's death in 1870. The excerpt here was taken from the 2009 Modern Library paperback edition, which is based on the first 1870 London edition, published by Chapman & Hall.
>
> All letters from Dickens to others. These were taken from *The Selected Letters of Charles Dickens*, ed. Jenny Hartley (Oxford: Oxford University Press, 2012).
>
> *The Life of Our Lord*, which was not published during Dickens's lifetime. The excerpt here was taken from the 1991 edition published by Thomas Nelson.

Where any of the editions have deviated from the original British spelling, I have ignored the deviation and retained the original, to maintain consistency and to keep as close as possible to Dickens's own text. I have, however, changed single quotation marks to double ones, and put periods after "Mr" and "Mrs," for example.

The illustrations, from early editions of Dickens's novels, were taken from the *Victorian Web* (victorianweb.org). These images may be used without permission for any scholarly or educational purpose.

The Gospel in Great Writers

The Gospel in Dorothy L. Sayers
A master of the detective story delves into mysteries of faith, doubt, human nature, feminism, art, and more.

The Gospel in Dostoyevsky
Passages from Dostoyevsky's greatest novels explore the devastating, yet ultimately healing, implications of the Gospels.

The Gospel in George MacDonald
Discover the spiritual vision of the great Scottish storyteller who inspired C. S. Lewis and J. R. R. Tolkien.

The Gospel in Tolstoy
This rich, accessible introduction shows how the teachings of Jesus inspired some of Tolstoy's best literary work.

The Gospel in Gerard Manley Hopkins
Discover in Hopkins's own words the struggle for faith that gave birth to some of the best poetry of all time.

The Gospel in Dickens
Short, readable excerpts reveal the Christian vision and values that suffuse Dickens's work.

Plough Publishing House
151 Bowne Drive, PO Box 398, Walden, NY 12586, USA
Brightling Road, Robertsbridge, East Sussex TN32 5DR, UK
4188 Gwydir Highway, Elsmore, NSW 2360, Australia
845-572-3455 • info@plough.com • www.plough.com